£2

THE BLUE

HARRY COLE
Bermondsey,
when he was fourteen, during the war,
became a cricket-bat maker, soldier,
stonemason and, in 1952, a policeman. For
thirty years, until he retired in 1983, he served at
the same police station in London.
He is a qualified FA coach (he has run
numerous junior football teams), a referee and
a keen cricketer. For many years he had a
regular column in the *Warren*, the police
magazine. His other books are *Policeman's
Progress* (1980), *Policeman's Lot* (1981),
Policeman's Patch (1982) and *Policeman's
Patrol* (1983), and his two-volume auto-
biography, *Policeman's Prelude* (1984) and
Policeman's Story (1985).
Harry Cole is married and has a daughter. In
1978 he was awarded the British Empire Medal
for voluntary work. Since leaving the force, in
addition to writing he has taken up after-dinner
speaking.

HARRY COLE

The Blue Apprentices

FONTANA/Collins

First published in 1986 by Fontana Paperbacks,
8 Grafton Street, London W1X 3LA

Printed and bound in Great Britain by
William Collins Sons & Co. Ltd, Glasgow

For Zena

CHAPTER ONE

'Right!' boomed Inspector McCormack. 'In twenty seconds you can turn over your papers. But don't forget to read the questions through thoroughly. There is always at least one mad-arse who answers the wrong question. Usually it's the only one they make a good job of.' He stared pointedly at the new wall clock. 'Five . . . four . . . three . . . two. Turn your papers over—NOW!' There was a rustle of papers and a scraping of chairs. Two rulers and a pen clattered to the floor. Somewhere at the back of the class someone threw a fit of coughing, but throughout it all Helen Rogers remained impassive. She stared at the closed question paper, unable to bring herself even to touch it. Her arms remained paralysed at her side.

Michael Butler realized instantly that the situation was serious—he had never seen so much of Helen's thighs before. Whenever that young lady sat down there would always be a generous expanse of upper leg to be seen. She would, however, then bounce twice and smooth down her skirt, always in one polished movement. She had now been sitting stone-still for ten minutes and not once had she bounced. Those black tights were going to be one hell of a distraction. He turned his paper over and dragged his vision from the dark-nyloned legs. 'Define Section One of the Firearms Act of 1968.' He momentarily closed his eyes in concentration. What the hell do I remember about the Firearms Act? To his astonishment, when he opened his eyes once more, they were again focused neatly on Helen's right thigh. The inspector too had noticed the girl's inaction. Sadly for him he had missed out on the legs, but then training school instructors were supposed to be above that sort of thing. He slowly rose from his desk and tiptoed to the second row back. 'What's the trouble, Miss Rogers?'

he whispered in a muted tone that still managed to reach every corner of the room.

The girl raised her head in a series of short, stilted moves. She opened her mouth but no sound came forth. The inspector took hold of her left hand and slowly placed it on to the paper. Then, gathering her fingers and paper into one huge fist, he turned over the intimidating sheet. This simple movement seemed to trigger off the necessary mechanism. Her right hand instinctively dropped to her lap where, after two quick bounces, she smoothed the skirt into one straight, knee-length line. Then, picking up her pen, she appeared to both read and answer the question at the same time. Michael Butler shook his head. He now found the whole situation totally demoralizing.

Class 16A were in the final week of their four-month course at the Hendon Police College. It had not been particularly easy for any of them, but for some, particularly the distracted Michael, it had been absolute purgatory. Great reams of acts and sections had to be learned word-perfect, and for someone who could barely remember the registration number of his moped, Michael found this particularly difficult. To his credit, he had stayed the course. Since that first day, some sixteen long weeks ago, five of the nineteen students had packed their bags and returned home to mum, at least two of them in tears. This exam was now to decide whether Michael was to join them. It was the final test of the course and the results always came through mercifully quickly—by mid-afternoon at the latest. To fail was not necessarily a disaster. It would simply mean a back squadding for two weeks with a chance to take the exam once more, this time with the intake behind. To fail that exam, however, *would* be a disaster. For Mickey there would be no question of a back-squadding. He had stupidly decided that he passed today or he did not pass at all. He realized now that this was a totally illogical stance and he secretly wished he had not taken it. However, in a moment of bar-room bravado, he had clearly stated his intention and now he felt stuck with it. Giving one last hopeful glance at those now concealed thighs, he dropped his gaze to the next question. 'Name the statutory defence for Section One of the Firearms Act.' He groaned silently, things were getting worse.

'Okay! Pay attention, you lot!' The inspector's voice cut into the general classroom hubbub as he strode purposefully through the door. Beneath his arm was a thick folder of question papers. 'These are your results from the morning exam. Firstly the bad news. Coxon, Ryan, Gellatly and Smithers, none of you scored the required sixty per cent. You will each be back-squadded to the intake behind from tomorrow morning. As for the rest of you, Helen Rogers—once she got going—was top student with ninety-six per cent, and you, Butler—' the inspector sighed deeply and shook his head—'have managed to amaze me once again by passing yet another exam. But if I were you I would not ask what my marks were. God only knows how you do it!'

'Aw, go on, sir, tell me. I like a bit of excitement. What were they?' asked the now buoyant Michael.

'Well, you got the date wrong for a start, yet still managed sixty per cent!'

'I never had a moment's doubt, sir, not a moment's!' Michael grinned smugly.

The failed quartet bravely congratulated the successful majority and then did the decent thing by leaving immediately for their new classroom. This move cleared the air for some real heady conversation. Every Hendon recruit who has ever passed the final exam is convinced that from that moment, the remainder of their police career will all be downhill. The atmosphere was euphoric.

The group by this time had been given both their postings and their warrant cards. Five of them: Helen Rogers, Michael Butler, the class captain Gerald Newton, David Ducker, a sports fanatic, and finally Angela Helms—who at nineteen was the baby of the class—were to be posted to Cabul Lane Police Station in the 'MP' district of south

7

London. Of the rest, three single men were bound for Chelsea, and the four married men were to be posted close to their homes in north London.

It was customary college practice for each successful group to wine and dine their instructor at the end of the course. It is on these social occasions that all those maddening little habits, with which each instructor flagellates his class, become quaint little quirks in the now forgiving mind of the student.

The evening had begun pleasantly enough and, under the watchful eye of Inspector McCormack, everyone had been on their best behaviour. Perhaps the biggest surprise had been the girls. Five females had begun the course, but with two resigning and a third back-squadded, both Angela and Helen had the field to themselves. Helen, in particular, took advantage of this. At twenty-eight she was at least five years older than anyone else in the class and this maturity stood her in good stead. She was a particularly dark-haired girl, almost gypsy-like in appearance, with a full, round figure. Her hair—usually worn in a tight bun beneath her uniform hat—hung shoulder-length and free. Two large golden earrings swung sensuously from her lobes, and her low-cut, tight green dress bit intriguingly in at her waist. In short, she looked a real woman. Angela, on the other hand, was very much the opposite. With her slim figure, bubbly hair, freckles and pretty white dress, she looked even younger than her nineteen years.

The group returned to the training school around eleven o'clock, and the inspector bade them good-night. The Chelsea-bound lads and the four married men then adjourned to play cards.

'I don't feel like going to bed,' Angela complained. 'Is there nowhere else we could go?'

'My uncle runs a basement club just off Wardour Street,' offered Gerald. 'If we all think it's worthwhile, I'll give him a ring.'

The five had drunk just enough to make the suggestion

sound sensible. 'Getting there will be a problem,' Michael pointed out. 'We'd need two taxis, and the return fare would cost a fortune.'

'Well, there's always my football team's old van,' said David. 'I use it for toing and froing to the college. It's not very comfortable but I dare say we can manage.'

Helen appeared to have reservations about the whole plan, but Angela's enthusiasm, to say nothing of her imagination, ran riot. 'This club of your uncle's, Gerry, will it be full of "heavies"?' she asked.

'Eh?' queried Gerald in genuine puzzlement. 'What on earth's a "heavy"?'

'You know—big-time villains and all that. I think *really* big villains are so sexy. It's one of the reasons I joined the police.' She closed her eyes in mock ecstasy. 'Those unbuttoned shirts and hairy medallioned chests send me wild. I can't wait to search them for concealed weapons.' Clasping her hands together she drove them down between her knees and faked a compulsive shudder.

'If what I have heard is true, the only "heavy" in my uncle's club will be Gladys, my aunt. Look—' stressed Gerald. 'If we *are* going, we need to make up our minds soon. It'll be time to come back otherwise.'

'Well, what are we waiting for?' Angela sang out. 'Watch out, heavies, I'm coming!' She raised her eyes suggestively.

After a few false starts and a great deal of smoke, they rolled sweetly along the Hendon Way. The Deadly Nightshade Club was not actually 'just off' Wardour Street at all. It was just off a street that was just off Wardour Street. In fact, most things about the club seemed 'just off'. This subsequently was to include the drink, décor, and Gerald's relations. Even the neon light above the door was faulty, reading as it did—

DEAD NIGHT HADE CLUB. BERS ONLY.
EXTENSIVE WIN   CELLAR.

They were greeted at the door—if greeted was the word— by Uncle Frank. The group had assumed that both Frank and Gladys would be benign, cheery characters who would fall rapturously upon their nephew's neck. The group were wrong. Gerald, it transpired, was the white sheep of the family. While he had been swotting it out in a police college, half of his relations had been sweating it out in a prison. At the last count there were six inside and three on bail. It was soon quite obvious where Uncle Frank's sympathies lay. He met them in the tiny red-curtained foyer with a gruff, 'Nah, wot's all this abaht?' He was a humourless middle-aged man with a menopausal face and a teenage toupee.

'Oh—er, these are some of my friends from the police college, Frank. We just thought we would like to celebrate. We passed our exam this week and now we are all fully fledged coppers, as you might say.' Gerald laughed nervously.

'Right, nah listen!' Frank pointed a stern, podgy finger at his nephew. 'One! Yer gits no preferential treatment. Two! Yer gits no discount. And three, on no account let anyone know that you're coppers. Don't *talk* like coppers, don't *think* like coppers, and above all don't *act* like bleedin' coppers. 'Ere, wait a minute—what's this?' He moved the warning finger from beneath Gerald's nose and aimed it in the direction of Angela. ''Ow old is she—twelve?'

Michael Butler was starting to bristle. Even Dave, normally the most placid of individuals, raised his eyebrows. 'Look, mate—' began Michael who, incensed as he was, could scarcely avert his gaze from the ill-suited toupee.

'Oh, I'm sure it will be all right,' Helen cut in smoothly. 'We only want a quiet celebration drink, Mister—er, may we call you Frank?'

Seeing Helen for the first time, Frank changed his manner instantly. 'Hello, dahlin'!' he leered. 'Where'd you spring from? Blimey, the law's really looking up if it's recruiting class birds like you! Let me take your coat. This way everybody.'

If he was pleased to see Helen with her coat on, he was ecstatic when she slipped it off. Mickey later claimed that the toupee stood on end.

'You know, this really is a dive,' Helen whispered as they filed down the narrow staircase. The noise from the disco

10

built up like approaching rapids. 'I'm not sure we should be here at all. It would be ironic if we were arrested before we had even begun our police career.'

Each of the group had differing ideas of what the club would be like, but none was prepared for its claustrophobic modesty. Red regency stripes were everywhere. Everywhere that one could see, that is, for it was only the flash of the disco lights that gave any visibility at all. The club was little more than a room and not a very large room at that. The clientele in the main appeared to be tourists, Japanese mostly. There were, however, two crowded, noisy tables of football supporters, their language in every respect indicating an origin north of the border.

At one end of the room, running the disco, was a tall, spindly black man dressed completely in white. At the other, was a truly massive blonde in a quite ludicrous red lurex dress. She stood behind a bar that was, in comparison, so small that she appeared to be wearing it around her hips. As she leaned forward, her voluminous breasts rolled over the bar-top like escaped sea lions.

'I haven't seen Aunt Gladys since I was a toddler,' side-mouthed Gerald. 'But that's just got to be her behind that bar.'

'Well, if that's her *behind* the bar,' asked Michael, 'who are the two people on top of it? I admit I like a good pair of "bristols" but they must go about two to the hundredweight!'

'Shush! Don't be rude!' Helen nudged him.

'Guess who this is, Gladys,' Frank yelled, cupping his hands because of the noise. Gladys looked nonplussed.

'It's Gerald—you remember? Your sister's boy.'

The puzzled look vanished from the old blonde's face and realization dawned. 'Oh, it's young Gerry! Here—' she ordered, her eyes narrowing and her voice falling. 'Didn't he go off and join—'

'Yeh, 'e did, but we won't talk abaht that, if you don't mind,' Frank cut in, casting furtive left-and-right glances. 'We've got a business ter run.'

'Well, you'll have to get some more chairs for his little friends,' Gladys said kindly. 'Perhaps Gerry will give you a hand. Meanwhile, what'll the rest of you boys have to drink? Oh!' she exclaimed, her gaze falling for the first time on the two girls. 'These with you, Gerry?'

'These, my dear,' Frank interrupted in an excited whisper, 'are two young *police* ladies. 'Ow abaht that then?' He placed an over-familiar arm around the girls' waists, then patted each of their buttocks. Helen gave a start and was patently not pleased. Angela, on the other hand, sqeaked a little 'Ow' and raised herself up on her toes.

'Let go of the arses and get hold of the chairs, Frank, there's a good lad,' Gladys ordered icily.

While Frank and Gerald disappeared into the store-cupboard, Michael rather nobly decided to order a round of drinks. 'Three pints of lager and two vodka and lemonades, please, Gladys,' he requested pleasantly. 'Oh, and get one for yourself and for Frank.'

'That's very kind of you, young man.'

Michael made a think-nothing-of-it gesture.

'That'll be sixteen pounds, please.'

'That'll be what?'

'That'll be sixteen pounds,' repeated Gladys through tightening lips.

'Hang on a minute, will you?' requested Michael anxiously as he turned towards the group. 'We're going to have to organize a "whip",' he announced urgently.

Four reluctant hands dived into pockets and handbags and eventually the ransom was paid.

Meanwhile, Gerald was making some rather interesting discoveries in the storeroom. Probably the room's greatest asset was that it at least contained a decent light. This in turn caused him to notice several cases of the cheapest form of sparkling wine. Alongside these cases was a small cardboard box of 'Vintage Champagne' labels. In fact, in the far corner of the room was a narrow shelf that was stacked high with wine labels of every year and vintage. By the simple process of switching labels, a customer could be served a wine—expensive, of course—from most of the chateaux of the world. The words EXTENSIVE WIN CELLAR took on a whole new meaning. Six cases of *vin ordinaire* and a packet of labels provided a wine cellar the equivalent of anything else in town. Reading his thoughts, Frank shrugged and philosophically observed that 'It all tastes the same in the dark.'

Not the least of the revelations in the storeroom, though, was a slim, almost skinny, redhead. She would have been an inconsequential figure in every respect except for one thing. With the exception of a G-string, two spangles and a pair of sneakers, she was totally naked. What, Gerald understandably wondered, was a near-naked redhead doing in Uncle Frank's storeroom? If the light had not been so good he might have thought she was a blow-up doll.

In fact, she was not doing a lot. She was simply changing her shoes. Those sensible, flat-bottomed sneakers were in the process of being discarded for the more glamorous, sling-back, high tapered heels that were more in keeping with the rest of her adornments. Yvonne de Millau, or to use her social security title, Tracy Crutchlow, ignored Gerald's presence and went straight for Frank.

'It don't get no bleedin' warmer in 'ere, Frank. I fort you were gettin' an 'eater above that door?'

'Sorry about that, Tracy, luv. I've been a bit tucked up lately. Same routine tonight, is it?'

'Yeh, but I ain't doin' no bleedin' encores, I'm late on me rounds as it is. I'm due up the road at the San Remo in twenty minutes.'

'Oh, by the way, Trace,' said Frank. 'This 'ere's me nephew, Gerry. Gerry, this is Tracy—she's the cabaret.'

'Oh—er, pleased to meet you,' stammered Gerald. 'What is it that you actually do?'

'Trace is an erotic dancer,' Frank interrupted proudly. 'She's the sole entertainment for 'alf a dozen clubs in the area. Ain't you, Trace?' Trace nodded loftily.

Gerald looked studiously at the girl and decided that he had never seen anything less erotic in his life.

13

'What're the punters like ternight?' Tracy asked as she adjusted a spangle.

'Japs mainly. Then there's a few of 'is mates.' Frank pointed at Gerald with a chair. 'But you might 'ave ter watch the two tables of Jock football supporters near the stairs. They're gettin' a bit boisterous.'

Leaning back, Tracy performed two practice poses at her reflection in the basement window, turning first right then left. 'Give me just two more minutes, Frank, and *do* get your bleedin' disc jockey to play me proper music ternight, will yer? Christ only knows what 'e played last night, but it was like takin' orf me knickers to "Land of Hope and Glory".'

Picking up the chairs, Gerald staggered back into the vibrating darkness of the club. As his eyes accustomed to the gloom, he saw that his friends were in animated conversation at the bar. Before he could set down the chairs, Michael was on to him.

'Got ten quid, Gerry?'

'Whatever for?'

'We're having a whip.'

'A *ten-quid* whip?'

'Have you seen the prices in this place?' asked Michael tersely. 'Your bloody family must all be millionaires! Three drinks each and we'll all be skint. I know he's your uncle and all that but I think the booze in this place is one great con!'

'You think the booze is a con? You just wait till you see the cabaret!'

'When's that due?'

'LADIES AND GENNEL*MEN*!' announced Frank, exactly on cue. 'I 'ave great pleasure in intro-doosin' to you —straight from her engagement at the Lido in Paris—the fabulous rage of the left bank. I give you Mademoiselle Yvonne de Millau!'

Gerald looked hopefully at the disc jockey, secretly wishing for at least one good verse of 'Land of Hope and Glory', but Donna Summer's voice cut quickly in with

14

'Love to Love You, Baby'. The lights if anything went even dimmer, and the 'rage of the left bank' shimmered stick-like into the room.

Gerald had hoped that Yvonne de Millau in the dark would be a stunning improvement on Tracy Crutchlow in the light, but it wasn't to be.

'Oh my gawd!' moaned Michael in sheer disbelief. 'Is that it?'

''Fraid so,' Gerald nodded with a wide grin. 'You'd better lie back and enjoy it, it's costing enough!'

In the absence of a table, the group's chairs were arranged into a tight, cramped semicircle. 'I have no wish to appear catty,' whispered Helen, leaning across to Gerald. 'But what on earth is she?'

'My Uncle Frank says she's an "erotic dancer".'

'In comparison to your aunt, perhaps she is,' shrugged the girl.

Mademoiselle de Millau was by now well into her act. An act that seemed to consist mainly of rubbing herself against the backs of most of the seated male customers. The spangle that had given her trouble in the storeroom finally fell off, but no one seemed to notice. The football supporters at the next table were becoming increasingly restless. 'Git 'em orf, lassie. Orf I say! Orf! Orf! Orf!' became the main cry.

To the accompaniment of joyous whoops from the Scots, Tracy popped a fastener somewhere near her bony left hip and the deed was done. Her thin arm held aloft the triangular wisp of material. She leaned back with arms and legs spread wide, jerking quickly backwards and forwards. The light, what there was of it, concealed all but the dancer's frail outline. Her tiny breasts and close-shaven vulva vanished into a shadowed obscurity. She appeared a sexless creature, neither male nor female.

The whoops of the Scots changed to hisses and boos, then the first glass of beer was thrown. Considering the lack of vision in the place it was an impressive shot, too, striking the nude fair-square in the chest. The contents of a second

15

glass soared through the air, this time by no means as accurate. Perhaps it was a Freudian mistake, for instead of smacking against poor Tracy's frail diaphragm, it cascaded down Helen's ample cleavage. Michael was on his feet almost before the beer had struck. Before anyone could stop him he had reached over the nearby table and hauled out the only beer-less occupant.

To be fair to the Scot, he did not need encouraging. He almost jumped the table, scattering colleagues as he did so. In comparison to the dedicated fitness of Dave Ducker, Michael was almost sedentary, yet he possessed a tall, natural athleticism that was easy to see. His opponent on the other hand, whilst some three inches shorter, was of an altogether stockier build. 'Nae look heeere, Jimmy,' came the thick Glaswegian snarl. 'Ye'll be gittin' yerself into all sorts o' bother wi' that wee temper o' yours.' As he spoke, he eased himself forward until they were almost face to face.

When the head-butt finally came, Michael was more than ready for it. His three years in the Army had finally stood him in good stead. He had seen these face-smashing butts in bar-room brawls from Cyprus to Berlin. Swaying quickly to his left, he fetched up his powerful right fist with all the strength he could muster. It was not a pleasant sound. The sickening squelch of a busted nose is fortunately not heard by its recipient. The Scot reeled back, cuffing away the blood and mucus.

Michael's reaction was certainly excessive, but as the ten Scots rose instantly to their feet, each of the young police-officers realized the implications. There were now only two choices: run—although they would never have made the staircase—or fight. If they were to fight then it had to be done swiftly, preferably whilst the opposition was still restricted by the table. Dave Ducker was in first. His powerful, stocky body seemed to sprout arms like pistons. Several of the Scots collided with each other and at least two fell to the floor.

'Get the girls out!' Dave called gallantly, but at least one of the girls was too busy delivering a kick to a Gaelic crotch to heed.

'Right, you lot!' bellowed Uncle Frank, trying a bluff. 'The law is 'ere! Pack it up nah, d'you 'ear me? Come on, pack it up I tell yer!' The deception had no chance of working, yet it suddenly reminded both Dave and Gerald that in fact they now *were* the law. Gladys switched on all the lights, and the Japanese turned their chairs around as if the brawl was just another part of the cabaret. Meanwhile, the real cabaret, or what was left of it, stood calmly drying herself in the storeroom doorway.

The police inspector, his sergeant and ten constables, sat patiently in the police van. The nearby San Remo Club was due for a raid at midnight and they were marginally ahead of schedule. Punctuality was essential because they had two plants in the club.

'There's bleedin' murder going on at the Nightshade, guv'nor,' mentioned a passing pedestrian in as offhand a manner as one can best explain a mass slaughter.

The inspector groaned. He had been waiting three months to amass enough men to raid the San Remo. Now that he had sufficient numbers he looked like being sidetracked by a stupid fight at the Nightshade. He promised himself that whenever he had a free moment he would endeavour to make Frank's life quite unpleasant. He did toy momentarily with the idea of carrying out the raid first and looking in at the fight later. With sufficient delay, it is surprising how many 'murderous' club fights can be quite tranquil by the time police arrive. 'I suppose we *could* leave the disturbance until after our raid, Sarge?' he suggested.

'Yes, *you* could,' agreed the sergeant, slipping back the responsibility to where it belonged. 'But if *you* did, it's a dead cert that you'd find no drugs at the Remo and two bloody corpses at the Nightshade.'

There was nothing else for it, he would just have to split forces. 'Okay,' asserted the inspector. 'Take a couple of lads along to the Nightshade but don't hang about there too long, the Remo can sometimes be quite hairy. We'll keep in touch on the bat-phone.'

The sergeant and two PCs slipped out of the Transit, quickly covering the sixty or so yards to the Deadly Nightshade. As they tumbled down the stairs they heard the last of Frank's beer glasses striking the mock-stone wall. The battle quickly petered out on the trio's arrival and fetched a round of applause from the Japanese. There were cuts and bruises in abundance but other than the original busted nose, no serious injuries. The club, on the other hand, now resembled the council tip.

As instructed, the sergeant reported back via his personal radio. 'Good,' acknowledged the inspector. 'Square it up as soon as you can and join us here, we're going in now.'

There was little 'squaring up' to be done. Club fights are ten-a-penny and, as usual, even those close to the scene had seen nothing, done nothing, sustained nothing and, in short, not even been there.

'Yes, I s'pose you *could* say we had a little trouble,' agreed Frank grudgingly to the sergeant. 'But as you can see, it's fine now.'

The sergeant nodded and looked around the beleaguered room. 'This is *fine*, is it?'

'Oh, yeh!' assured Frank with open arms. 'A quick sweep round and you wouldn't know the place.'

'How about this lot?' The sergeant pointed at the two groups of protagonists. 'D'you want them out?'

'No, no,' Frank laughed through the tightest of lips. 'They are all in the same party. They just got a little boisterous, that's all.'

'It's okay, Sarge, we're going anyway,' Gerald announced, seizing the opportunity of a safe conduct. 'Ready, everyone?'

The sergeant stared at him thoughtfully for a moment. 'Okay, but wait for me upstairs in the foyer. I'd like a word before you all leave.'

Swallowing the last of the insults from the Scots, the group filed silently up the staircase and huddled together in the tiny foyer entrance. In their absence, the sergeant and the two PCs confirmed once more that *absolutely* nothing had happened. The Japanese meanwhile waited patiently for the second act.

At last satisfied, the sergeant sent his two constables on to the Remo and joined the recruits in the foyer. 'Gather round me close and listen carefully,' he murmured angrily. 'You just happen to be the biggest bunch of prats I've met since I've been in this force. You're Hendon recruits, aren't you?' There was no response to his question. 'You are! It's written all over you!' he insisted.

'Yes, Sergeant, we are,' agreed Helen shamefacedly.

'Well, at least one of you has the guts to own up.' The sergeant sighed despairingly. 'By rights—after that little lot—this should be your last day in the job, do you realize that? Instead of which you've got away with it. No one down there wants to know and, lucky for you, the Japanese seem to think it was some bloody medieval pageant! Christ knows how you're going to get back to the training centre—or explain those bruises tomorrow morning—but that's your problem. I would just suggest you all put your hands together and thank whatever God was looking after you tonight.' His personal radio suddenly interrupted with an almost indecipherable message. 'I'm on my way, sir,' he acknowledged. Before leaving the foyer he turned once more to the group. 'And remember—You have never been here, neither tonight or any other time—understand?' Without waiting for a reply, he stepped out into the street and was gone.

The drive back to the college was a very subdued trip indeed. As they passed Hendon Central Station, Angela spoke for the first time since leaving the club. 'All right, so the evening went flat, but we're leaving here tomorrow and I'm going to do the one thing I promised myself if ever I should pass the blooming exam.'

'And that is?' asked Michael with almost bored indifference.

'I'm going for a swim.'

'A swim?' he echoed. 'At this time of night? The school pool will be locked.'

'I don't intend to go in the school pool.'

'Well, where are you going then?' he asked, as the rest of the group began to take an interest.

'I am going to dive into the school fishpond! The first day I entered this place I was dying for a swim. I was going to do it then but I chickened out. If I don't do it tonight I'll never do it. So in ten minutes' time it's just me and the goldfish.'

'But it's too shallow,' protested Gerald.

'No it's not,' said the girl. 'It's five feet deep, I can swim easily in that.'

'It'll also be perishing,' Michael pointed out.

'Well, I'm not staying in there all blooming night! A dive in, a quick swim across and then out. It'll all be over in less than a minute. Coming, anyone?'

They all looked at each other as if she had taken leave of her senses. 'But where's your costume?' asked a worried Helen.

'At home.'

'So what will you swim in?'

Angela shrugged. 'My lipstick, I suppose.'

The fellows perked up immensely.

They were soon faced with the final problem of actually entering the college now that it was well after midnight. Dave parked the van some distance from the school, and the group walked quietly to one of the entrances. It was the practice at the time to staff security points with particularly young students. These youngsters, having passed their exams, were still below the statutory age for serving police-officers. They were therefore utilized on various security positions around the complex until they reached the age of eighteen and a half. An old schoolfriend of Angela's was scheduled for the gate that night and a smooth passage was hoped for. They were not to be disappointed and within a few minutes had gathered expectantly around the fishpond.

Michael had decided that if the swim was to be as brief as Angela had declared, then he was not going to miss a second of it. He therefore gave it all his concentration. Even so, he was still surprised at the speed of her strip. One moment she stood on the path fully dressed, the next she was on tiptoe, nude and poised, on the low wall of the pond. Snatching a quick breath, she entered the water as smoothly as a seal. Helen picked up Angela's quilted coat and ran with it to the far side of the pond. She held it open as the goose-pimpled, pert-breasted girl slipped shiveringly into it.

'Wish I'd thought of that,' said Michael regretfully.

The hasty disappearance of Angela into the residents' block was the signal for the party to disperse. They each said their 'good-nights', and both Michael and Gerald crept to the third floor where they occupied adjoining rooms.

'I reckon that sergeant was right, Gerry,' confided Michael. 'We were bloody lucky tonight. Even that daft cow's swim seems to have gone unnoticed. I think we've come out of this smelling of roses.'

'Not altogether, I'm afraid,' Gerald answered sadly.

'Why? Whatever's the matter?' enquired Michael anxiously.

'I must have lost my warrant card in the fight at that club.'

'Then ring them and ask them to look for it. He's your bloody uncle after all!'

'I have rung him. I phoned from the call-box downstairs while you were ogling Angela.'

'And?'

'The worst possible result. Apparently, a police inspector who was raiding a club nearby decided to check back on the early disturbance at my uncle's place. One of the Japanese gave him the card.'

'We must be able to come up with some sort of story, surely?'

'How? We weren't issued with the cards till late in the afternoon. It then gets discovered by, of all things, a

21

blasted police inspector. This is on the same day in a club where there has just been a serious disturbance.' Gerald paused and shook his head sadly. 'You know, I just have a gut feeling that tomorrow will be my last day in the force. Pity, I think I would have enjoyed being a white sheep. Good-night, Mick.'

CHAPTER TWO

In spite of everything that had happened in the last few hours, it was the smell of the polish on the chief superintendent's desk that upset Gerald most. It churned his egg-on-toast breakfast like a coffee-grinder. A knot of nausea bubbled angrily beneath his chest.

'Are you seriously trying to tell me, Newton,' the chief superintendent was saying menacingly, 'that somewhere around midnight you went to this club—no, I can't call it a club – this sleazy bloody clip-joint? You there became involved in a fight and lost your warrant card? Not satisfied with that you then returned in the early hours of the morning and broke into the school—and you did all this on your own? Is that what I'm supposed to believe? Well, is it?' he glared.

'Yes, sir.'

'For what purpose were you using your warrant card in this—this—place? Drink? Women? Showing off?'

'I wasn't using it for anything at all, sir. I must have just dropped it.'

'Do you not think it strange that your card was found in a club that was being searched for drugs? A club, I might add, that you had just vacated. A club that had previously housed a serious disturbance? Do you not perhaps think that could be a mite unusual?'

'I was definitely on my own, sir,' insisted Gerald. 'I must have dropped my warrant card when I pulled out my wallet to buy some drinks.'

'*Some* drinks, Newton? *Some* drinks? So you weren't on your own after all!'

'Well, I met a girl in there but I entered the place on my own.'

'Hmmmm, I see.' The chief superintendent leaned back

in his chair and studied Gerald thoughtfully. 'This girl—was she a "tom"?'

'Sir?'

'A *TOM*, Newton. A whore! A prostitute! A lady of easy virtue, if you wish. Was she trying to separate you from your money?'

Gerald was fast becoming confused. He had trapped himself with this fictional young lady and he was not sure of his safe way out. Poor Gerald, there was none. He was now lined neatly for the drop. 'Well—er, I don't really know, sir.'

'Well, let me put it this way, son. Do you think that a respectable young lady would venture into such a place on her own?'

Gerald shook his head.

'How much money did you have on you?'

'About a tenner, sir.'

'A tenner, eh? As much as that!' said the chief superintendent, unable to resist a little sarcasm. 'You entered a clip-joint, picked up a tom, bought two drinks with a whole tenner in your pocket. You were hardly geared to set the West End ablaze, were you? I take it you intended to have sex with this girl?'

Gerald did not answer.

'Come on, we are both adult people. It's not as if you are married, is it?'

That's true, thought Gerald, I am single. Perhaps it might be a good idea to play up to this all-chaps-together line.

'Yessir, I did hope that sex would materialize. I've been at the school for four months and, well—after the exam, I did feel like a bit of female company, sir.'

'There you are,' said the chief superintendent matily. 'That didn't hurt now, did it? So, only having ten quid about your person, you gave her your warrant card—eh?'

Gerald became instantly alarmed. 'No! No, sir, it wasn't like—'

'Did you give it to her as security against a good screw, or did you hope she might think it was an American Express?'

'No, sir, no! It wasn't like that at all!'

24

'You must think I've come down with the la
rain, lad! You are in this sordid little mess righ
neck, and what I want from you now is a l
classmates who were with you.'

At that moment, Gerald finally realized that he and the Metropolitan Police were doomed to part company. The only matter still to be decided was should he take his colleagues with him? There would be scant satisfaction in that. There would be much more pleasure to be derived out of frustrating the bumptious old sod in front of him.

'I attended that club on my own, sir, and I left the place on my own. Other than that I have nothing more to say.'

'Well, I have! I am beginning to think it may be no bad idea if you resigned from this force. Perhaps it is as well that the flaws in your character have emerged now and not when some totally innocent party is depending upon you. I will therefore ask you for the last time—Who was with you at that club?'

'I will therefore *tell* you for the last time—no one!' snapped Gerald.

'It's a great pity, you know,' sighed the chief superintendent condescendingly. 'You were the class captain and your course record was an excellent one. Yet as a result of your stubborn attitude, there are now men going out to division who should not be in this force at all. Do you not realize that?'

'The only thing I realize, sir, is that I am leaving and the rest of my class are staying.'

'I take it by that you *are* resigning?'

'Yes.'

'Very well. Collect your personal belongings and report to the admin office as soon as possible. That is all.' The chief superintendent picked up a pen and bowed his head, indicating clearly that the audience was now at an end.

Gerald walked slowly back to the residents' block. It would seem quite strange to leave the place—he felt that he had been there years. Waiting for him outside his room were his compatriots from the previous night. There had

25

an hour's mechanical delay before their coach was
ady to take them out to division.

'What happened?' Helen asked anxiously.

Gerald briefly recounted the gist of the interview.

'Well then, there's no problem,' said Angela. 'We'll
simply go and tell him the whole story.'

'No!' Gerald exclaimed with an insistence that surprised
them all. 'You'll do nothing of the kind! Look, I'm leaving
now and that's definite. I have resigned and there is no
going back. It's done, finished, finito! If you go in there and
confess all, it won't just be you four who'll get the chop, it'll
also fall on your friend on the gate. All due respect to you,
Angela, but the sight of your bare arse in the fishpond will
have been small consolation to the poor bugger if he gets
the sack.'

'It's not on, Gerry,' David cut in. 'We can't possibly
leave you to carry the can for the rest of us.'

'I am *not* carrying the can! I am simply leaving of my own
accord—honest, Dave. I realize now that I could never
work under such restrictions. It's just not for me. What will
you gain if you go in there and confess all? Nothing!' he said,
answering his own question.

'He is right, you know,' whispered Helen softly. She
walked the two paces towards him and slipped her arms
around his neck. She tilted her forehead until it rested upon
his chest. Gerald instinctively put his lips to the top of her
head.

'Come on now, I've lots to do,' he urged. He hooked a
finger under Helen's chin and tenderly lifted her tearful
face. The sobs, strangely enough, came from Angela who
had sympathetically buried her face into Michael's broad
shoulder.

They escorted Gerald to the admin office and began their
goodbyes. 'Chief superintendent wants to see you four
urgently,' called the admin sergeant, looking up from his
typewriter. 'You'd better get your skates on, he's not in a
very good mood.'

'Don't forget now,' reminded Gerald in a whisper.

'Don't you let me down. Say as little as possible and stick to it. Good luck.'

The chief superintendent's attack was fairly predictable. It revolved around poor Gerald being left to face the cold outside world because of the cowardly refusal of 'some people' to own up. The new concern being expressed for the departing class captain was hardly in keeping with his earlier treatment.

'Say little and stick to it' had been no bad advice. There was, of course, no doubt whatever in the chief superintendent's mind that all five had been in the club. He also had no doubt that they were not going to admit to it. Given sufficient time, he would have concentrated upon the older girl. She was obviously the most emotional and therefore the most vulnerable. On reflection though, he thought the matter had turned out quite well. After all, within a few hours of receiving a complaint, he had been able to present a sacrifice. No one could bitch about that. Gerald had lost his Metropolitan Police warrant card and the Metropolitan Police had lost Gerald. All in all, a fair swop.

'Okay, I'll waste no more time on this matter. But—' He paused and adopted his very strict stare. This was an expression that he kept for recruits whom he believed were getting the better of him. 'DO not delude yourselves into believing this matter has been forgotten—it hasn't.' The last sentence was as rehearsed as the stare.

The small, grey, single-decker coach pulled slowly away from the residents' block. Its complement of young passengers waved a sad goodbye to a couple of indifferent cleaners. Gerald's resignation had completely overshadowed what should have been an exciting time. The steady rain that had been falling all morning added a depressing dimension to a sombre day.

This 'delivery run' was never a favourite with the civilian drivers, meandering as it did through the worst of London's traffic. The first drop at Chingford was easy. But then came a tortuous run via Tottenham and the Isle of Dogs to

Chelsea. It was early afternoon before the bus reached Chelsea Police Station. There was still an hour's journey to the last call of the day at Cabul Lane.

'What do you reckon it's like there?' asked Angela to no one in particular. 'I've never been to south London before. They say it's quite rough.'

'I used to work around Cabul Lane,' said David matter of factly. 'I did a paper-round there.'

'Did you?' asked Helen in a surprised tone. 'Did you actually live there?'

'For a short time. I was fostered to a family a short distance down the market.'

'What was it like?' interrupted Angela with genuine interest.

'The area? Or being fostered?'

'Both really, I suppose.'

'The area's okay. There's a load of rubbish spoken about many parts of London. I should know—I've lived in enough of them. It's no better and no worse than any inner-city area anywhere in the country.'

'And what about fostering?' Angela persisted.

David shrugged. 'My mother died when I was two. My dad was killed a few years later. I seemed to spend most of my life in other people's houses.'

'Yes, but what's it *like*?' repeated Angela.

'What do you mean—what's it like? How do I know what it's like? I would only know what it was like if I had experience of anything else—and I haven't. It's just— well, it's all right, that's about all I can say.'

'Perhaps you delivered my papers,' said Helen, trying to change the subject. 'I used to live around here too.'

'I always thought you came from Dorset,' said Michael.

'I do! But it was ten years ago that I lived here and then it was only for a short while. I was a bit daft at the time, I suppose. I moved in with a feller. I was only eighteen at the time and we were going to get married. He was the manager of a carpet shop and occupied the flat above it.'

28

'What happened—about the marriage, I mean?' asked Angela.

'We didn't get around to it,' shrugged Helen.

'Why?'

'The very best of reasons, I suppose.'

'You were too young,' said Michael.

'No! He was already married,' Helen answered wryly. 'Although there's no doubt I *was* too young as well.'

'If I had my way,' broke in Michael philosophically, 'I would ban all marriages under the age of thirty. I just don't know why people rush into the bloody thing. Every one of my friends who got married in their teens have broken up—every one!' he emphasized. 'Long engagements, that's what we need. A nice five-year engagement gives them plenty of time to get sick to death of each other.'

'We'll be there in a few minutes,' announced Dave, glancing at familiar streets. 'It doesn't seem to have changed much. How about your carpet shop manager, does he still live in the area?'

'I don't know, I haven't seen or heard from him since.'

'I bet he's got half a dozen kids by now. You'll probably have to escort them across the road.'

Helen smiled ruefully. 'It would never surprise me—he was a bit like that.'

The coach slowed for a throng of pedestrians crossing to a market. 'We're here,' announced Dave. 'Welcome to Cabul Lane nick, everyone.'

Cabul Lane Police Station was a grey-bricked, nineteenth-century building, situated in a short street just off the main road. The back yard of the station had been of ample size when it simply housed six horses and two handbarrows that were used to wheel in the Victorian inebriates. But the yard, like the building itself, had never quite made the transition into the twentieth century.

'I'll never be able to get this bus anywhere near that dump,' complained the driver. 'You'll all have to get out and carry your gear for the rest of the way.'

'Oh! Thanks a bunch, mate,' said Angela through gritted

teeth as she struggled with two suitcases, a large canvas holdall and a folded spare uniform. 'The tip is under the seat.'

'I don't know why you've got so much luggage,' said Michael, shaking his head. 'You must be the smallest copper in the force and you've got the most bloody clothes!'

The late-afternoon shoppers showed complete indifference as they scuttled in and out of the burdened quartet. Reaching the steps of the station, they found the usual long queue of customers stretching from the front counter. At the suggestion of a passing PC—who did little else to help—they made their way to the heavy wooden gate at the rear of the station. This led directly into the back yard. As they struggled through the huge gates, the angry, persistent bell of an approaching police van could be heard as it swung in from the main road. It reached the gateway just as the zip of Angela's holdall burst open. A dozen or so of her more intimate garments fluttered brightly in the strong breeze. The van screeched to a halt and once more the bell rang out impatiently.

'All right! All right! I'm being as quick as I can!' yelled the flustered girl as she gathered up the tumbling wisps. Yet again the bell cut into the gusty afternoon air, but this time it brought a running, shirt-sleeved sergeant from within the confines of the building.

'It's the Weasel!' called the driver as he launched himself from his seat and into the interior of the van. The vehicle rocked on its springs as thuds and yells could be heard. The jacketless sergeant wrenched open the rear double doors. The four recruits could now see everything clearly as the struggle was silhouetted against the windscreen. The van driver had dived to the assistance of a fair-haired copper in the rear of the vehicle who appeared to be receiving an almighty battering at the hands of the van's other occupant —a tall, powerfully built, bearded individual.

The figure at the rear of the van reached in and seized the struggling prisoner by the collar. 'C'mere, you greasy bastard!' he grunted. This action caused the prisoner to

30

kick out with renewed energy, and from the way that the driver suddenly reeled back it was very apparent that at least one boot had found its target. Both officers in the van were now almost incapacitated.

'D'you think we should help out?' asked David, somewhat ponderously.

Michael, however, was already on his way. Although the sergeant had managed to pinion the prisoner's arms, his legs were still unfettered and were lashing out in all directions. Michael's rugby tackle caught the youth knee-high in a tight armlock and, although his struggles continued, they lost much of their early intensity. The van driver meantime had slowly regained his feet.

'Right! We've got him now,' grunted the sergeant. 'Cuff him, Frank, and let's get him in the bloody charge-room.'

Michael was curious to see the face of the cause of this mayhem and, from his crouching position at the prisoner's feet, unwisely looked up. A rapid burst of phlegm-ridden spittle splattered untidily across the bridge of his nose. With a roar he released his arm hold on the 'Weasel's' knees and leapt to his feet. The punch he threw was ferocious rather than accurate and the quickly turned head of the prisoner caused it to glance from his bearded jaw. Eric Neville Tomlinson, a police sergeant of some twenty years, had never before been the victim of an assault. Michael Kevin Butler, a police constable for all of four months, redressed that little peculiarity within thirty seconds of arriving at the station. The blow itself was bad enough, but the weight of it caused the sergeant to topple backwards from the rear of the van, together with the prisoner and the blow's perpetrator.

Help by this time was arriving from several quarters, including, of course, the bewildered new trio who were already wondering just what they had let themselves in for. The dazed sergeant was led gently into the doctor's room, and the aggressive prisoner was rather less gently propelled into the charge-room. In the main, the barrage of questions thrown at Michael basically boiled down to one main theme: 'Just who the fuck are you?'

31

Peter Hill, alias 'The Weasel', now sat subdued in the corner of the charge-room with his greasy head held firmly in his equally greasy hands. The nickname of the Weasel was by now totally unsuitable. At six feet and fourteen stone, he had really outgrown it. It dated back to his early teens when he had first come to the attention of police. Then, just four years or so previously, he had been a thin scrag of a rebel who had decided to kick against every form of authority, mainly his teachers and his father. It had seemed then that he was destined to grow up somewhat below average height and well below average build. Yet within those few years he had filled out into a miniature giant. He may have become larger but he certainly hadn't become cleaner and the hair on his head and face had now amalgamated into a lank, greasy mess.

The Weasel was well known to most of the neighbouring stations. His customary practice was to become drunk and then attack—verbally to begin with—anything he saw as authority, ranging from bus conductors to doctors. He was particularly severe on anything in uniform. Although frequently drunk, his capacity for alcohol was surprisingly small. Two pints would be enough to make him argumentative, three would turn him into a roaring belligerent. These moods did not last long though and would pass just as quickly as they had begun. Peter would then revert to his customary self—a sullen, uncommunicative youth greatly in need of a wash.

This aversion to washing stemmed, understandably, from his current abode. He shared a flat with four other semi-vagrants in an old block soon for demolition. This accommodation was little more than a squat but, because of its condition, the council allowed it to be occupied for just a nominal rent. Possessing, as he now did, a permanent address, Peter was usually bailed just as soon as he was sober.

It could be said that in spite of his lifestyle he had led something of a charmed existence. He had yet to be imprisoned for any length of time, and his treatment by police during his many apprehensions had been far more circumspect than his conduct may have warranted. Even that very day he was to be charged for being drunk and disorderly and not with the more serious offence of assault on police. It was true that most of the bruises and grazes that he had inflicted had, after examination, proved to be superficial, but many miscreants had been put away for less.

There was, in fact, a reason for this tolerance. A tolerance that had been all but abandoned by the haymaker that Michael had so inaccurately thrown. Kathy and Ron Hill, who had seemingly failed so miserably with their youngest son, had in fact succeeded admirably with his graduate older brother. It was possible that Peter could never have reached the same high standard and had therefore decided not to try. Whatever the cause, it was unquestionably killing his mother. If it was killing his mother, it was not doing his father much good, particularly in his capacity as chief inspector at Cabul Lane Police Station!

It seemed, therefore, that Peter was putting more effort into destroying his father's career than any other project that had taken his interest since he had set fire to the Scouts' hut for the third occasion. It was the need to combat this destruction that was felt so strongly amongst the street-duty men and women of Cabul Lane. This feeling may have not been quite so determined had Ron Hill not been about the most respected senior officer south of the Thames. Even so, everyone realized this benevolence could not last. Sooner or later, respect or no respect, Peter-the-Weasel Hill was due his comeuppance. It was not to be this day, however, for within two hours of being charged, he was yet again bailed and sullenly left the station.

It is doubtful if any four recruits, or perhaps one should say three, had ever made such a combined impact on a police station before. Michael obviously held pride of place by smashing the sergeant between the eyes within seconds of arriving. The general enthusiasm for Angela's undies was only bettered by the lip-pursing approval for the

33

statuesque Helen. The blow to the sergeant's face, although hard, at least had some of the sting removed by the Weasel's beard. It had also landed fair-square and, although a couple of black eyes were confidently forecast by several suspiciously over-sympathetic constables, at least no cuts were sustained.

One of the first requirements of any recruit to a police station is the obligatory interview with the superintendent. This will usually take the form of a pep-talk in which the pet theories that all superintendents nurse can best be inflicted upon the captive audience. These theories are as many and varied as the superintendents themselves. However, it would be fair to assume that most of them deal with such matters as appearance, attitude to the public, and presenting the force at all times in the best possible image. Some superintendents have even been known to fetch up such controversial themes as *crime*, but, in the main, this subject is taboo. Superintendent Heath on the other hand was unique. His special subject was one which he honestly believed had been badly neglected for years throughout the force. He claimed it was synonymous with all that was wrong with present-day policing. 'After all, if we look after the pennies, young man,' he would say, irrespective of what sex he was speaking to, 'the pounds will look after themselves.'

Few recruits would have a clue what this meant. They would sensibly nod in agreement whilst promising faithfully to back him to the hilt. Then, just as they were about to leave, he would spring it on them. This revolutionary theory about the running of the force would be expounded and driven home with a true Yorkshire fanaticism. 'Do you know what is wrong with this force? Well, do you?' he would glower.

Not wishing to be presumptuous in the presence of one so sure of himself, especially when that 'one' is a superintendent, they would all shake their heads dumbly.

'Well, I'll tell you what is wrong with this force! Teacups! That's what's wrong—bloody teacups! Teacups are indicative of every flaw this job has.'

Now the average police recruit, of either sex, joins the force basically because if they did not, they would be unemployed. There are a few, a precious few, who join because that is their destiny. If this latter group are so rare, then those that even *begin* to understand the teacup theory are minuscule. Of the four who stood in front of him that afternoon, at least two of them thought he meant he actually *read* the things. Angela seriously wondered if every time she drained a cup she would be expected to study the formation of leaves in the bottom.

'You just watch them,' continued the superintendent, punching home every syllable with a podgy finger. 'Show me a person who returns his empty cup to the counter and I will show you the backbone of the force. But how many times does a police car drive into this yard and the driver dump his cup just anywhere? Every blasted shift, that's how often! But it won't last—oh no! I'll have them yet. It's the small things that count in the long run. Remember—if you look after the pennies, the pounds will look after themselves. Right, close the door and see the clerk on your way out. He will give you your postings.'

Sergeant Sid Meecham, the superintendent's clerk, sat at his desk adjacent to the superintendent's office, checking the annual leave register. He glanced up as the bewildered four filed back into his room. He recognized the puzzled expressions from the scores of previous interviewees.

'Afternoon, all. This is usually the moment when someone will say to me, "What the bleedin' hell was that all about"—Yes?' All four nodded in unison. 'Well, if you don't know, you're in excellent company. Anyway, here are your postings.' He rummaged through the mass of papers on his desk before finally discovering a typewritten memo. Peering over the top of his spectacles, he went into a short explanation. 'The station works a four-shift system, or "reliefs" as we call them. I have decided to split you into pairs—it will mean you will know at least one bugger. Suit you?'

'Yes, thank you, Sergeant,' breathed Helen gratefully.

'Hmmm,' murmured Meecham, almost to himself. 'You could just be a problem to me, girl. I can feel it.' He took an exaggerated deep breath and continued. 'Miss Helms, you will be WPC 590 MP and you will, together with David Ducker—who will be PC 627 MP—join "B" relief, under Inspector Dunn. You may find him a bit stern at first but there isn't a better duty officer in the whole of the Met.' The sergeant again checked his memo before resuming his briefing. 'You, Miss Rogers, will be WPC 486 MP and will, of course, join this young man here who will, from henceforth, be PC 171 MP Butler. You will both join "C" relief under the good offices of one Inspector Wilson. "C" relief are early-turn tomorrow morning—parade at six forty-five sharp; and "B" relief are night-duty tomorrow night—parade at ten forty-five, equally sharp. Any questions?'

'How about our accommodation, Sarge?' asked Dave.

'Well, you two fellows will be over at Gatton Road section-house, and you two young ladies are up at White Stone Park.'

'Sergeant?' queried Helen.

'Oh yes, I'm sorry, you don't know where that is, do you? Well, it used to be a police nursing home, hence the rather Victorian name. It's a detached old house standing in its own small grounds, bit like a seaside guesthouse. Only one-star though, I'm afraid. The one advantage you girls have over the fellows is that your place is within a good walking distance of the nick. In fact, it's actually on the perimeter of our manor—best part of it too!'

'Are we—er, strictly segregated?' asked Michael predictably.

'Twenty years ago you wouldn't have been allowed on the pavement outside the place!' said the old sergeant, shaking his head wistfully. 'But now you can play Wee Willie Winke with every plonk in the hostel providing you don't do it on duty, and other than their fathers, no bugger will give a damn. Answer your question, son?'

Michael reddened. 'I—I didn't mean that to sound like it did, Sarge. It's just that all four of us are good friends and I wondered if we could visit each other, that's all.'

36

'Oh yes, you can visit all right and I'm pleased that subject came up. Before I commit these postings to the official list, are any of you four emotionally involved with each other so to speak? I ask this because it is *not* a good policy to work on the same shift with someone with whom you have a close relationship. It's not like a bank, you know. It can be quite tough out there at times and we want no avenging angels just because the light of your life has got herself a thick lip. Speak now or belt up.'

There was a long silence before Helen finally spoke. 'We have no special relationships, Sergeant, but can I ask a question?'

'Of course.'

'Sergeant, what is a "plonk"?'

'A plonk, young lady, is *you*—a WPC. You will find that out here, on the districts, you will be referred to as a plonk on most occasions. I can't honestly tell you *how* the name derived but I would guess it has an obscene origin and relates to the part of your anatomy that sits down. ANY more questions?' He looked from one to the other. 'No? Very well then, I'll arrange for the van to drop you off at your respective accommodations. That is, providing of course that the van driver speaks to you, Butler.'

Three-quarters of an hour later, the girls waved their farewells as the van drove away from White Stone Park leaving them with their baggage in the hallway. The old building was much as they had imagined, with small, compact bedrooms and a bath and toilet on each landing. It seemed a fairly quiet place with just the television in the smaller of the two lounges disturbing the tranquillity.

The rain had ceased and, although it was now quite dark, London had a clean-washed air about it.

'It's quite a nice evening now, Angie,' commented Helen. 'Let's have a quick look around the garden before we turn in.'

'Let's look tomorrow in the daylight,' replied Angela unenthusiastically. 'I'm not mad keen on gardens and, in any case, I've changed my shoes.'

'Well, I'll just have a quick peep by myself. I'm early-turn in the morning and it'll still be dark when I leave. Won't be long.'

'I'm going to have a hot soak,' Angela said wearily. 'It's been a hell of a long day. Look in on your way to bed —yes?'

'Will do.'

Helen stepped out on to the gravel path and was instantly delighted how fresh and clean everything smelt in the late autumn air. The hostel was situated upon a hill and a surprisingly good view of the lights of central London could be seen between the tall bushes and branches. She wondered if she would be able to see St Paul's and if it would be illuminated. Moving between two dark trees for a better vantage point, a flash of light caught her attention. She glanced back towards the hostel where she could clearly see Angela in the bathroom. Quickly checking the garden, she saw that it was surprisingly secluded and in no way overlooked. Just as well with that full-length window, she thought. As she turned once more towards St Paul's she was fractionally aware of the faintest of footsteps before every light in the world went out.

CHAPTER THREE

The police van had threaded its way through the evening traffic, depositing both Michael and Dave at the Gatton Road section-house. In comparison to many such abodes the building was almost contemporary. A spacious red-brick structure, it offered more than the young men had dared to hope. All in all, the first impressions had been of rather pleasant surprise.

On the van driver's instructions, they reported to the warden's office. Once there, 'Old Cyril', an ex-artillery corporal and now section-house warden, allocated them their rooms. There were thirty or so of these units on each of the five floors of the building and the pair were delighted to be allocated adjoining rooms. These consisted of a bed, washbasin, and a limited amount of bedroom furniture. The building housed single police personnel from all over south-east London. With most of the residents from different shifts and at a variety of stations, there was a constant toing and froing.

One of David's first actions was to enquire about the laundry facilities. Like many single men he had an accumulation of sports clothing, much of it in need of a wash. 'Is there a launderette or something close by?' he asked the warden.

'It's not a launderette that your tracksuit needs,' cut in Michael, pinching his nose in mock reproof. 'It's an incinerator!'

'*Is* there a laundry?' Dave persisted, pointedly ignoring his friend's sarcasm.

'There is if you look lively,' announced the old soldier, glancing up at the clock. 'You could just about make the Coin-op Wash afore it shuts.'

'Well where is this Coin-op Wash and how long have I got?'

'Two streets away and it closes at nine.'

The young recruit gave an exaggerated sigh and sat down. 'It's a waste of time then, it's almost that now.'

'Why don't you listen, boy?' growled the warden irritably. 'If you stop fart-arsing about and get your skates on, you can be along there in two minutes. You don't even have to wash the stuff yourself. Unless you're a real tight sod, Brenda will do it for you. You just give her a couple of bob and collect it tomorrow.'

David was practically out of the door before the warden had stopped speaking. 'Don't you want to know where it is?' Cyril called after him. The young man skidded to a halt. 'It's the second turning on the right and Brenda is the manageress. And don't you dare upset her!' called the old soldier once more to the fast-departing figure. 'She's an absolute bloody diamond!'

'Get the coffees in, Mickey,' sang out David over his shoulder as he ploughed through the shiny black puddles. 'I'll be back in four minutes.'

Brenda Flynn turned the second key in the lock and gave the door a trial push as she did so. Through omitting that little procedure she had once been called out on a bitter wet night and had no desire to repeat the experience. The day-long rain had deterred the early evening customers and caused Brenda to close shop a little before time. The alternative, she felt, would be a rush of late washers all taking advantage of the improved weather. She had barely turned away from the door when she heard the running footsteps.

Dave took the situation in at a glance and stopped a few paces short of the doorway. 'Oh,' he murmured, staring obviously down at his watch, 'I was told you were open until nine.'

'Why? What've you got there?' asked Brenda, pointing to his holdall and ignoring the obvious innuendo.

'Just some sports gear.'

40

'*Just* some sports gear?' she echoed. 'Muddy and smelly, no doubt.'

Dave was about to make a retort when he remembered Old Cyril's words and decided upon a different approach. 'I was recommended to see you by the section-house warden. He said you were a diamond. Twenty-two carat, in fact.'

She felt herself blush and was instantly annoyed by her own reactions. Compliments had been scarce in her life and she could never take them easily, particularly when they came second-hand.

'Look, don't patronize me, just tell me what it is that you want,' she snapped, with a degree of irritation that she knew was out of proportion.

'I just want some sports gear washed, that's all. But if it's too much trouble . . .' He gave a shrug.

'What an infuriating young man you are! Are you always like this?'

'Like what?' Dave said sharply, also beginning to become very annoyed.

'Like . . .' She paused and shook her head rapidly as she searched for words. 'Like . . . like . . . *supercilious*. That's what!'

'I'm not even sure I know what that means,' answered Dave, now rising to the bait.

'Well, it *could* mean you were a pompous, stuck-up sod. In fact, I'm beginning to think that's just what it *does* mean!'

Dave stared at her for a moment and was surprised to find his annoyance rapidly subsiding. He raised his hands in mock surrender. 'I give in, can I start again, please?'

She smiled just the tiniest of tired smiles. 'Okay, start again. But please, don't patronize me, eh?'

'Look, Cyril not only said that you were a diamond but also that you would possibly wash my sports gear and that I would be able to collect it in a day or so. Now, have I got that part right?'

'Yes,' she sighed wearily. 'You've got it right. C'mon back to the shop. I'll not wash it tonight though, but at least

I won't have to carry it to and from home.' Rummaging in the deep nylon pockets of her shapeless blue overall she finally produced the key and reopened the door. 'Just put it over there on top of the machine. D'you want to pick it up here or from my home?'

'What's the difference?'

She shook her head. 'None. It's just that sometimes you coppers can't get here during shopping hours. If I know you are calling I'll keep it at home. It's of no great consequence, I only live two minutes away.'

Dave knew that, if anything, it would be easier to pick up the laundry from the shop. He also knew he did not want to do this. There was something about her that intrigued—almost fascinated—him. He had to know more about this woman—for woman she certainly was. He guessed her age as around forty and could hardly help noticing the thick gold ring on her finger. Her flat-soled sandals and ill-shaped overall did nothing at all for a plumpish figure. Yet she was not without a certain beauty. There were times in conversation when she would turn her head suddenly. Then a mass of tumbling fair hair would swing sensuously around to reclaim its position alongside her cheeks and neck. This, together with her deep-green eyes and wide, handsome face, appeared beauty enough. David waited as she locked the shop door for the second time that evening.

'Look,' he faltered. 'I've—er, made you late, I'm afraid. Let me walk you home.'

'Good heavens, son, it's only round the corner.'

He smarted inwardly at the word 'son'. 'Well, I'll need to know where to come when I pick up my clean gear.'

'It's 99A Sutterden Street, just above the greengrocers, but if it makes you happy you can come along now. Don't come empty-handed though, you can carry the shopping.'

The weight of the two shopping bags surprised him. 'However many in your family? These weigh a ton.'

'Why is it that men always complain about the weight of shopping? Women just accept it. Would you like me to take it back off you?'

42

'O' course not,' said the young man bravely. 'It's not *that* heavy. It's just that I thought it was rather a lot for you to carry.'

'You get used to it,' she murmured matter of factly. 'In any case, I'm hardly a delicate girl.'

'So how many are there?'

'How many what?'

'In your family,' he persisted.

'Oh, just the four of us. The three kids and me.'

He wanted to ask about the obvious missing member but lacked courage.

She answered for him, however. 'I'm a widow and have been for four years—satisfied?'

He struggled for words. 'I'm . . . sorry, it's just that— well—'

She cut him short. 'Don't be, I'm not. None of us are.' She gestured towards a brown-painted door at the side of a greengrocers. 'That's it, that's "Flynn Towers", or at least the west wing of it. You can drop those shopping bags now.'

'I've fetched it so far I may as well carry it upstairs—yes?'

She stared at him for a moment. 'You're a strange lad. Most boys of your age would have dumped it and run. Perhaps I should take you home and give you to my Sandra for her birthday—she'd love you.' She gave a brief smile, then added, 'C'mon then, but watch the stairs, they're dangerous.'

Sandra Flynn looked up at the clock as she heard the front door close. 'Is that you, Mum?' The double set of footsteps had caused her just a little anxiety.

'It certainly is, love,' came back Brenda's voice. 'Who were you expecting—Prince Charming? Because if you were, you're in luck. He's not only here but he's carried home the shopping!' The door swung open and the couple entered. 'Put the bags down anywhere. This is Sandra—my eldest, she's nineteen tomorrow. Sandra, this young man is —Oh, I'm sorry but I don't know your name.'

Dave shuffled uncomfortably. 'It's David—Dave Ducker.'

'That's a letdown, Mum! Dave Ducker? You told me he was Prince Charming!' Dave felt himself crimson.

'As far as I'm concerned, young lady,' declared Brenda, 'anyone who carries two bags of my shopping up them stairs definitely *is* Prince Charming!'

It was easy to discern the family likeness of mother and daughter. While the girl was much fairer—in fact, almost blonde—she moved, looked and sounded just like a streamlined version of her mother. She was, in effect, a very attractive young lady. David was invited to stay for tea and discovered that of the two youngest children, nine-year-old Danny was asleep in bed, while fourteen-year-old Jackie was sharing her homework with a friend next door.

While Brenda left the room to make the tea, Sandra began to make small talk. She asked about his interests, his taste in music and if he had a current girlfriend. He gave polite but almost noncommittal responses. As the girl talked, he searched the room with his eyes but was unable to find what he sought. There were photographs by the dozen, on shelves, cupboards and walls, but although every stage of the three youngsters' lives was encapsulated in the frames, not one adult male could be seen. Brenda featured in the occasional picture and looked particularly devastating in some of the earlier ones, but of the father, her husband, there was never a sign.

'Can I ask you something?' asked Dave, cutting suddenly in on the girl's chatter.

'Anything you like,' Sandra responded cheerfully. 'And no. I don't have a *current* boyfriend. Although—'

'What happened to your father?'

There was a rattle of teacups from behind him, followed by a thud as the door swung fully open and collided with the short rubber doorstop.

'Why'd you ask?' demanded Brenda in a flat, unemotional voice.

Dave turned and reddened. 'I dunno, I never knew my own family and I just wondered . . . .'

'There's no secret,' said Brenda in the same flat tone.

She placed the tray on the table without once looking at it, while staring defiantly at the young questioner. 'My husband was a brutal bastard who beat the daylights out of us—Sandra, Jackie, little Danny. It didn't matter which, he did it to us all. Some of the things he did to those two girls were evil. Four years ago—a week before Sandra's fifteenth birthday—he got his comeuppance. He walked drunkenly into the traffic just one time too many. No tears were shed in this house, I can tell you. Do you have any idea what fear is? Do you?' Without waiting for a response she continued. 'Fear is drunken footsteps coming up the stairs, that's what fear is. It grips your guts and ties 'em in knots. D'you know, we've actually wet ourselves before he even opened the door? Did you know that?' Her eyes finally left the young man's face as she fussily arranged the cups to her own satisfaction.

'I'm sorry,' whispered Dave. 'I really am. It was none of my business and I shouldn't have—'

'Forget it—please?' Brenda requested, with a softening of voice. She gave a wry grin. 'I keep having a go at you, don't I? I'm not usually like this, honest. It's just that whenever we talk about Tom's accident, people can never really understand how relieved we were. I always feel that they think we were bloody-minded or something. Or perhaps, even worse, that we pushed the poor bugger into the traffic!'

'If it's any consolation,' offered Dave, 'I must have been fostered with at least a dozen families and although most of them were as good as gold, there were at least three that I would have willingly pushed under buses.'

Brenda gave her biggest smile of the evening before knuckling away a solitary tear from the corner of her left eye.

The next hour slipped quickly by as the trio swopped family history. Their conversation was only interrupted by the return of Jackie. If Sandra was a copy of her mother, then her sister was straight out of the same mould.

'I'd better be going,' Dave announced, glancing reluctantly at his watch. 'My mate will be wondering what's happened to me.'

'When would you like your cleaning back?' asked Brenda.

'Is Thursday okay? I'll need it for the weekend.'

'Well, Thursday is early-closing day but if you'd like to ring the bell downstairs any time after two in the afternoon. I'll have it ready for you,' Brenda offered.

'If he calls for it around six o'clock he can stay for tea, can't he, Mum?' asked Sandra quickly. 'He'll be able to tell us about his first few nights as a real policeman then.'

'Yes, that's a nice idea,' agreed the older woman. 'Why don't you come?'

'I'd like that,' Dave said gratefully. 'I would like that very much indeed.'

Sandra accompanied him down the winding staircase and opened the street door. He wished her good-night but she cut him short. 'Don't I at least deserve a birthday kiss? After all, I'm nineteen in another—let me see—hour and thirty minutes.' She tiptoed and eased herself forward, raising her lips towards his face. At first he seemed to draw back but then he responded to her invitation with just the faintest of dry- lipped brushes. 'Is that *it*?' asked the girl in genuine puzzlement. 'Is *that* a birthday kiss?'

'Er—I'm sorry,' he stammered. 'I wasn't ready. I think I must have been surprised.'

'Would you like to try again?' asked the girl helpfully.

'I—I think perhaps I w–would.'

This time she took the whole initiative. In one smooth movement she eased herself towards him, slipping her arms slowly but firmly around his neck. Tilting her head provocatively to her right, she deliberately let both her perfume and body-warmth precede her moist, open-mouthed kiss. The only thing to be said in Dave's mitigation was that he did appear to try. True, he did not appear to try very much but there was definitely the resemblance of an effort.

'I think you were marginally better when you weren't ready,' laughed the girl without a hint of rancour. 'You are

46

going to find life very difficult in the force, young Constable, very difficult indeed. G'night.' She kissed her own right index finger and, tapping him lightly on the tip of his nose with it, closed the door.

Dave pushed through the glass swing-doors of the section-house and noticed the warden curled up with his pipe in his cosy small office. The old man roused and took the briar from his mouth with a dignified air of regality. He pointed it at the youngster like an accusing finger. 'Your mate's been looking everywhere for you. He thinks you've been lost, seduced or abducted. He seemed quite worried. Perhaps you'd better pop into the TV room and assure him you're alive. Did you see Brenda?'

'Uh-huh,' answered Dave noncommittally. 'Like you said—a diamond.' This unanimity seemed to reassure the warden and he lay back once more in his chair and closed his eyes.

The TV room was like a wood-panelled study, except there was not a book to be seen. Armchairs were scattered in irregular lines and cigarette ash surrounded the empty glass ashtrays that lay in abundance on the floor. The dark-brown décor and complete absence of lighting made visibility difficult. However, as Dave's eyes slowly adjusted to the darkness, he could see six or seven heads distributed amongst the chairs. On the coloured screen, a creaking coffin lid was being lowered. This gloomy scene slowly faded and the next sequence featured a horse-drawn hearse climbing a hillside in bright sunshine. The improved light from the television immediately bathed the room in a pale-yellow reflection. Mickey Butler lay back with his eyes shut and his feet on the arms of the chair in front of him.

'Oh yes!' announced David in a voice high with irony. 'It's easy to see you really *are* worried. You must have lost consciousness through sheer anxiety.'

Michael sleepily opened one eye. 'Eh? Oh, it's you! Where the bleedin' hell've you been? Your coffee's cold.' He pointed to a shadowy cup of mud-like substance, a good third of which appeared to be fermenting in the saucer.

47

Opening both eyes he leaned forward and squinted closely into Dave's face. 'Here, just a minute! You've got lipstick on your mouth. Where've you been, you dirty little sod?'

'The launderette, but don't let it worry you, it's nothing at all like you think. Look, I'm tired and it's been a long day. I'm going to bed. Are you staying here to watch that rubbish? If so, I'll say good-night.'

Michael rose to his feet and gave a long stretch and yawned. 'No, I'll turn in too. I've got an early start in the morning.' He nodded indifferently towards the television. 'Dracula has already bitten into Ingrid Pitt's neck *and* she's flashed her tits twice so there's not much more to see. You still haven't explained that lipstick on your kisser though.'

David had no intention of discussing the Flynns and in any case he had suddenly been hit by fatigue. He bade a good-night to his friend and closed his room door. The bed was firm but comfortable. Sleepily he ran over the day's events in his mind and smiled at the recollection of Michael's thumping of the station officer. He liked Michael a great deal but he was pleased that the pair of them were on separate shifts. Before he finally dropped off he began to accumulate thoughts of Brenda. He lay quite still in that darkened room as she encroached on his recollections. For almost an hour he flitted between sleep and wakefulness. At times she appeared so real he almost spoke to her. He had become dreamy with desire. A desire to hold her, to touch her hair with his face and perhaps even explore her soft body. Tomorrow he would be a policeman and that bothered him. Rules and laws, rules and laws. That was all they had taught him, rules and laws. Well, Brenda had broken a law, the law of trespass. She had trespassed in his mind and he was unable to move her out. She would have to be punished. Yes, of course, that's it—a punishment! As the last curtain of sleep began to envelop his mind, he thought of the penalty she must pay. A cuddle! That's it, a cuddle! But *what* a cuddle it would be! A cuddle so passionate and intense that she would have no choice but to give herself to him. He was about to place his arms around her waist when he slid reluctantly into oblivion.

48

CHAPTER FOUR

The short-stay ward was little more than an extension of much of the borough. Cramped, old-fashioned and down-at-heel, just a gallon or two of emulsion paint differentiated it from the workhouse. Helen lay in the first bed on the left and already considered she was suffering from too much attention. The blow that had smitten her had strangely not hurt at all, although there was a slight stiffness and ache around the base of her neck. She had, however, lain unconscious for almost an hour in those bushes before being discovered semi-naked by an anxious Angela. It would appear she had recovered remarkably well, being coherent and intelligible from the moment she had recovered consciousness. She felt quite well and had answered all the questions in an assured manner, yet they had still insisted on a twenty-four-hour stay in hospital for, as they put it, observation. Nurses appeared to queue to check her pulse, her blood pressure, or gaze at her dark-pupilled eyes. In spite of these interruptions, the only discomfort she was experiencing was from the several deep scratches across the small of her back. It would seem that these had been caused by brambles as she had been dragged into the bushes.

Seldom had such a brand-new recruit made the instant acquaintance of so many officers. Such numbers had called that the ward sister had become definitely tetchy. Detective Inspector Bromley was due his second visit in four hours and this time he was to be accompanied by a woman detective sergeant. He had explained to Helen on his previous visit that he would be needing a written statement. He had hoped that the four-hour interval between the two visits would assist the girl to remember more details of the attack. Sadly, the idea had not worked. She remembered no more about the incident on his second arrival than she did when she first found herself lying spread-eagled in those damp bushes.

A harassed nurse approached the bed with the third bunch of flowers of the day. 'There's a lady and a gentleman to see you. They are just having a quick word with Sister.' She paused thoughtfully for a moment then added almost to herself, 'Well, actually, Sister is having a quick word with them. I'll give you some curtain screens.'

'Why do I need screens if I'm only having visitors?' asked the puzzled patient.

'I think that Doctor will be with them and no doubt she'll want to examine you again.'

'No doubt she will,' echoed Helen with a note of irritation.

'Look, love,' said the nurse in a quiet, friendly voice. 'So you've been attacked. You're not the first, you know, not even in this ward. Believe me, everyone who has called on you so far has done so with your welfare at heart. We've had girls in here who have been beaten so badly that their own families couldn't recognize them. In many respects you've been very lucky, so just bear with everyone for a little longer, eh?'

'I'm sorry,' murmured Helen. 'It's just that I feel such a fraud. There's absolutely nothing wrong with me and it seems such a waste of everyone's time. But you *are* right, of course.'

'Good girl,' smiled the nurse as she closed the last of the drapes.

Soon the sound of approaching footsteps was followed by the swish of the curtains as the female doctor and the two police-officers appeared suddenly at the bedside.

'Morning, Miss Rogers,' said the inspector brightly. 'This is Detective Sergeant Keegan. She's going to take a statement from you. Dr Sproston you already know and she is just here to help out with any technicalities that may arise. All right?'

'All right,' agreed the girl.

'Before we start, can you remember any more detail than you did this morning—anything at all?'

'I'm sorry, no.'

'You seemed to be in no doubt then that you weren't sexually assaulted. Are you still of that opinion?'

'I'm sure of it.'

'Even though you were unconscious at the time?'

'Even though I was unconscious at the time.'

'Is that possible, Doctor?' asked the inspector.

'Well, we gave the patient a thorough "internal" and took samples from her. There was not a trace of bruising or of any interference on her whatsoever.'

'Okay, so we've established she wasn't raped but how about indecent assault? Is there any evidence of that?'

'The same rules apply. There is absolutely no evidence of interference anywhere on her body. Of course, it would not be possible to prove any *superficial* indecency. The patient herself would be the best judge of that. Yet she says she has no discomfort at all, other than the bramble marks on her back.'

'Teeth marks?'

'None.'

'Forgive me, Doctor, but have you searched everywhere?'

'Every inch of her.'

Helen could feel herself reddening. 'Do I get a say, sir?' she asked curtly.

'What is it that you *want* to say, miss?'

'It's true I'm not a virgin but neither am I a fool. If anyone had been tampering with me don't you think I would know it?'

The inspector shook his head. 'No, I don't necessarily think you would. Tell me, exactly what items of clothing were you wearing when you recovered consciousness?'

'Coat, cardigan, shirt and tie, I think.'

'Nothing else?'

'Well, I don't know if you want to include my bra.'

'Did you have it on?'

51

'Partly I did.'

'Partly?'

'Yes, it was in place on my right breast but it had been removed from my left.'

'So there you were, minus shoes, tights, skirt, half a bra and knickers, lying in the bushes for the best part of an hour and you claim you were not even touched? And how did he get the bra from your left breast for heaven's sake? Divine intervention? Good heavens, girl, just the physical act of tearing off your clothes is an indecent assault!' Helen shook her head determinedly but made no reply. 'Why are you so reluctant to come to terms with this? I grant you that if you had been raped you would know it. All I am saying is that you would not know if you had been sexually handled or abused whilst you were unconscious. You see, you are not the first young lady this has happened to on this manor recently. In fact, there have been two others, both nurses.'

'Did they see him?' asked Helen sharply.

'No more than you did.'

'What was the result of their injuries?'

'The first had a fractured skull and the second one a broken collarbone. So you see, you were very lucky.'

Helen nodded slowly in dumb agreement. 'These nurses, were they . . . were they touched in any way, sir? Sexually, I mean.'

The inspector looked thoughtful for a moment but then replied, 'Seemingly not, except perhaps for one thing.'

'And that is?' asked the girl.

The inspector glanced at the detective sergeant who now leaned forward and spoke for the first time. 'Your clothes, Helen, did you get them all back?'

'I think so,' said the girl uncertainly. 'They are in that plastic bag in the bedside locker. They told me that the Scenes of Crime Officer is calling later today to examine them.'

The detective sergeant picked up the bag and tipped the contents on to a newspaper at the foot of the bed. She spread them out by using a closed biro-pen.

52

'Is anything missing, love?'

'Yes,' said Helen instantly. 'My panties are not there. They are blue with my initials on the left top. They are part of a set that I had for my birthday.'

The detective sergeant looked instantly at the inspector and that gentleman gave a groan. 'That's all I need. It looks like we've got a raving nutter prowling around the manor who'll batter girls into unconsciousness just to pinch their bloody drawers! Why can't he simply nick them from a washing line like all the other perverts?'

'Can I make a suggestion, Inspector?' asked the doctor.

'Be my guest,' replied Bromley.

'Well, does a nurse going off-duty look so very different to a WPC going off-duty? Particularly when the nurses' home and WPCs' hostel are in the same road. Those sensible shoes and black stockings are almost an identical trademark for both sets of girls.'

'That's a very good point, Doctor,' agreed Bromley. 'An attack on two nurses could have been a coincidence but three is an obsession. We now *have* three. It could be simply a case of mistaken identity—he thought he was attacking a nurse!'

'Do you want me to begin this statement now, guv'nor?' asked Sergeant Keegan.

'Yes—and leave nothing out. I want absolutely everything she can possibly remember in that statement. One day we are going to capture this bastard and I want him away for a long stretch. Coming, Doctor? We'll leave these two constabulary ladies to their girl-talk.'

The statement—as far as it went—was a pretty useless document. All that Helen was able to recall was that one moment she was in the garden dressed—and the next moment she wasn't.

'You know that Mr Bromley thinks you are holding something back, don't you?'

'But I'm not! Honest I'm not!' protested the girl.

'Okay, love,' said the detective with little conviction in her voice. 'You know best.'

Helen dropped her gaze to the bedcover and clenched her fists. 'It's just that, well . . .'

'What is it, love?' cut in the detective, sensing a breakthrough. 'You can tell me off the record if you like.'

Helen gave the deepest of sighs. 'I'm twenty-eight years of age and so far I have made a complete botch of my life. I think the police force is going to be the last chance for me. I'm sure I'm going to like it and I think I can be good at it. What I *don't* want is for the story to get around that some bastard has raped me before I've even started!'

'There's nothing to worry about,' assured the detective. 'Mr Bromley is now quite convinced that you weren't raped.'

'Mr Bromley? Huh!' snorted Helen. 'Mr Bromley is the least of my worries. Anyone who knows anything about this case—and the other two cases for that matter—knows only too well that I wasn't raped. But that won't stop the stories circulating though, will it? How do you think I am going to feel on my first day at the station?'

'I honestly feel you're worrying unnecessarily. It won't be like—'

'Won't it?' cut in Helen, her bitterness rising. 'Won't it? Not much it won't! "How about that one over there!" they'll say. "Someone had her over in the bushes on her first day in the WPCs' hostel!" They'll say, "A right raver that one! I bags second chance!"'

'Look, love,' said the sergeant softly, as she placed a restraining hand on the waving wrist of the now distressed girl. 'Being a "plonk" is very different to any other job you'll ever do. It doesn't matter what anyone tells you, there is *nothing* like it anywhere. It can be a great life but it *is* full of ups and downs. You are right in one respect though —blokes *will* talk, but what do you care? Stuff 'em! You are a very good-looking girl—but I don't suppose you need me to tell you that—okay, then use it. Providing you have a bit of backbone and a sense of humour you'll have them eating out of your hand in no time. You are also lucky in one other respect. Cabul Lane is a busy little nick and with few exceptions you have a great bunch of coppers there. You just walk on that first parade with your hat on straight and a good bra under your shirt and you'll knock 'em dead! See, you're smiling already.'

'It all sounds a bit too easy but I suppose you're right,' nodded the girl.

'I am, you'll see.' The detective began to gather up her papers. 'Well, that's your official visits over. Your boyfriend can come in now.'

'My boyfriend?' echoed the puzzled Helen.

'Well, I assumed it was your boyfriend. There's been some dishy young man sitting outside in the corridor for well over an hour. Shall I show him in?'

'Not before I've borrowed your mirror!' perked Helen as she rearranged the shoulders of her nightdress. She was still fussing with the nightie when her visitor entered the ward— or, more precisely, two visitors. 'Mickey!' greeted the girl with delight. 'I *am* glad to see you.'

Yet another bunch of flowers made an appearance as Michael Butler walked swiftly to the bed. 'The lady detective said it was okay—' he began.

'Yes, it's fine, Mick! It's fine! I'm just sorry you had to wait so long.' She opened her arms to him and they embraced as if reunited after an eternity. Dropping to the bed, he kissed her firmly and not without passion. 'It's really great to see you looking so good, Helen, it really is! I wasn't too sure what I'd find.'

'But surely this is your first day on the streets, Mick? Shouldn't you be at work?'

'It's five in the afternoon,' he pointed out. 'I came straight up here when I finished at three o'clock. Angela said you could receive visitors.'

'Oh, Angela! She should have told you I was being discharged soon. I'm fine, Mick, honest I am. You shouldn't have bothered—but I'm really glad that you did!' She hugged him again, this time with her eyes open. It was then that she noticed the second visitor. Standing at the foot of her bed, with a smile that was perilously close to a

55

leer, was a tall, pale-faced, lank-haired man in his early thirties. Her dislike of him was so instant she stiffened. The sudden movement disturbed Michael from his pleasant indulgence. He turned his head towards his companion and it was very obvious that he had completely forgotten his presence.

'Oh—er, Helen,' he faltered, rising to his feet. 'This is Reg Patterson. He's a PC on "C" relief at Cabul Lane. He's been showing me around beats this morning and he insisted that as you were a newcomer to the relief, he would like to meet you. Reg, this is Helen Rogers.'

'It's lovely to meet you, my dear,' greeted Reg. Dropping a coat on the foot of her bed he moved swiftly to the bedside and made to kiss the girl. She turned her head sharply and a cold kiss landed high on her cheek. Instinctively she tugged up the neckline of the nightdress that she had so painstakingly arranged just seconds before. She may have frustrated his mouth and to a lesser degree his eyes but she was totally unsuccessful with his hands. They lingered lovingly around her abrased back. 'That hurts!' she snapped icily.

'Oh, I'm so sorry, my dear,' smarmed the newcomer, but his hands did not withdraw, instead they moved to her waist.

'Please!' The word sounded like a command.

In slowly withdrawing his hands from her waist, he still managed to brush the sides of her breasts with his fingertips.

'I just thought I'd pop in, my dear. After all, we're one big family on "C" relief, y'know. I am so very pleased that you have made such a recovery. Perhaps I'm indirectly responsible. I have said several silent prayers for you this morning.'

Helen looked with some desperation towards Michael who stood watching the proceedings with mild interest from the foot of the bed. The only support she received from that quarter, however, was an unhelpful grin and a deep, exaggerated shrug. As usual in her relationship with him, her mood had changed from one of potential passion to that of maddening frustration.

'Michael!' she glared. 'Would you get *Mister* Reg Patterson a chair, please. He'll find it far more comfortable than the edge of my bed.'

It seemed that Michael finally understood the message because the grin faded and he came to life with a start. 'No, we won't stop, Helen. I just wanted to satisfy myself you were okay. I'll let you get some sleep and I'll pop in again tomorrow when I finish early-turn.'

'Yes, I'll join him, my dear,' confirmed Reg predictably.

'Oh no! Please don't, they are sending me out later in the evening. I shall be back in my own bed at the hostel within a few hours.'

'It's okay,' assured Michael. 'I'll call there instead.' He bent over and kissed her lightly on the forehead. 'Look after yourself. I'll see you tomorrow.'

Just as Helen was fearing a nauseous goodbye from Reg, the sister sped into the ward. 'That's enough now! This is an observation ward and my nurses have work to do. The young lady will be released shortly and there will be time enough to see her then.' To underline the urgency she picked up Reg's coat from the bed and thrust it towards him.

Helen watched with a mixture of relief and anxiety as the sister ushered both visitors to the door. She needed a quick confidential word with Michael but timing was everything. If she spoke too soon they might *both* return—too late and he would not hear her. The ward door was about to swing shut when she made her move. 'Oh, Mickey!' she called in a voice that betrayed more than a little of her unease. 'One last quick word? It won't take a moment, Sister, honest.'

'A moment then, but definitely no more. This is a hospital, not a debating chamber.' The sister then turned her attention to Michael. 'Quick now, look lively!'

Michael scuttled back to the bedside with a puzzled expression across his handsome face, a face that Helen felt like both kissing and battering but not necessarily in that order. 'What's the matter?' he asked with genuine concern.

She gave him a tight, clenched-teeth smile. 'If you bring that bloody creep anywhere near me again, I'll knife you!' she hissed sweetly.

Michael coughed on a disguised chuckle and raised one finger in acknowledgement. 'He's a smoothie, eh?'

'Out now, young man, d'you hear me—out!' came the now familiar voice of the sister.

He left the bedside and, as he sauntered once more to the door, gave the sister a long, knowing wink. 'God, but you're lovely when you're angry, Sister!' He half-turned towards the bed. 'In fact, you both are!'

At half past eight that evening, almost twenty-four hours to the minute since she was attacked, Helen Rogers was told of her discharge from the observation ward of the Royal Friary Hospital.

'You appear none the worse for the incident,' said the young doctor, 'but if you feel any repercussions—any at all—come straight back and see us. Your police station is providing the transport and they have just phoned to say they are on their way. As soon as you get your things together you can go.' Helen reached for her clothes as, for the tenth time that day, the screens were swished around her bed.

'Helen! Where are you?' The familiar girlish voice of Angela Helms could be heard approaching the bed.

'I'm in here, Angie!' responded Helen as she happily parted the drapes.

Bert Bones, the old station van driver, had his best treat for years as a nubile young lady clad in little but police-issue tights smiled expectantly at him for almost a second.

'Eeeek!'

The drapes were whisked back into place with a speed that seriously left him wondering if he had imagined the whole scene.

'I think you'd better wait outside, Bert,' suggested Angela thoughtfully. 'I don't think she's quite ready yet.'

'Angie! I thought you were supposed to be starting night-duty this evening?'

'I am, but I wanted to make sure you were settled back at the hostel before I left for work. I've fetched you another pair of panties and once we've tucked you up snug for the night, Bert is going to drive me back to the station.' For the second time in as many minutes the old van driver's heart gave an assortment of bumps.

The trio had just boarded the police van when a small estate car screeched to a halt and flashed its headlights irritably. A small, dapper individual bounced from the driver's seat and hurried to the waiting van.

'D'you have a WPC Rogers on board, Bert?' he asked.

'Yep,' answered the driver, nodding his head towards the darkened interior. 'What d'you want her for? I'm just about to take her back to the WPCs' hostel.'

'I want all of her clothing,' said the Scenes of Crime Officer matter of factly. 'Where is it?'

'I'm wearing it!' came the worried reply from inside the van.

Bert fingered a switch and pale white light lifted a little of the gloom in the rear of the vehicle.

'I do hope you're not, miss,' said the SOCO in a tone of reproof. 'I've got to take everything away for a thorough examination.'

Helen shook her head in disbelief. 'D'you know, it seems that everyone I've met in the last twenty-four hours has either asked me to take off my clothes or taken them off for me! Well, they are not coming off in here, you will have to follow us back to the hostel.'

Ignoring Bert's quiet comment of 'Shame', the SOCO gave a resigned shrug and wandered back to his car shaking his head. 'The DI is not going to like this at all—not at all,' he kept repeating.

The two vehicles manoeuvred their way out of the crowded hospital car-park and some ten mintues later eased to a halt outside the White Stone Park hostel.

'Okay, young ladies, here we are,' sang out Bert from the front of the vehicle. 'If you want to be on time for your first night-duty, Angie, you have exactly—' He glanced at his watch. 'You have eleven minutes.'

'Won't you come in and wait?' asked the girl politely.

'Oh, I'm not sure if I can take the excitement,' said the old driver. 'I've had young ladies waving to me wearing just their tights, the SOCO demanding a strip-off in my van, and now I'm being offered a full eleven minutes in the plonks' hostel! Where will it all lead? Most blokes only get in that place through the window.'

'Well, we're going to spoil you,' said Angela, kissing him lightly on the cheek. 'You're such a sweetie that you can come in through the door.'

Angela slipped an arm around Helen's shoulder and escorted her into the building. 'I've spoken to several of the girls in here and they have all promised to keep an eye on you for a day or so. How do you feel now you are back in the place?'

'I don't know—apprehensive, I suppose.'

A tall, towelling-robed redhead suddenly emerged from a bathroom. 'There's one good thing to come out of it, love,' she said. 'A couple of workmen came this afternoon and fixed up a floodlight at the back of the hostel. Although they weren't all that popular with the girls trying to sleep.'

A forced cough interrupted the dialogue as the SOCO loudly cleared his throat.

'Oh yes,' said Helen, 'I'd forgotten about you. You want my clothes, don't you?'

The tall redhead stared at the SOCO for a moment then patted him familiarly on the crown of his head. 'Well, I've heard that it makes you go blind, but I didn't know it stunted your growth as well. You randy little sod, you!'

By the newcomer's attitude, the two girls guessed that the diminutive SOCO was in the habit of being teased by the WPCs. It certainly did not seem to bother him, and his previous authoritarian manner noticeably changed. He hung his head in mock penitence then buried it deeply into the redhead's fluffy, ample chest.

The cry of the van driver interrupted proceedings. 'Miss Helms, we have exactly six minutes to get you to Cabul Lane Police Station. If you are late on your first night,

Inspector Dunn will chew your balls—' He stopped as he realized the implications of his words and fluttered both hands in nervous embarrassment. 'Or—er, whatever is the equivalent female punishment.'

Kissing Helen quickly on the cheek, Angela bade her a fond goodbye and ran eagerly towards the open street door. 'Come on then, Floyd!' she called to the van driver. 'Let's go get 'em!'

CHAPTER FIVE

Inspector Ted Dunn sat in the most comfortable chair in the collator's office and gazed thoughtfully at the young constables assembled before him. The strict formality of his own early days in the force had long gone. Nowadays even the youngest of recruits would sit draped casually across chairs and tables while attending this pre-duty briefing parade. The tide of informality had swept through the force to such an extent that it was now common for constables and sergeants to refer to each other by their Christian names. He would wince every time he heard it. Constables, he considered, were constables and sergeants were sergeants. They were not Teds and Freds or Damiens or Carolines and never could be. He often wondered what the old-time coppers would have made of it all. To be caught in the station canteen even for a few minutes on the coldest of days would mean a week's posting on the draughtiest traffic-point. But now! If the average inspector discovered a skiving PC in the canteen, the chances were he would probably say, 'Hello there, Nigel, would you like a coffee?' And that was another thing—all these pansy names! When he first joined it was Berts, Bills, Jacks and Tommys and even the occasional Vic. If there should have happened to have been a woman police-officer at the station—and they were *never* girls, always women—then she would be Beryl or Doris, or possibly Betty or Joyce. He considered that people with unsuitable names should never be allowed in the force in the first place. He would never forget that matrimonial dispute that had gone so wrong six months ago. The husband, a sixteen-stone navvy, had arrived home very much the worse for Guinness and given his wife her usual Friday wallop. The situation was a weekly occurrence and had been so since their marriage some thirty years previously. Unfortunately, a new neighbour had called the police. A panda car had arrived and once the dust had settled five people had been arrested, three others were incarcerated in the Royal Friary Hospital, and two more spent the entire night at the station making complaints about the police. Ted Dunn considered the Christian names of the first two officers on the scene to be totally responsible. As he complained later to his wife: 'How can those idiots at Scotland Yard expect me to police a manor like Cabul Lane when they send me such pansy names as Ashley and Sasha!'

Ted Dunn had deliberately left a gap between himself and the lower ranks. The result was that he was easily the most respected figure at the station. The PCs and WPCs in particular thought the world of him—even those with the most suspect of names! Every so often he would rebel against this admiration and insist that everyone's hair was too long, or that their uniform was scruffy or their punctuality lax. He considered it his task to lead from the front and never permit anyone to do anything he would not do himself. If he thought his subordinates wrong he would come down on them like a ton of bricks, but if he thought they were right—or even acted for the right reasons—he would back them in any situation. Which explained why he had remained an inspector for so many years.

Dunn gave the nod to his sergeant, Bill Truscott, and the parade was soon underway.

'Right! Pay attention now, you lot,' announced Truscott. 'Painter! That means you. In fact, it particularly means you!'

Paul Ford, alias Paul-the-Painter, was the unofficial station painter and decorator. He could frequently be seen in his off-duty moments chugging around the manor in his old three-wheeled van. In spite of the fact that he must have painted half of the small business premises in the area, he would vehemently deny any involvement. This was primarily because the carrying out of such work was a discipline offence and could easily result in dismissal. His pro-

63

testations, however, would have been more impressive if the latest delicate shades had not figured so prominently down the cuticle of his fingernails and on the hairs of his nostrils.

'I swear he's a bloody paint-sniffer,' Truscott would say. 'He's definitely got the first sign of it—his brain's gone soft.' Now Truscott raised his voice an octave. 'Okay, here are your postings for the night.' The sergeant quickly worked his way down the list of beats and panda patrols. He finished with the time-honoured question: 'Anyone not posted?'

Dave and Angela exchanged glances, neither confident enough to speak.

'How about you two?' asked Dunn, eyeing them thoughtfully. 'Are you with us or not?'

'Yessir!' answered the girl.

'Then bloody speak up, lass!' He glanced at some papers in front of him. 'Ducker and Helms, is it?'

'Sir!' they both acknowledged.

'Christian names?'

'Angela, sir.'

'David, sir.'

'Hmm' growled the inspector. 'Bearable I suppose. How old are you, miss?'

'Nineteen, sir.'

The inspector shook his head in disbelief. 'Post them, Sergeant.'

The sergeant quickly amended his clipboard. 'Ducker, you are with 691 Ford on four, five and six beats until your grub break at two o'clock. From three o'clock you will join him again, this time on panda one. And if he trys to get you to wash down any ceilings, let me know.' He switched his attention to Angela. '590! You will be with 307 Dawson. You'll be on panda one until grub break, then on four, five and six beats. And watch him closely because he's a randy sod. Incidentally, Dawson, when you finished with that panda last night it was like a bloody dustcart. Fag-ash all over the place. I shall be having a quick shufty at it sometime during the night and I don't expect to see old newspapers, teacups and cigarette packets everywhere.'

'Sergeant!' acknowledged Dawson.

Truscott quickly went through the day's noteworthy crimes and the details of a couple of missing persons. 'Finally,' he added, 'pay some attention to the vicinity of the nurses' home. Yes, I realize you do very little else, Dawson, but I would prefer your duties to be constabulary rather than carnal. Anything further, sir?'

The inspector raised his head wearily. 'Only a three-page memo from the superintendent concerning . . .' He paused for several seconds and almost imperceptibly shook his head. ' . . . concerning teacups. I've no intention of wading through this lot, but for Chrissake, after you've had a teabreak, *eat* the bloody cup if you have to but I don't want to see them anywhere but in the canteen. Does everyone understand that?' There was a mass head-nodding. 'And if I find one in your panda, Dawson, I will personally stuff it right up your rectum. . . . You may well wince, young man! Right, out you go—and don't forget the nurses' home!'

As the members of the night-duty departed through the door, Dunn looked wonderingly at the slight figure of Angela Helms. 'Pretty kid that one, isn't she, Sergeant?'

'She is that,' agreed Truscott.

Dunn sighed an old policeman's sigh. 'She don't look much like a copper though.'

'That's a fact,' said the sergeant. 'She looks more like an off-duty Brownie.'

The 'off-duty Brownie' was studiously following her mentor for the night. This is always a problem for the new recruit. He or she rarely has a clue where to go or what to do, and then there is always the terror of being forgotten. As a result, they cling leech-like to the person they have been posted with and rarely leave their side. Many is the new young plonk who has followed her guide diligently to the door of the Gents—which was exactly where Alan Dawson was heading. 'Wait in the yard for me, love,' he said hastily. 'I won't be a minute.'

Still full of her first briefing, Angela decided to put the delay to good use. 'Excuse me, which is panda one?' she asked a departing off-duty constable. He nodded towards a blue-and-white Austin that stood in a darkened corner of the yard. If Sergeant Truscott would be carrying out an inspection during the night, perhaps she should have a quick tidy up before they commenced work.

Zipping his trousers, Alan Dawson walked up the short flight of steps that led from the male lavatory to the station yard. Pretty though the girl was, her company was the last thing he wanted tonight. He glanced quickly around the yard but could not see her. Bloody typical! The one night he wanted to be on his own, he was lumbered with a dozy plonk who was already lost! He could just imagine Inspector Dunn's reaction if he was to enter the front office and announce that within ten minutes of starting work he had already lost a new recruit. Still, perhaps she had also visited the lavatory. In his experience of plonks that seemed to be where they spent most of their time.

Angela had removed a fair amount of debris from the front seats of the car before deciding to tidy up the rear. On opening the door, her attention was drawn to a stout cardboard box that lay across the back seats. Crouching to pick up a chocolate wrapper she nudged the box, causing it to topple on to her foot.

Alan Dawson was about to enter the front office when he first heard the screams. They weren't ordinary screams, they were taking-a-leg-off-and-slowly-disembowelling screams. In addition, they were uncomfortably close. 'Oh no!' he thought. 'The box! She couldn't have—could she?' But he knew deep down she had.

The three ear-piercing screams had fetched people running from all corners of the station. It was all quite needless really, because the four-foot-long python that was currently wrapped around Angela's left ankle was actually quite harmless.

'Let me get this straight,' said Dunn in a despairing attempt to stay calm. 'You're telling me that you are just looking after it for a friend—a python! A bloody great python! *And* in the back of a police car! You know, of course, you have nearly unbalanced that girl, don't you?'

'Well, it's only a *small* python, sir,' protested the downcast Dawson, as he coiled the snake back in its box.

'It's four feet long!'

'I know, sir, but that's not very long for a python, sir.'

'Not very long? Are you mad? When a five-foot-five-inch plonk opened that box in the dark, it must have seemed like the bloody Loch Ness monster!' Turning to Sergeant Truscott he continued: 'Whatever's gone wrong with this job, Sergeant? I've got a superintendent who collects dirty teacups at one end, and a PC who thinks he's a bloody snake-charmer at the other!'

'I think he's a frustrated dog-handler, sir,' responded Truscott who had scarcely been able to control his delight at the whole situation. 'The guv'nor wouldn't let him have a dog so he's got himself a snake. Probably within a year or two we'll have official police pythons.'

'Well, I tell you this, Sergeant Truscott, he's got just ten minutes to get rid of that bloody snake before I get him deemed for insanity. Did you hear what I said, Dawson?'

'But I *was* getting rid of it, sir,' protested Alan. 'The owner is a friend of mine who has gone away on holiday. I just said I knew someone who would look after it for him until he gets back. I was going to drop it off just as soon as I left the station tonight.'

'I suppose it never occurred to you to do this noble deed in your own time?'

'I was going to, sir—honest. But I'm afraid I overslept.'

'Dawson, it is now twenty minutes past eleven. If that snake is not safely tucked up in a different bed by half past, I am going into the taxidermy business.'

'Sir?'

'A taxidermist, son—you know what they do, don't you?'

'No, sir,' said the puzzled young policeman.

'Taxidermists *stuff* things, Dawson—need I say more?'

'No, sir! exclaimed Alan, now receiving the message quite clearly. He gathered up the box and ran towards the panda, stopping and turning just short of the car door. 'Er —590 Helms, sir—shall I take her with me?'

Dunn closed his eyes in disbelief. 'Tell him, Sergeant, will you, please,' he murmured quietly to Truscott. 'I swear that young man is barmy.'

'With pleasure, sir,' said Sergeant Truscott politely as he turned his attention to the young constable. 'No, you insensitive prat! Miss Helms is currently recovering from a hefty touch of the vapours. I very much doubt if she'll speak to you for the rest of her service let alone ride in your bloody panda tonight! Will you just get that python out of this police station double-quick?'

Seconds later, the panda roared out of the station yard. 'D'you know, Sergeant,' said the old inspector wearily. 'At this very moment there are thousands of folk out there who are sleeping content in their beds because of the blind faith they have in the Metropolitan Police. My God! If only they knew! Why couldn't the fool keep a cat like normal people?'

'Perhaps he did and the python ate it. You never know, sir, with any luck it might even eat Dawson. If we were lucky enough for that to happen, perhaps we could slip it quietly into the superintendent's lavatory for a real win-double.'

'You're trying to cheer me up, Sergeant Truscott, aren't you? Come on, let us go and have a look at that hysterical female.'

Angela Helms was, in fact, anything but hysterical. True she had given voice to a crescendo of screams at the serpent's first embrace, but then, to Angela, every snake was a king cobra. As she herself understandably put it: 'If a girl suddenly discovers she has a life expectancy of two minutes, she is entitled to scream.'

'So you're all right, miss?' asked Dunn with no little concern.

'Fine, sir.'

'Very well then. If you are quite sure you're okay, Sergeant Truscott here will arrange another posting for you.'

'Can't I go back on the panda with PC Dawson, sir?'

'Back on the panda? With that lunatic?'

'If that's all right, sir.'

'Yes, yes, just keep him out of my sight for the rest of the night though, will you?'

In effect, Alan Dawson could not have been nicer. He apologized at length. So much so that Angela eventually felt obliged to cut him short. 'Let's forget it, eh?' she asked. 'After all, only my dignity was hurt and the rest of the relief seemed to think it uproariously funny. I suppose now it's all over I'm beginning to feel that way myself.'

Before Alan could reply, the car radio spluttered to life. 'Panda one, panda one. 27 Earlrose Street disturbance. See informant—a Mrs Barbara Hobbs—at the door. Message ends 23.40.'

'Received. Panda one out,' responded the young man.

Angela had difficulty hiding her excitement. She adjusted the angle of her hat and smoothed down her uniform with the palms of her hands. 'This is my very first call and it's just like the television. Haven't you got a blue light or klaxon or something we could switch on?'

'Well, firstly it's not a bit like television. It's almost certainly a domestic dispute because they account for about half the calls that we deal with on the pandas. And secondly, blue lights and klaxons are only for the area cars and I'd have to be an advanced driver for that and I'm not that good. We just use the headlights and the horn.'

27 Earlrose Street was one of a row of flats above a line of shops in the local market. Entry could only be gained via a service road at the rear. On reaching the corner of this road, Alan switched off the headlights and rolled quietly up to the location. 'I have a nasty feeling I've been here before. I am sure it's a husband-and-wife dispute and he's a round-faced bloke of about forty with a bald head. If that's the case, he's really obnoxious . . .' He shook his head. '. . . and we've got grief.'

'Why?' asked the puzzled girl.

'Basically because there's sod all we can do. You'll find husband-and-wife disputes an absolute bloody nuisance. Remember, whatever you do, don't nick anyone.'

'Why?' persisted the girl, desperately trying to remember any lesson at training school that might have dealt with such a situation.

'Because your entire evidence will be provided by the other partner, usually the wife, and they will always—but *always*—go bent on you at court. Anyway, let's go and see what this is all about.'

Access to the flats was gained via a steep, narrow flight of concrete steps that led up to a walkway. The flats in turn faced on to this walkway. Number 27 was immediately at the top of the steps.

'This is the place right enough,' sighed Alan. 'She'll be waiting on the steps and—'

'Here, mate, here I am!' Sure enough, a slightly built woman in her early forties sat halfway up the flight.

'It's me husband again, mate. He's had a few jars an' he's pickin' on me boy. He's only sixteen an' he's scared to death of his dad, bless him.'

'How about you?' asked Alan. 'Has he touched you?'

'No, mate, no. He never touches me, mate. Like I said, it's only the boy.'

'You mean he's assaulted him?'

'Well, no, not actually *assaulted* him, more like "had a go at him" as you might say.'

'So what do you want us to do?'

'Speak to him about it, mate. He's always pickin' on me boy when he's had a few. I don't think it's fair.'

'I can't make him love your son, I'm afraid,' said Alan. 'If that's all it is then there's nothing I can do. I'm sorry.'

'Well, that's a bloody fine state of affairs, innit? It seems like you wouldn't care if he killed someone. When I phoned your station they said you'd have a word with him for me. I thought he might take notice of you, mate.' With that she seemed to become aware for the first time of Angela's presence. 'Perhaps you'll have a word with him, mate?' she asked the girl. 'I'm sure he'll take notice of you. You being a policeman-lady an' all that.'

'Look!' cut in Alan. 'If I do have a word with him and he tells me to "sod off", there's nothing I can do. So that's all it will be, just a word and nothing else.'

'That's all I'm asking for, mate! I don't want to cause no trouble for anyone, honest I don't.'

Alan shook his head in resignation. 'My heart's not in this,' he murmured, almost to himself.

Angela stayed with the woman a yard or two back from the door as Alan gave a short, sharp push at the white plastic doorbell. This provided the first surprise. Instead of provoking an angry buzz, it triggered instead the seemingly endless verse of 'My Bonnie Lies Over the Ocean'. Alan stepped back in surprise, while Angela suppressed a giggle.

'It was me husband's choice, mate,' whispered the woman. 'He loves all them classics.'

Nothing seemed to happen, so, warily, Alan pressed the bell again. This time a twenty-five-second burst of 'Greensleeves' filled the late-night air. A light came on in the hallway and a stocky figure was silhouetted against the glass door. The door was vigorously pulled back with such force that it crashed against the interior wall. A glowering, belligerent, balding figure with heavy-framed spectacles stood with folded arms. 'Yeh? Whadda you want?'

'I would just like a quick word with your son,' said Alan.

'Well, yer can't have one. Fuck off!'

'Your wife is concerned for his welfare. All I want to do is to have a quick word with him and I'll leave. It won't take a minute—please?'

'If you don't fuck off I'll throw you down those stairs.' The man began to sway forward.

Suddenly a young man appeared in the passage behind him. 'It's okay, policeman, don't worry, I can handle

71

him. It's just that the old lady gets herself in a bit of a panic. He's no problem, I can cope. But thanks all the same.' The figure, although young, was a very powerful lad and indeed did look as if he could cope.

'Fine!' said Alan, ignoring the panting drunk. 'So you would be quite happy for me to leave?'

'A' course.'

This conversation had been carried out over the shoulder of the father who still stood at the door. The young constable then unwisely turned to the woman.

'And how about you, dear, are you happy now?'

'Yeh, thanks, mate, thanks a lot.'

'Well, I ain't fuckin' happy!' the husband roared.

'No, I didn't think you—' Alan's words were cut short by a vice-like grip around his throat. He cursed his own stupidity.

Angela ran forward to help, but it was over almost before she moved. As the hands had closed around his throat, Alan had instinctively tugged at the gripping wrists while stepping back and slightly to one side. The whole balance of the man depended upon Alan standing still, but as he moved so the assailant lost his balance and fell forward. In an effort to check his fall, the man relinquished his hold on the young constable's throat. For the first few steps Angela had the impression the man was flying, but it could not last and he crashed to the floor somewhere around the sixth concrete step. Unfortunately, he did not remain there but continued to bounce and roll down every single remaining step. He ricocheted from the last one and came to a halt partially upside-down against the brick wall of a pram shed. It had been like watching a truck hurtling down a mountainside.

The woman screamed as she and the two police-officers converged at the top of the staircase at the same moment. Angela was marginally first and she skimmed down the staircase three steps at a time. Crouching beside the groaning, inverted figure she was appalled at the apparent extent of his injuries. His knuckles had scraped the sides of both walls and, seemingly, so had his face. The flesh on both areas was a mass of grazes and abrasions. His spectacles and watch lay in pieces and his shirt and trousers were ripped. Meanwhile, blood oozed from at least three cuts.

'I don't believe it!' she cried, looking up at Alan who was approaching. 'It's not possible to get that hurt falling down a flight of steps!'

Between the two of them they righted the upturned victim and sympathy poured from the anxious Angela. Reassuring words tumbled forth as she held his injured hands and did her best to make him comfortable. Meanwhile, Alan, who had not spoken since the unfortunate man had begun his dive, climbed to his feet and made a quick examination of the staircase and landing. Then, turning to the still prostrate but conscious figure, he uttered his first words.

'You're nicked!'

Angela was totally dumbfounded. 'Whatever for?' she exclaimed.

'Assault on police,' explained the young man.

'But just look at him!' protested the girl. 'He looks like he's been hit by a truck!'

'Exactly!' agreed Alan. 'That's why I'm nicking him. Can you imagine my position if I don't? Supposing he goes along to a doctor looking like that and tells him that it was done to him by a copper at midnight on a dark staircase. Where does that leave me? Or, for that matter, you! No, he's definitely nicked. Let the magistrate sort it out in the morning.'

'But—' began Angela.

'But nothing! How d'you feel, Mr Hobbs—can you stand up?'

All belligerence had totally disappeared from the bemused Mr Hobbs. He had yet to fathom just how he had managed to travel from his front door to an upside-down position at the bottom of the staircase—and in such a short space of time.

'Thanks for your help, mate,' said the woman acidly. 'But I didn't expect you to chuck him down the bleedin' stairs.'

'He did *not* get chucked down the stairs!' snapped Alan. 'If you remember, lady, I did point out to you that this was a matter in which the police should not get involved. It was *you* who insisted that I should take action.'

'I just thought you would have a quiet word with him, mate. I didn't want you to break his bleedin' neck. What happens to him now? He oughta go to hospital and not a police station. In any case, he hardly laid a hand on you. I can't possibly see as that can be said to be an assault, nohow I can't.'

In spite of Mrs Hobbs' inability to 'see' the assault, the fact was that twenty minutes later Arthur Bertram Hobbs sat dejectedly in the Cabul Lane charge-room, listening to PC 307 Dawson 'telling the tale' to the station officer.

'What have you got to say about that, Mr Hobbs?' asked the station officer. 'This officer says you put your hands around his throat and therefore he arrested you. Is that correct?'

Mr Hobbs nodded an agreement—he was sobering fast.

'Well, we'll get a doctor to look at your injuries and then I'll bail you. You should be back home within an hour or so.'

As opposed to most cases of assault on police there was a great deal of sympathy for the prisoner. He did indeed look a pitiful sight. Dr Patrick Byrne, the police surgeon for the district, instantly recognized Hobbs as one of his own patients.

'Arthur!' he exclaimed. 'What on earth are you doing here?' When the reasons for Arthur's incarceration were explained to the good doctor, he shook his head in disbelief. 'But I've known him for years! He's as good as gold normally, although he certainly should not have been drinking—he's very diabetic. But it's totally out of character.' The couple entered the 'Surgeon's Room' and, an hour and three stitches later, Arthur Hobbs emerged a definitely brighter man.

'He's very lucky,' marvelled the doctor. 'I've had to put a few stitches in his earlobe and give him a tetanus injection, but everything else is either a graze or a bruise.'

'Not to me watch and glasses it ain't,' complained Arthur. 'What'll happen now, Sarge?' he asked, turning to the station officer.

'You'll be at court at ten in the morning, then a remand to a later date,' explained the sergeant.

'Why a remand?' asked Arthur. 'Why can't they deal with it then?'

'Because of the time factor. Most not-guilty pleas are remanded in the first instance.'

'But I'm pleadin' guilty,' announced Arthur. 'An' futhermore I'd like to apologize to whoever it was that I assaulted.'

'Er—it was me,' interrupted Alan shamefacedly.

'You!' cried Arthur. 'There don't look much wrong wiv you, son!' He gazed all round the charge-room before finally spotting Angela. 'How about you, miss? I've seen you before, ain't I? Wasn't you on the staircase when I "brutally assaulted" this young man? I didn't by any chance give you a belt, did I?'

'No,' replied Angela. 'You were a perfect gentleman to me, Mr Hobbs. I just felt sorry for you, that's all.'

'Felt sorry for me?' echoed the prisoner. 'Bleedin' hell! I'll tell you what, miss. If you felt sorry for me you're gonna make a rotten bleedin' copper! Still, it takes all sorts, I s'pose, even in the police force.'

Further conversation was interrupted by Mary, the night-duty telephonist, who entered the charge-room clutching a piece of paper in one hand and her knitting in the other.

'Are you free, panda one?'

'Uh-huh,' nodded Alan.

'Well, I've got one for you.' She handed the paper to

75

him. '219 Wharf Road, domestic dispute. Her live-in boyfriend is smashing the place up. I can show you dealing?'

The young man gave a weary sigh. 'Come on, Angie-baby. This time it's your turn to throw him down the stairs. I'm just going to stand by and look sad.'

CHAPTER SIX

When David first woke, it was some time before he could remember just where he was. All he could think of was the bruising pain in the lower part of his abdomen. He felt he had slept for a month, yet had abstained from urinating for about the same length of time. There is something about night-work that causes the strongest of bladders to pulsate after an hour of daytime sleep. Newcomers to shift-work try everything. They will not touch a sip all night and will then squeeze out the faintest of dribbles just a second before climbing into bed. It makes not the slightest difference, nothing does. They would be equally successful if they had downed eight pints of draught Guinness whilst putting on their pyjamas. Dave had climbed into bed at a quarter to eight that morning and, after what seemed like an eternity of sleep and a barrel of beer, had staggered along to the bathroom at half past nine. He experienced no difficulty in returning to sleep, it was just that he woke every subsequent hour in the erroneous belief that he had slept all day.

After the fourth awakening, he lay for some time staring at the ceiling. Images of Brenda flooded his mind. He slowly closed his eyes and let his thoughts wander. They would take him wherever he wanted to go, with whomsoever he chose. Brenda, then, it would be. They would hold hands and walk, laugh together and talk, whisper and perhaps make love. He found himself sighing her name. A name for which he had never cared much. But now it was a beautiful name, a beautiful name for a beautiful woman. Oh, Brenda, Brenda!

'Dave! You awake?'

He sat up with a start. Surely not, it can't be. Or could it? He turned towards the door—it wasn't.

'Mickey, it's you.' Even the bed seemed to groan in disappointment. 'What the bloody hell do you want?'

'Have you managed to collect your football club's old van yet?'

'Yes, it's downstairs in the car-park. Why?'

'I thought it would be a good idea to pop over and see how Helen is progressing. You can also tell me about your first stint of night-duty.'

Dave sighed. 'Okay, if we *must*, but what's the time?'

'Four o'clock, I've just finished my early-turn.'

'I don't think I'm going to like night-duty, Mick. I don't know if I'm coming or going—and I'm not even sure what day it is.'

After a mid-afternoon breakfast and a quick shower, the pair arrived at the doors of the old hand-painted red van. If anything, Mickey thought, it looked even more decrepit than the previous ill-fated occasion that he had travelled in it. The first problem was to start the thing. After a few well-chosen obscenities, a quick kick and a forty-yard push, the tired old engine spluttered reluctantly into precarious life. The noise inside was deafening.

'D'you know the way?' yelled Mickey, with a pained expression.

'Of course! I dropped Angela off this morning after we had both finished nights. Hey!' Dave added as an afterthought. 'I almost forgot, she made an arrest in her first couple of hours on duty. How about that!'

'What for?'

'Assault on police, apparently.'

'Angela was assaulted?'

'No, you berk. The fellow she was *with* was assaulted.'

'Badly?'

'No, hardly at all. By all accounts half of the nick thought she was going to get up a collection for the prisoner! Oh, by the way, she was also attacked by a python.'

Mickey stared at his friend for a moment in complete astonishment. 'A what?'

'A python—it's a snake.'

'I *know* what a bloody python is!' Michael's eyes narrowed suspiciously. 'Are you having me on?'

'No, of course not! You know what a daft cow she is, don't you? Everything happens to Angela!'

'"Everything happens to Angela?"' echoed Michael. 'Well, how about the other one? Between the pair of them, and within two days, those couple of plonks have been knocked unconscious, stripped half-naked, attacked by a snake and nicked a geezer for assault on police. By comparison that makes me and you extremely boring.'

'Yes, I suppose it does,' agreed David reluctantly. 'I walked the streets for bloody hours last night and never saw a thing.'

They had reached the end of the quiet road in which the hostel was situated, when Michael leaned forward dramatically. 'Hang on a minute!' he ordered. 'Pull over to the side for a moment. Just behind that lorry will do.'

The urgency in his tone caused Dave to follow the directions unquestioningly. 'What is it, what can you see?'

'See that red Cortina? Just ahead of us on the other side of the road?'

'Yes.'

'It's Preacher's car.'

'So who's "Preacher"?'

'He's a real weirdo from "C" relief. You haven't met him yet. He came with me to see how Helen was yesterday and had his hands all over her in less than a minute.'

'That's weird? I should be so weird!' responded David ruefully. 'But in any case, why shouldn't his car be there? Perhaps he's visiting, just like us.'

'Well look at it, man, look at it!'

David was experiencing great difficulty in focusing on anything at that moment. He had yet to adjust to the nocturnal hours of night-duty. His senses were still half-asleep.

'I can't see anything wrong. It looks okay to—There's a bloke in the back with binoculars and he's looking at the windows at the side of the hostel!'

'It's Preacher right enough,' confirmed Michael.

'What do you think he's doing? Shall we go and ask him?'

Michael thought for a moment. 'No, let's pretend we haven't seen him. We'll carry on to the hostel as if nothing has happened.' He shook his head. 'There's something really strange about that geezer. The rest of "C" relief swear he carries those binoculars with him on night-duty to gaze in bedroom windows. So far no one has caught him at it.'

'Well, we have.'

'Not really. It's a long way from being dark, in fact the sun's still out. It'll do no harm to bear it in mind though. Come on, let's see what the girls have to say.'

Keeping their gaze dead ahead, the pair drove past the Cortina, and the van coughed to a halt a short distance beyond the hostel. Sliding shut the door of his van, Dave was unable to resist a quick glance in the direction of the suspect car. There was a sudden flurry as the watching figure slid quickly down between the seats. As they walked through the front gate of the building, a tall, well-dressed, grey-haired man in his early forties emerged from the front door of the hostel carrying a briefcase. He gave them a slight nod of acknowledgement before easing himself into a smart blue Rover car and driving swiftly away. Helen had experienced a delayed reaction to her attack, and the doctor had been called.

On entering the hall, the smell of fried bacon pervaded throughout. Through an open door they spotted the cause of the aroma—Angela Helms was about to tackle a king-size breakfast. She smiled a welcome and, by the use of a fork, directed them to two chairs on the opposite side of her table. 'Hi, boys,' she greeted. 'What on earth are you doing here?'

'Well, there's a fine welcome, I must say!' complained Michael. 'We've come to see *you*! I've come straight from work, Dave here has come straight from bed—and that's all the thanks we get.'

'I'm sorry, boys. It's just that I'm not used to such

attention. In any case, I saw Dave when he fetched me home this morning and I'll see him again in another four or five hours when he takes me back tonight. Of course, it's *always* a pleasure to see him,' she added hastily.

'We thought we saw a doctor as we came in. We wondered if Helen was all right.'

'Doctor? Oh yes—er, doctor. That's right. He—er, called to give her a routine check-up, that's all. Nothing to worry about. In fact, she's fine. She'll be starting work at the end of the week.'

'Where is she?' enquired David.

'She's up in her room. I'll tell her you are here when I've finished my breakfast.'

'Angie, for the life of me I can't understand how you can eat so much when you have just woken up,' said Dave, wrinkling his nose in disgust. 'I just don't know how you do it. All I have had is a slice of toast—and I had to force myself to eat that.'

Michael slid back his chair. 'She's not only got more clothes than anyone I know, she also *eats* more than anyone I know. I can't work out why she's not a bloody giant,' he said, rising to his feet. 'Whilst you're polishing off that lot, Angie, perhaps Dave and me can call on Helen. We know her room.'

Choking on her fried bread, Angela waved Michael back to his chair. 'No, boys, no! Leave it to me, eh? Helen's having a little "woman's problem" at the moment and she's asleep. She's asked me to wake her about six o'clock and it's almost that now. She won't thank me, you know, if I let you go up there when she's not looking her best. Be fair, fellows.'

Michael raised his hands in surrender. 'Anything you say, Angie. But perhaps while we're waiting you'll tell me all about your snake?'

Some twenty minutes later, after having first deposited the young men in the lounge, Angela returned to collect them.

'It's okay, Helen is awake now, come on up.'

They were agreeably surprised at the girl's appearance. Other than a little puffiness around the eyes, she appeared in good spirits. Angela made a pot of tea and they began to discuss their first impressions of the force. It was Michael who raised the subject.

'Have you seen anything of Preacher Patterson since you were in hospital, Helen?'

'Yes,' agreed the girl quietly. 'I have seen him twice. He came back after Angie had left for night-duty last night, and again before she woke up this afternoon.'

It was obvious from Angela's expression that she was as surprised as either of the two men.

'Can I ask if you invited him?' enquired Michael.

'Good God, no! The man gives me the absolute creeps. He became quite unpleasant last night, so when he came back today I just exploded and told him to sod off—and he did. He left without so much as a word.'

Michael walked over to the window and peered out into the now darkening street. 'I've got news for you, love—he's still here.'

'What!'

'He was outside when we arrived. He was just sitting in his car staring at the building.' Michael had decided not to mention the binoculars, feeling that they gave the whole situation a somewhat sinister twist. 'I think it's time I had a word with him.'

'Mickey, please,' Helen implored. 'Please don't. I don't want any more trouble, Mick. I'm a big girl now and can handle the likes of Preacher Patterson. Just leave him to me, huh?' She rose from her bed and walked slowly across the room towards him. Her dressing gown gaped and her movements were blatantly sexual. She knew her words would never keep Michael from a confrontation so she was instinctively using her body. To Helen it was a natural alternative. The fact that two other people were present mattered not in the slightest. David felt his pulse rate leap, and even Angela watched in fascination. Michael, on the other hand, ignored the whole show.

'Helen, I'm not going to do anything rash, I promise. I'm simply going to let *him* know that *we* know what he's up to.'

'But you *will* do something rash, Mickey!' she cried, her voice rising in temper. 'You will do something rash because that is what you always do! You know you do!'

Angela gave a quick, imploring glance towards David and the movement seemed to prod him into life. Tearing his eyes from the protesting girl's nightdress, he uttered his first words for some minutes.

'She's right, Mick. It'll be best if you stay here. I'll go.' Michael made to protest but a vice-like grip fell on to his wrists. '*I'll* go, I said,' murmured David in an ominous whisper.

The three of them watched from the window as Dave strode briskly across the road and wrenched at the door of the car. It did not open. They saw him shield his eyes from the reflection as he gazed for some seconds at the interior of the car. He then turned towards the building and gave the trio an exaggerated shrug. He checked the temperature of the bonnet with the palm of his hand and it was cold to the touch. Finally, after staring up and down the road a few times, he came back into the hostel.

'There's no trace of him,' he announced. 'There's condensation on the outside of the windows and it looks like it's been empty for ages. I suppose we definitely did see him, did we?' he asked Michael, scratching his head in perplexity.

'We saw him all right, and I'll see him again in the morning. He and I are both on the same shift so he can't escape that one. Come on then, Dave. If you want something to eat before you go to work we had better make tracks.' On reaching the door, he turned once again to Helen. 'I'll see you again tomorrow, kid, but if there's anything you want me to do for you, just ask, eh? I don't really need that cabaret act, you know. 'Bye!'

The young men had barely left the confines of the building before Angela turned somewhat angrily to her friend.

83

'Why didn't you tell me about Patterson? If I'm going to cover up for you, Helen, it's no good you leaving me in the dark. Surely you can trust me?'

'I'm really sorry, Angie, honest I am. I know you deserve an explanation and I'll give it to you—'

The rest of her words were interrupted by a dramatic call from downstairs. It was David's voice and it was urgent.

'Angie! Angie! Quick! Quick!'

Angela raced from the room, closely followed by Helen. There at the foot of the stairs was David. In his arms he carried the semiconscious and groaning figure of a girl. A fair-haired, dark-coated, black-shoed girl, with blood seeping ominously from a scalp wound.

The yells and groans had caused WPCs to race from every corner of the building. Their apparel was as colourful and varied as the girls themselves; one even sported a ghostly white face pack.

'Here! Put her in my room!' offered one WPC with a tightly wrapped towel piled high on her head.

David turned sideways to negotiate the door and laid his charge gently on the bed. The movement caused her coat to part and the anxious watchers noticed that her clothing was ripped and shredded, with her black tights beribboned around her ankles. It was painfully obvious that whoever had attacked her had used a very sharp knife—and not been too careful with the blade. Lacerations ran up from her knees to just below her breasts. As David bent to examine the first of these wounds, so the girl opened her eyes clearly for the first time. She let forth a scream that cut into every corner of the hostel and then immediately went into a fit of uncontrollable shakes.

'It's all right, it's all right!' blurted Helen as she raced forward to throw her arms around the hysterical girl. 'We're with you, love, he won't hurt you, shush.' She cradled the sobbing body into the soft bodice of her night-gown.

'We've got to do something about her scalp,' said the face-packed WPC. 'It's awful. Keep talking to her, Helen, whilst we look at her.' A sharp intake of breath indicated that the head wound was obviously a bad one. Helen soothed and rocked her patient like a baby, occasionally planting the lightest of kisses on the unbloodied parts of the now quietly weeping girl's hair.

'An ambulance is on its way,' called a female voice from outside the room.

'Look at her right ear,' whispered one of the helpers urgently. 'What is that coming out of it?' A golden fluid seeped slowly down the girl's right lobe.

'Lay her down, Helen,' said the face-packed girl softly. 'Gently, though, gently. I think her skull is fractured.' As her head touched the pillow, the girl whimpered slowly and closed her eyes in pain. 'Turn her slightly,' ordered the white-faced helper.

The movement seemed effective as a faint smile of relief momentarily crossed the girl's face. She then closed her eyes and slid her hands from the arms of Helen's soft dressing gown.

'She's passed out,' said Angela. 'Perhaps it's just as well, just look at those cuts!'

There were five lacerations in all, at least two of them being particularly deep. The girl with the face pack turned towards David. 'What happened? How did she get like this and who is she?'

David made no response. It was as if he had not heard. He just stood staring at the bleeding wounds, with unchecked tears streaming down his full, pink face.

'Davy!' cut in Angela sharply. 'Come on, pull yourself together. What happened?'

The young man faltered for a second, then quickly passed the backs of his hands across his cheeks. Two great moist patches smeared halfway towards his ears.

'We were walking down the road towards my van when I heard a moaning sound coming from the bushes in the front garden of the old derelict vicarage. She was lying in the long grass. She kept repeating the same words over and over again: "Oh, please don't. Please don't." That was all she

85

would say. Mickey dashed off to see if he could find whoever did it. I felt completely useless, I couldn't do a thing. I was just so ashamed and I kept saying "I'm sorry, I'm sorry".' He shook his head in despair. 'Whoever would want to do a thing like this, Angie? Who?'

'I don't know, Dave, but I think you'd better go out there and help Mickey to search, don't you?'

He nodded and moved towards the door. On reaching it, he turned once more to Angela. 'I hope to God Mickey's not found him, Angie, I really do. Because if he's found him — whoever he is—I'll kill the bastard. And what's more, I'll do it with pleasure.'

As David ran out into the street, he practically collided with Michael returning to the hostel. 'Any sign?' he asked his panting friend.

Michael shook his head. 'I don't even know who I was looking for. I've run up about two dozen streets and seen about twenty different people. Any one of them could have done it.' He shrugged. 'How's the girl?'

'She's a mess,' answered the distressed David. 'And such a nice kid, too.' He shook his head despairingly, then added as an afterthought: 'Which way did Preacher go?'

'Eh?'

'Preacher—which way did he go?' He nodded towards a vacant spot at the north kerbside. 'His car's gone.'

'I don't know,' replied Michael thoughtfully. 'In all the excitement I'd quite forgotten him.'

The sound of approaching klaxons soon told them that Preacher might have gone but others were on their way.

'Mick! How could Preacher come back and collect his car and yet not be aware that something was wrong? He must at least have heard the commotion. Did you notice if the car was here when we left the hostel a few minutes ago?'

'No. The last time I remember seeing it was when you put your hand on the bonnet. You and I walked in the other direction when we left the hostel. I'll tell you what though — that creep has got to know *something* about what has gone on here today.'

The two-tone cry of the ambulance was echoed by an approaching white police car, and both vehicles screeched to a halt within seconds of each other.

'She's inside and you'll need a stretcher,' Dave told the enquiring ambulance driver.

Forty minutes later, with the victim in the casualty ward of the Royal Friary, the two young men, plus Angela and a now fully dressed Helen, were on their way to an interview with Detective Inspector Bromley at Cabul Lane Police Station. As they alighted from the police van in the station yard, they encountered the female detective sergeant who had interviewed Helen the previous day.

'Hello, love,' she greeted. 'I can't stop, I'm on my way up to your hostel again. It all happens there, don't it? The DI's in his office on the top floor. Go straight up, he's expecting you all.'

The quartet had climbed just two of the eight flights when Helen suddenly stopped. 'Please wait,' she asked the three friends. 'I want you all to do something for me. Please, it's so very, very important to many people.'

'What is it?' asked David, concerned. Even Michael raised his eyebrows.

'I think I know what's coming here,' murmured Angela quietly. 'In fact, I'm sure I do.'

'Please, I desperately need your help. Angie's guessed it anyway. But it's particularly important that you two boys back me up.'

'I'm bursting with curiosity,' announced Michael impatiently.

Helen glanced quickly up and down the staircase. 'It's the—well, it's the doctor you saw.'

'Doctor?' echoed Michael.

'Yes, you know, the one you saw when you first arrived at the hostel today? The one who had just visited me, remember?'

'Oh yes! I'd forgotten all about him,' said Michael. Suddenly his eyes opened wide. 'Helen! Are you going to be a mum?'

'Don't be silly, of course not!' snapped the girl irritably.

'Well, it has been known before, you know. Well, anyway, what about him?'

'You said that you had forgotten him—yes?' Both lads nodded. 'Well, would you mind "forgetting" him once again then? All the time, for example? He had nothing whatever to do with anything that happened at the hostel this evening and to mention him would only cause many people a great deal of unhappiness. Would you do that for me? Please, boys.'

'I think it's a lot to ask the two fellows, Helen,' said Angela quietly. 'At least I *know* the truth. If you want them to cover up for you and stick their necks out, I think you should at least tell them why.'

Again Helen glanced nervously up and down the staircase. 'All right, but please, please trust me. He wasn't a doctor at all. He's a friend of mine and has been for some years. He's also a local married man. I asked Angie to phone him for me when I was in hospital. If the DI finds out that he was in my room just before that poor kid was assaulted, he is certain to interview him. Apart from anything else, I'm not sure just where that would leave me. Look, I'll tell you everything about it after we've seen the DI—yes?'

'You do get yourself into some scrapes,' said Michael, shaking his head. 'Come on, Dave, let's go up for the interview. I don't know about you, son, but I haven't seen a doctor since that one at the training school lifted my dick with a spoon and told me to cough.'

David winced and nodded agreement. 'I can feel that spoon now, Mick, it was like ice.'

'It's getting to be a habit interviewing you young ladies,' greeted the DI. 'But, if you don't mind, I would like to speak to the two lads first.'

The questions were at first predictable. No, they had not seen the attacker. No, they had not seen a weapon. No, the girl had not said who had attacked her. No, they had not noticed anything suspicious.

'Well, only if you count Preacher, of course,' Michael said.

'Preacher?'

'Yes, PC Reggie Patterson, sir. He was there when we arrived at the hostel, but he had left by the time the girl was attacked.'

'You are sure of that?'

'Well, no, not absolutely sure, of course, but we think he was.'

'What was he doing there?'

'Well, Preacher is something of a lurker, sir. I believe he creeps around the manor quite a bit.'

'Did you speak to him?'

'No. I don't think he was even aware we saw him.'

Further conversation was interrupted by the ringing telephone.

'Yes . . . yes . . . Whereabouts? . . . Okay! I want the SOCO there immediately and the whole area ribboned off . . . Yes . . . I'm coming straight down . . . ten minutes at the most . . . fine!'

The DI replaced the telephone with one hand and reached for his coat with the other. 'I'm sorry to get you four here for nothing, but I won't have time to speak to you now until tomorrow. I'll be in touch.'

'Good news, sir?' asked Michael hopefully.

'We've found a weapon—it's a start. Apparently it's a Stanley knife. Villains use them when they don't actually want to kill the victim. It makes one hell of a mess though. It also means you were very lucky, young lady. Your underclothes must have come off easily. That poor girl you saw this afternoon had hers cut away!'

Helen plunged her hands between her knees, hunched her shoulders and shuddered.

'Come on,' called the DI as he hastened through the door. 'I'm going back to your hostel, I'll drop you off.' The detective inspector led them briskly across the yard towards his small saloon car. 'I hope you're all going to fit in here, my springs aren't too great as it is.'

89

'Hey!' exclaimed Angela, nudging Michael in the ribs. 'There's your mate in that car.'

A tired-looking, middle-aged man was about to slide into the driver's seat of a large Ford across the far side of the yard. A sullen, glowering individual sat immobile in the rear.

'Eh?' queried Michael, at first not understanding.

'It's your mate,' she repeated. 'You know, the one that you thumped in the van, or, more correctly, the one that you missed.'

'Oh, so you've already met the Weasel, have you?' asked Bromley as he switched on his engine. 'He's just been nicked yet again for drunk and disorderly. I don't know what's going to become of him,' he said, shaking his head sadly. 'His old man's a diamond of a chief inspector but it's taking its toll, I'm afraid. That's him in the driving seat. He's aged ten years since Christmas. It's the third time this year he's been called in to take the sod home.'

The two senior officers acknowledged each other with nods before speeding away in opposite directions.

As they came to a halt outside the hostel, the DI uttered his first words of the journey. 'Look, I don't want any of you to mention anything we have spoken of so far, particularly concerning Patterson. Understand?'

'Sir!' acknowledged the quartet dutifully.

The DI then joined three other detectives in huddled conversation and the four friends trooped into the building.

'We have very little time, Helen,' said Michael. 'Dave and Angie will have to leave soon for night-duty. Do you want to talk to us *now*?' he asked pointedly.

She nodded wearily. 'I'll make some tea and we'll have it in my room. Go upstairs and I'll join you.'

Ten minutes later, with Angela sitting in the only chair in the room, the two young men eased themselves down to the floor while waiting for Helen to take the stage.

'You may remember I told you about an affair I had on this manor some ten years ago? Well, I didn't quite tell you the whole truth. I *did* leave him—in fact, I have left him several times—but of course I went back, I always do. I don't know what it is about him. I have had many other blokes but somehow they are just not him. So, I swallow my pride and back I go.'

'It was that fellow we saw, wasn't it? The one we assumed was a doctor. I thought he didn't look like any carpet salesman,' said Michael.

'He's not, although that part was actually true. He *was* a carpet salesman when we first met. Now he owns the place! He's no one's fool, my Tony, he's got six shops in south London alone! I worked in the office with him to begin with. Then, when he began to do well, I became his secretary. Oh, it was all very cosy, except that I wanted kids, plus him for seven days a week and not just five. You see, I'm jealous, I'm possessive and I'm emotional—all the things that a good mistress shouldn't be! But the point is, I *was* a good mistress.' She smiled ruefully. 'I had enough practice, I suppose. Things came to a head about a year ago. I had a brief relationship with a police sergeant—married, of course, aren't they all? Anyway, this sergeant suggested I should try the force. I'd never thought of it before and I don't know why. It seemed to have so many advantages. I thought it would get me away from Tony, I'd have a change of job and a change of area. I thought I might even meet someone who could make me forget him. All the time I was at training school things were fine. You lot were all terrific to me. Then we were posted and what happened? They posted me to Cabul Lane, the one damned place in the whole of London where I did not want to go! Do you know that when we drove down Cabul Road on Monday afternoon to report to the station, I actually saw him through his office window—Did you know that?' Tears welled in her eyes, and Angela, who had now joined her on the bed, slipped a comforting arm around her waist.

After a moment, she lifted her wet face from Angela's shoulder and continued: 'When I found myself in hospital, I pretended that if I could get him to visit me there would be no harm in it. Perhaps we could have spoken about old times like two adult, sensible people.' She shook her head. 'Some chance! I even told myself I was almost over it. The second he walked into that ward I knew, of course, I wasn't. I was as much his woman, his mistress, his plaything if you like, as ever I was. Girls like me don't let go it seems.'

'But how about his wife?' asked David. 'She must have known, surely? I mean, ten years is one hell of a time!'

'I don't think she *does* know. You see, within those ten years they have gone from living in a converted storeroom at the back of the shop, to a detached house in Tonbridge. That's good going by any standards. I think she's so grateful for that she'd forgive him anything, or at least delude herself that nothing was happening. Then there's his kids. He's a selfish, vain bastard, I know, but he genuinely seems to love his kids. No, he'll never leave them.' She sighed. 'I suppose I've known that almost from the first time I met him. Anyway, he came to see me at the hospital and, as you know, he also came round here this afternoon. He gave me six kind words and I was eating out of his hand. You see, that's your visiting doctor, Michael—just a bloody carpet salesman and his sordid little whore!' She turned sobbing into Angela's clean white duty shirt.

'Look, kid,' said Michael as he joined the two sitting girls on the edge of the bed. 'I think you're beautiful and I'd break the neck of anyone who ever said the things about you that you've just said about yourself. But even more than that, I'm on your side. D'you understand?'

'Me too,' cut in David, kneeling down on the thin, faded carpet at the girl's feet and placing both hands firmly on her knees.

Helen lifted her wet face and looked firstly down at David and then at Michael. 'I've often said all men are bastards,' she said, 'but . . . well, perhaps some are not quite such bastards as others.' She rose to her feet and made an effective effort to control herself. 'Come on now, off you go, otherwise you two are going to be late for night-duty. Thanks for listening to me, I feel a whole lot better for telling you everything—honest.'

'You sure?' asked David.

'Yes, I'll be fine now, don't worry.'

'Well, Angie had better leave with me in my van. I'll not have sufficient time to change for work and get back here to pick her up. Is that okay, Angie?'

Angela nodded. 'I'll get my coat.'

The trio gave Helen a long goodbye kiss and soon they were gone. She stared at the closed door for some minutes before easing her head down to the pillow and quietly sobbing herself to sleep.

The distance from the hostel to the section-house was some six miles and the shortest route was via the straight but busy Greyheath Road. After travelling four of these miles, during which time Greyheath Road was studiously avoided, Michael felt he should at least know the reason.

'Just a change of scene really—nothing more,' answered David casually.

The truth about the detour was, in fact, a little more than that. It was David's boyish hope that by approaching the section-house from a side street he might possibly catch a glimpse of homeward-bound Brenda.

'Davy, stop!' Angela's dramatic demand cut in on his third wistful fantasy of the journey. 'What car does Preacher drive?'

'A Ford—red Cortina, I think.'

'I'm sure I saw it in that little cul-de-sac we just passed.'

'Leave it out, Angie!' complained Michael. 'If we're not careful we are going to make Preacher the phantom flasher of south London!'

'I tell you it was his car, I'm sure of it. He had a yellow front index plate and it hung down on one side.'

David gave a quick glance at Michael. 'He *does* have a yellow plate and it *does* hang down.'

The old van did not take kindly to dramatic stops, particularly when followed by dramatic accelerations. It ground its teeth in a series of ominous noises before spluttering reluctantly back to the junction.

'There! What did I tell you!' cried the triumphant girl.

93

'She's right, Mick,' Dave said excitedly. 'It's Preacher's car sure enough—and he's sprawled out in the back seats again!'

Michael was the first out of the van and he sprinted up to the rear of the Ford and seized the nearside door handle. Throwing it open with a flourish, he stopped dead. Preacher was sprawled across the back seats right enough, or at least he thought it was Preacher. But then it was difficult to recognize the face as belonging to anybody, primarily because it was no longer a face. It was a red pulped ball with little bloodied bubbles popping from the hole in its centre.

CHAPTER SEVEN

David lay in bed and, for the ninth time that morning, impatiently checked his watch. He groaned to see that it was just a little after midday. When he had slipped between those sheets at eight o'clock, he was convinced he would sleep all day. Yet for most of that time his thoughts had raced at such a speed as to render sleep impossible. So much seemed to have happened. Was it just a week ago at the training school that he had been anticipating a dismissal for brawling?

The last bulletin he had heard about Preacher had not been good. 'Touch and go,' the surgeon had said. 'Seems to lack the will to survive.' If only he hadn't looked so awful. Did people always look like that after an assault? David's experiences so far had upset him terribly. If Preacher had really inflicted those wounds on the young nurse, then he deserved all he had received. Yet David found he was as distressed by the perpetrator's injuries as he had been by the victim's. He clearly remembered telling Angela that he could kill whoever had cut up that girl and at the time he honestly believed he could. The state of Preacher's face had changed all that. He was now seriously wondering if he could cope.

David had a feeling that most recruits ease themselves sensibly into night-duty, particularly if they have never before worked nights. Yet in addition to the problem of Preacher, there was Helen to contend with. What was to be done about her? He was very fond of the girl and was genuinely worried. In spite of this concern, he had been so tired that morning that he should have slept both long and deep. Yet he hadn't. The reason for this restlessness had nothing to do with either Preacher or Helen. It was entirely to do with a plump mother of three, twenty-one years his senior and not out of his thoughts since he had first set eyes on her. Today was the day he had planned to see Brenda Flynn and the mere thought of it was driving him to distraction.

David had no set plan for the day. 'Ring the bell after two o'clock for your washing,' Brenda had suggested. 'Call around six o'clock and stay for tea,' Sandra had added. Very well then, he would compromise and call at four o'clock. Having finally made the decision, he turned away from the window and made one last despairing effort to sleep. It was futile and within seconds he knew it. As a result, he rang the bell of the brown-painted door at exactly two o'clock. He nervously smoothed down the front of his windcheater as he heard footsteps approach the door. There was a pause, then a squeak as the door swung inward on rusty hinges.

'Hello, son! You're early, aren't you? I've only been home a few minutes.' Again the word 'son' grated his pride. 'I suppose you want your washing?' Brenda continued. 'Wait here and I'll pop back upstairs and get it for you — tracksuit, wasn't it?'

David was appalled—this wasn't the plan at all! He had not lain awake all morning simply to be left standing at the door. He must say something, something really clever and sophisticated. He opened his mouth but nothing emerged. Brenda suddenly turned as if a thought had just struck her. 'I thought you were nights?' she asked.

'I . . . I . . . I am,' he blurted.

She glanced quickly down at her watch. 'Well, what're you doing up so soon? Couldn't you sleep—or do you have a heavy date?' she asked with mild interest.

'No . . . no . . . I don't have a girlfriend,' he said quickly. 'It's just that . . . well—'

'You couldn't sleep then, eh? Come to look at you, you do look a bit washed out. Come on up, I'll make you a cup of strong tea. By the way, if I was you I'd keep quiet about not having a girlfriend. I think my Sandra's got quite a crush on you and she is a rather impetuous young lady.'

He followed her up the four twisting flights of stairs and by the time they had reached the last flight he felt sick with frustration. He desperately needed to reach out to touch her and speak to her freely. All he had managed so far had been bumbling, stuttering sentences that had embarrassed him deeply.

'Sit yourself down.' She gestured to a wide, comfortable-looking settee. 'You can drop off if you like. You certainly look as if you could do with a sleep. Would you like a shortcake with your tea?'

'A shortcake,' thought the young man. How mundane! How could he possibly think of anything as commonplace as a biscuit? Especially when the woman of his dreams was about to slip out of her blue nylon 'Coin-op Wash' overall.

She reached up for the white plastic coat hanger that hung lopsided on the living-room door. 'Sandra's always complaining that I only take off my overall when we have visitors. She's right, of course, it just never occurs to me when I'm on my own.' She smiled down at him with her hands on her pleated-skirt hips. 'Now, do you or don't you want a shortcake?'

The words, 'I don't want a bloody shortcake! I just want you—I love you!' congregated in his mouth, but somehow they escaped his lips as, 'Yes please, I'd love a shortcake.'

She disappeared into the adjacent kitchen. 'You still haven't told me why you couldn't sleep,' she called from behind the partially closed door. He made no reply and the door swung open as she emerged, carrying a tea tray. 'I never know how anyone works nights anyway. It seems so unnatural to me.'

'That's it!' decided David. If she mentioned it once more then he would tell her. After all, he had been mentally preparing himself for two days to call on her and, now that he had, he was tongue-tied. It was quite ridiculous and he was determined to fight it.

'You're quite welcome to come back for a cooked tea this evening, you know,' Brenda was saying. 'Sandra would never forgive me if I kept you to myself this afternoon and you left without seeing her. Actually, if you don't mind me pottering about in the kitchen, you could doze where you are, at least until young Danny gets home from school. I wouldn't rate your chances much after that.'

David took a deep intake of breath and climbed to his feet. 'Brenda—' he began, as the piercing whistle from the kettle called from the kitchen.

'Ooops, just a minute, I'll make your tea.' She faded once more into the small kitchen. David silently cursed the kettle and wondered if he could summon up enough courage for a second attempt. 'Now, you were saying? Oh, do sit, Dave, you make the place look untidy.' Brenda had re-emerged carrying a well-cosied teapot.

The young man clutched his fingers so tightly that they ached. He started to sit down, then, changing his mind, bobbed straight back up again.

'Davy, what's the matter with you?' she said, placing the teapot on the tray. 'You're up and down like a yo-yo.'

'Brenda . . . Brenda, please, Brenda, I've got to talk to you.'

Concern flooded her face. 'Of course!' She moved swiftly alongside him and sat on the settee, tugging on his forearm as she did so. 'What is it, son, what's the problem?'

'Well, that's part of it—"son". Why d'you keep calling me son?' he said, lowering himself to her side.

'I had no idea it upset you! Anyway, you could easily *be* my son. After all, my daughter is about the same age as you. Is that all that's bothering you then?' she asked puzzledly.

Her question at last did the trick. It removed a blockage from the young man's vocabulary that caused words to deluge in a torrent. He swung towards her and grasped both her hands in a firm grip. The unexpected movement caused a fleeting glimpse of alarm to cloud the woman's face.

'Brenda, right from the first time that I met you I've been in love with you. I know that sounds ridiculous, even laughable, but I can't sleep, eat, or even think about anything else but you. I know what you're going to say to me and I know that you are right, but it doesn't make me feel any better.' His words suddenly began to thicken and he knew he must stop because tears were just seconds away. 'I'm sorry, Bren', really I am, but—' He turned his face swiftly from hers and dropped his gaze to the padded settee cushions. 'Well, now you know.'

He relaxed his grip on her hands and she instantly slipped them from his palms, but surprisingly she then returned the gesture by covering his hands with hers.

'Davy, love, you *don't* know what I'm going to say because—well, I don't suppose I know what I'm going to say myself. I think if I was nineteen again I'd be just like my Sandra. I'd set my cap at you and chase you until you lay down and surrendered. But I'm not nineteen—' She gave a long-drawn-out sigh. 'Sometimes I wonder if I ever was.' She shook her head in bewilderment. 'Davy, love, in comparison to you I'm an old woman— Ah ha!' she exclaimed, forestalling his threatened protestations as he quickly lifted his head. 'I didn't say I *was* an old woman, I just said that in comparison to you I was. Oh, I'm flattered right enough, in fact I couldn't begin to tell you just how much I'm flattered.' She leaned back, away from him, and straightened herself up. She stared down, firstly at her plain white cotton blouse, then to her skirt and her sensible black shoes. 'Look at me, Davy. I'm not the most sylphlike, fashionable creature you'll ever see. In fact, I'm practically fat! But, in any case, age is not my most important objection. Neither your age nor mine. I don't suppose I would feel any different if you were twenty-nine, thirty-nine or even ninety-nine. No, my big objection, Davy, is that I am empty. There's nothing left, the well is dry. I have no love left to give *any* man. Once it might have been a different story but not now. The love was beaten out of me, Davy, and it was beaten out of me by a man— my husband!' She removed her hands from his and cupped them under his chin. She tilted it up until his moist, sad eyes were now just inches from hers. 'Just supposing, Davy, that there was

99

a drain of if left. Do you really think I'd give it to you? No, Davy, love. If I couldn't give it to my kids, I'd give it to the cat, or perhaps to my job, or even to another woman! But never, never, to a man, Davy, not ever again.'

There was silence for a moment as they just stared at each other—the bewildered, almost frightened, youth and the dry-eyed, bitter woman. They were so close that the boy felt her breath on his face and he gulped at it hungrily. The clean fresh smell of the kitchen soap wafted up from her hands that were still cupped around his chin. He wanted so much to kiss her because he felt he would never be so close again. In spite of this desire he remained immobile, unwilling to risk losing even her temporary nearness for such a prize. His staring eyes inched slowly down the woman's face until they reached her mouth. Still no movement came from her. He studied her lips—they were full and generous, yet firm-set and determined. Then suddenly, almost imperceptibly, he saw the first movement. It was little more than a quiver really. Nevertheless, the straight, tight line between those two full lips had visibly widened. Terrified lest the spell should break, he neither blinked nor breathed. 'Oh, you sod, Davy,' murmured the woman as she slowly leaned forward and put her lips to his.

At first it was a timeless kiss, lasting forever. Not another part of them even moved. Brenda was the first to change this rule as she slowly slipped her hands from beneath David's chin. Her movements were so light that David was at first unaware of the transition. Soon, however, as her arms tightened lovingly around his neck, he too began to move. Becoming more confident by the second, he slipped his arms around her back and eased her gently to the wide, padded cushions. The position was hardly comfortable for Brenda and she reluctantly broke from the kiss and swiftly adjusted her position by lying full-length along the settee. David looked adoringly down at her and opened his mouth to speak.

'Shush, don't you dare say a word,' whispered the

woman quickly, as she pulled him down alongside her and offered up her lips once more. This time, David did not kiss her mouth but traced the outline of her lips with the tips of his fingers. She responded by kissing each of the fingers rapidly before finally seizing one with her teeth and drawing it deep into the soft, moist warmth of her mouth. So far, all of David's play had been instinctive. Perceptive though she was, even Brenda could not have known that never before had he been so close to a woman—or girl for that matter. Not too sure of the accepted rules, David decided to stick to instinct. It had, after all, been rewarding so far. Easing his fingers from her mouth, he let them slip lightly down her chin and throat to the neckline of her blouse. Lifting her head slightly, she pushed her face deep into his and, open-mouthed, began to devour his lips. Trembling and now fully aroused, he slid his hand further down the outside of her blouse to the swell of her ample left breast. Although Brenda began to shake her head vigorously, still she drew hard upon his lips. He checked his movements momentarily before resuming his quest. Soon he found a button and then two more. It had always looked easy in films but unfastening three blouse buttons with one hand, while looking in the opposite direction, was more difficult than he imagined, particularly with someone shaking their head so vigorously. Because of Brenda's possible change of mind, David felt he daren't stop. He therefore responded to her open-mouthed kissing, while still feeling blindly in the vicinity of her breast. Soon another button popped and his exploring hand told him that a sizeable part of Brenda's left shoulder was now clearly visible. Resuming the attack on her mouth, he slipped his hand beneath the thin strap of her bra and levered it easily from her smooth, rounded shoulder. He found it maddening that he was not able to see what he had so adroitly unfettered. It was obviously now decision time. Was he to persist with the passionate kissing, or should he pause for a look?

It was at this stage that his inexperience finally let him down—he paused for a look. It was spectacularly the wrong decision. Michael Butler was later to tell him exactly where he misconceived. 'If you *must* look, Davy, you should do so *before*. You can even look *after* if you have to. But never, never look *during*.'

Her mouth now free from restrictions, Brenda reasserted her verbal control. 'No, Davy, no!'

Crimson with embarrassment, she dipped her left shoulder and raised the strap back into place.

'I'm sorry, Brenda, really I am. I thought . . .' His voice trailed away.

'It's okay, don't worry about it, it wasn't your fault,' she assured him as she gathered the blouse around her. 'It was mine. I'm big and ugly enough to have known better.'

His apologetic air changed instantly. Seizing her wrists, he became verbally confident for the first time since they met. 'You're nothing of the kind! You're beautiful,' he cried.

As she opened her mouth to speak, he freed one wrist and clapped his hand firmly over her mouth. 'Shut up and don't interrupt,' he ordered. 'I don't say things that I don't mean and even when I first saw you, I thought you were a truly beautiful woman—now I'm sure of it. You can have a go at me if you like and you'd probably be quite justified. But you cannot, you *cannot*, denigrate yourself. I simply won't let you. You, nor anybody else. Do you understand that?' Without pausing for a reply, he continued: 'I'll leave now and I promise I won't bother you again, but if you think I was looking for just a cheap thrill then you're wrong. And I don't bloody care if you *are* older than me— you are still wrong! I love you, Brenda, and I know you think I'm just a kid but even a kid can love. I would have done anything rather than upset you, but I obviously *have* upset you and now I'm deeply sorry about it.' He took the hand from her mouth then slowly released her wrist. Standing up, he reached to the nearby chair for his windcheater.

'Davy,' she whispered, as he moved towards the door. 'Look at me, Davy.' He paused and turned his head. 'What is it that you see in me, Davy? I'm no beauty, I doubt very much if I ever was. I'm just a . . . .' She shook her head in a frustrating search for words. 'Well, I'm just a middle-aged mum. Come on, look at me now, Dave, lying here. Have you ever seen anything with less pride or dignity? Sprawled on a settee with my tits half out, snatching at a bit of romance before my kids come home for tea—and that with someone young enough to be one of them! Then look at yourself, Davy. What are you—nineteen? You've got your whole life in front of you and here you are declaring love for some old b—' She saw the anger return instantly to his face as he anticipated her words. 'Well, all right, Dave, but you know full well what I mean. You're a fine-looking boy, Davy, you could have the girls at your feet. My Sandra's not stopped talking about you for two days! Isn't that ridiculous? She's barmy over you and you want to bed *me*!' She gave a harsh laugh.

'You still don't understand, do you, not even now?' he said, shaking his head sadly.

'Oh, I understand right enough. I understand I'm not the hard-nosed bitch I thought I was. I understand that as you were undressing me, I wanted you inside me as I have never wanted anything before. I understood that right enough!'

'You felt like that?' he asked incredulously.

'Of course I did! And d'you know why? For the first time in my adult life I felt someone touching me who genuinely cared about me. Strangely enough, I don't doubt that you love me, Dave. I think you are quite seriously in love with me. But that is worse for me than the "cheap thrill" you spoke about. Do you know why?' This time she gave him a chance to answer.

'No,' he said, shaking his head in bewilderment.

'It is a disaster for me, Dave, because I could so easily—oh, so easily—love you in return.'

'Well there you are then!' he cried triumphantly. 'That proves my point!'

'To me that proves anything *but* your point, Dave. If I fell in love with you, I would fall on you like a landslide. I would bloody *eat* you, Davy Ducker. Don't forget I have a whole lifetime of love to catch up on. It wouldn't be just

103

sex, but hand-holding, pillow-talk and days out with the kids. In twenty years of marriage and three children I never knew one second of a love like that.'

'But you contradict yourself, Brenda. You reckon that I couldn't make you happy, then you say—'

'Oh, you'd make me happy right enough. For about a month, I would guess, then nature would run its course. It would have to, that's the way of things, Dave. You would suddenly realize that all of your friends were dashing around with rosy-cheeked, firm-busted dolly-birds, whilst you . . . What would you have, Davy, what would you have?'

He bent down and slid his hand gently under her still partially exposed left breast. 'I'd have a real *woman*,' he murmured as he lightly kissed her nipple through its smooth covering. 'Not perhaps a "firm-busted" one,' he whispered between kisses, 'but a real woman all the same.'

'But you'd leave me, Davy, you'd leave me, you sod. I bloody know you would.'

'Never, Bren, never! Never leave you—I promise!'

She closed her eyes as he continued to kiss her and this time there was no move to resist.

David may not have slept very well during the morning, but that afternoon in Brenda's flat he was out like a light. Or rather he had been. As he roused from these slumbers, he felt it wasn't just that his brain had closed down, but that his whole body had fossilized. He was sure that his left arm, in particular, would never move again. Wearily he opened his eyes and examined the offending limb. It refused to move for the very best of reasons. Lying solidly across it and pinning it to the carpeted floor, was a buxom nude beauty who was even sounder asleep than he had been. The gentle hiss of the nearby gas fire explained why they had not perished from hypothermia. Nevertheless, the damp perspiration from their exertions had dramatically cooled on their exposed bodies. It was doubtless this change in temperature that had stirred him.

A crumpled eiderdown lay in a heap alongside them. He reached across the sleeping woman and began to cover her with it. The sudden chill impact was instant. Her eyelids fluttered for a second then she opened them wide. For a brief moment she appeared to recoil but, as realization dawned, she smiled happily and nuzzled into him.

'I'll let you into a secret about me,' she murmured into his broad chest. 'No one else in the whole world knows it. Would you like to hear what it is?'

'Uh-huh.'

'Give me your hand then and I'll show you.' He slipped his hand into hers. 'You'll have to be brave, mind you,' she pointed out. 'Are you ready?'

'Yes,' he said, showing just a little uncertainty.

She gripped his hand firmly and swiftly moved it round to her buttocks. 'I suffer from a very cold bum!'

'God! That's absolutely icy!' he complained.

'I don't know what you're bitching about,' she pouted. 'I have to live with it!'

'You must have got it through sleeping on that floor. You are probably lying in a draught.'

'No doubt I am, but it would be just as cold in a desert heatwave.' She quickly rolled over and tucked her well-rounded bottom into his now warm lap. He let forth a predictable scream. She wriggled even deeper into him as she seized his hands and cupped them over her breasts. 'You know what they say—"Love me, love my bum",' she paraphrased.

'I think the word is "dog", but as your bum is as lovely as the rest of you, you're on to a winner, you bitch.' He began once more to caress her.

'Davy, are you sure you're a total novice at this game?' she asked dreamily, between purrs.

'I swear it.'

'Hmm, my marriage must have been worse than I thought then because this is absolutely wonderful.'

Further conversation was interrupted by the old brown chiming-clock that perched precariously on the mantlepiece. She suddenly sat bolt upright and the eiderdown tumbled away. David thought she looked like a magnificent, unveiled Victorian statue. 'That's never the time!' she shrieked.

'Of course it is,' said the young man, glancing at his watch. 'In fact, if anything, that clock's a little slow. I make it ten minutes past.'

'Not four, surely?'

'Of course four.'

'Christ! My Danny will be home in a few minutes. Quick, get dressed!'

She began to race around collecting up items of clothing and straightening cushions. David did not move an inch but lay back with his head on his hands, watching in total admiration. 'Brenda!' he announced finally. 'All voluptuous women should do their housework in the nude. You look superb—bloody superb!'

She swung round with her hands on her hips and her feet astride. 'Well, make the most of it, lover,' she said. 'Because we can't make a habit of this. Besides—' She leaned over him and kissed him lightly on the top of his head. 'That draught's playing merry hell with my bum. NOW GET UP!'

As a result of their mutual haste, the room was soon tidy, with both occupants decently dressed. There were still five or six minutes before Danny was due to arrive. The now overalled Brenda stood in the kitchen, peeling potatoes. David moved up behind her and slipped his arms around her waist. 'Brenda, when do I see you again?' he whispered.

She sighed heavily and laid her head back on his chest. 'Davy, I'm not at all sure that you should. If this afternoon was just a one-off affair, I think that we both could survive. But if we go in any deeper, one of us—no doubt me—is going to get really hurt.' She turned up her head and kissed his face. 'I don't want to be hurt any more, Dave. I've had enough hurt for one lifetime.'

He spun her around to face him with an intensity that

almost bruised. 'Listen!' he snapped, his eyes narrowing. 'If you tell me you never want to see me again—fine! But unless you do that, Brenda, I'm going to see you at every opportunity that I can. I want you, I love you, and I don't give a sod who knows it. You and I are going to walk down the street arm in arm, we are going to stop and just kiss, regardless of whoever is there. It doesn't matter a toss to me what other people think. We can even take the kids out for the day if you wish—just like you wanted.'

She gave a hollow little laugh as she shook her head in disbelief. 'Oh, wouldn't my Sandra love that! I can just see her—holding our hands and skipping between us! You'd be lucky if she didn't stick a knife in you—me too for that matter! Do you know your problem, Davy? I'll tell you. You make love like a man but you talk like a romantic ten-year-old.'

'Listen here—'

'No, you listen to me. If you have any feelings for me at all, then you've got to listen. I had fifteen years of hell with my husband. The only thing that kept me sane were my three kids. Once he was dead, it was only the four of us who knew what misery we'd suffered. It is because of this that we are so close. All I want is for my kids to be happy. I can't risk happiness for myself. It's not that I don't want it, it's just that happiness always lets me down. So there'll be no walking arm in arm down the High Street, Davy, no day trips to the zoo. You can get that out of your head for a start. I realize that you are infatuated with me and I think you honestly believe you're in love. I would also be a liar if I pretended I wasn't extremely flattered by your feelings. But—'

'It seems to me there's always a "but",' the young man cut in ruefully.

'You're learning!' she conceded. 'But—I've decided there is to be no starry-eyed romance between us. If it would help you to come around here—not very often, mind—but if it would help you to get me out of your system, then I agree. I can't lie to you, Dave. Making love with you was just so beautiful. It would be no hardship for me to repeat that from time to time, but there are to be no declarations of undying love. I don't want to even hear the word. Of course—' She paused and smiled for a moment. 'If you would like to lie to me a little and tell me I'm beautiful or such like, I wouldn't object to that, but absolutely no *love*, Davy, understand? No love.'

'But why, Brenda, why?'

'Because if you tell me you love me enough times and make me feel as I did this afternoon, then sure as hell I'm going to love you. And the moment I do that, Davy Ducker, I'm finished.'

'Mum! I'm 'ome, Mum! What've we got to eat?'

'That's my family, Davy. It's time you went, I'm afraid.' She gave him a quick kiss to the cheek. 'Keep in touch though, eh?'

CHAPTER EIGHT

The night bus throbbed past as Michael stood thoughtfully in the doorway of Dolcis shoe shop. He was enjoying the freedom of being 'out on his own', but as yet he knew little of the manor and needed to take stock of his bearings. He studied his pocket-geographia at some length and tried to trace the boundaries of numbers five and six beats. He had been engrossed in this task for some minutes when he was aware of soft but rapid footsteps. Glancing from his studies, he was rather pleased to observe Duggie Frobisher, a local villain of no mean reputation. Michael's pleasure at seeing the lad was primarily because Duggie was the only villain he actually knew.

Two weeks previously, while a passenger in the police van, Michael had listened in some fascination as old Bert Bones had read Duggie 'his fortune'. It seemed that the young man worked alone. He was a housebreaker by occupation and was already on bail for at least two heavy break-ins. He was a strange lad in many respects; most of his family had been the scourge of the manor for years. They were vicious, uncaring and gloried in their justifiable reputation for violence. The six male members and at least two of the females, formed an integral part of the notorious Robertson gang from Peckham. This was a gang that was into most aspects of protection, prostitution and the new venture—drugs.

Young Duggie did not conform to the rest of the family. This puzzled the family as much as it puzzled the police. He was something of a loner, yet in his own way, he could create as much misery and mayhem as any of his more infamous relatives—albeit without the violence. Bert Bones had given Duggie a 'good talking to' and, when Bert spoke, people tended to listen. They particularly listened when Bert had them by the shirt front. That night, Duggie had not only listened but made an about-turn and gone home. On the face of it he had been attempting nothing more daring than a late-night stroll. Bert had explained, however, that a late-night stroll by Duggie was a clear breach of the 'Cabul Lane Late-Night Strolling Act'. As such, he (Bert) was quite entitled to swing one on him. Duggie then said he was deeply indebted to Bert for explaining the workings of this little-known act.

Although quite happy with this, Bert still felt obliged to acquaint the suspect with a recent amendment to this act. He therefore explained that any renewed walk later in the night, or even a reported break-in the next morning, could well result in retrospective action being taken. In Duggie's own parlance, this would mean being 'stitched up and swifted in at the first opportunity'. Douglas Brewster Frobisher therefore went home and, more importantly, stayed there.

Michael felt he had a decision to make. Should he too speak to the lad, or should he ignore him? If he was to speak, it would, of course, be for no other reason than that Duggie was the only villain he knew. By the same token, was that a sufficient reason for *not* speaking to him? With discretion hardly being Michael's strong point, the decision was made for him. 'Here—just a minute!' he called. 'You there, Duggie. Where're you off to?'

Now, to query the activities of a bailed and convicted housebreaker at one o'clock in the morning in a heavily residential area, may have seemed understandable to the constable, but the same, however, could not be said for the suspect.

'You ain't got no right to keep pickin' on me,' Duggie muttered angrily. 'That's 'arassment, that's what that is. I can 'ave you for that! I'm goin' to speak to my pro-bay-shun officer abaht it next time I see her.'

Now words like ''arassment' and 'pro-bay-shun officer' can be guaranteed to confuse any recruit making his first official 'stop'. Michael was no exception; he would have almost been happier if Duggie had pulled a gun.

'Yes . . . well,' he faltered, without a shred of conviction in his voice. 'You just watch it, that's all.' He then nodded wisely as if he had personally solved half of London's crime figures.

Douglas Frobisher was nobody's fool and just as he had realized he was on to a loser with Bert Bones, so he knew a winner when he saw one. But the very last thing he wanted was to be searched. He had enough HBIs (housebreaking implements) scattered around his person to open a bank. It was therefore essential that he retained the initiative. He glanced at his watch.

'So, let me see . . . it's one in the mornin' in Cabul Road and I've been stopped by . . . PC 171, is it? I can't quite see in this light. Anyway, would you like to tell me, officer, just why it is that you're detainin' me? After all, if I'm goin' to allege 'arassment I ought to know why.'

Michael's mind was by now just a void. He realized he had forgotten everything he had been taught. He had a gut feeling he was being had over and he did not have the first inkling of what to do about it. He decided to cut and run. 'It's all right,' he finally blurted. 'I'm now satisfied with your movements. You can go if you want to.'

Having more sense than to overplay his hand, Duggie also decided to make a strategic withdrawal. 'Now don't get me wrong, officer. I'm not anti-police, far from it. I realize you people 'ave a difficult enough job to do as it is. It is just that when you're on your way 'ome after a long day's work, well, you just don't expect to keep gettin' stopped like this. If you're 'appy, though, I won't take the matter any furver. Good-night.'

Michael could not bring himself to make a reply. He watched with some frustration as Duggie strode smugly off towards Camberwell. After a short perusal of the map, he realized that the young crook's path led in the general direction of five beat. Allowing a suitable distance, Michael decided to follow. He was soon to realize that the white-coated, newspaper-reading detectives, who were never more than five yards behind the suspect in television plays, would have had their work cut out to keep track of Duggie Frobisher. It was not that the youngster was aware of Michael, he was not. It was simply that he was devious by nature and hardly, if ever, took a straight path to any planned break-in. As they threaded their way through the narrow maze of streets, Michael temporarily lost sight of his quarry on at least two occasions, but it was at the rear of Oxbury Square where he finally admitted defeat. The square was one of Cabul Lane's few affluent locations. It had become something of a trendy spot in recent times, with many professional classes taking up residence because of its accessibility to central London. As a last resort, Michael stood motionless in the centre of the square, straining for every sound. Other than the wind through the few trees, there was little to hear. After five fruitless minutes he was about to give up when he thought he glimpsed the merest flash of torchlight. It had been so brief he was not even sure he had seen it. It had come, he believed, from the bay window of the largest house in the square. He moved stealthily in that direction. Yes! There it was again and of equal brevity. As his eyes became accustomed to the shadows, he realized why the light had been so brief. It was not the *real* light he had seen at all, but the fleeting reflection. The real light was still probing the patio window of the house next door.

Michael's first instinct was to leap the fence and grab the suspect. He was, however, uncomfortably aware that he was already acquiring a reputation for impetuosity. Better do this one right, he thought. Positioned as he was, he could hardly call the station on his personal radio without alerting the wary burglar. The only alternative was to tiptoe silently out of earshot. One minute later, every unit on the Cabul Lane manor knew that Douglas Brewster Frobisher was in the process of screwing 18 Oxbury Square. Ten seconds after that, most of them were on their way to the scene. Time was running out for young Duggie.

Michael's first response was from Cabul Lane itself.

'Where exactly is he now?' crackled the station officer's voice.

'Not sure, Sarge. I had to leave him while I called you on the bat-phone.'

'What? You bloody idiot! Get back there and watch him! He's a slippery sod, that one. If you turn your back on him for a second you'll lose him for sure.'

As far as Michael was concerned, he now had the green light. There was to be no more cat and mouse. It was a case of straight in, nick him and straight out again. He raced back to the house and vaulted the fence with ease. There was a garden spade propped up against a wall and next to it was a huge glass patio door that had been rather expertly eased from its runners. This door was propped at a crazy angle to the wall and appeared in some danger of falling. Racing through the opening into the dining-room, Michael made for the staircase. On covering half of the flight, he clearly heard a window being thrown open. He burst into the back bedroom in time to see the curtain wafting gently in the breeze. Michael had both legs over the sill before he realized that whoever had opened the window had most certainly not left by it. There was a cluttered corner beneath it that would have broken the back of anyone fool enough to jump. He cursed his own stupidity.

'What the hell is going on in here?' The light clicked on and a balding, pyjama-clad figure, waving a sinister-looking club, burst through the door. At the same time, the retreating footsteps of Duggie Frobisher could be heard running across the room below.

'Police-officer!' Michael needlessly announced. 'Can't talk now!' He dived past the startled newcomer and collided with a red-satined bundle of pink, warm flesh. In spite of the drama of the chase, he still felt compelled to assist the terrified lady to her feet. 'You smell beautiful,' he panted as he resumed pursuit.

All of Duggie's movements so far had been with stealth. The only loud noise had been the opening of the window —an obvious red herring. His next movement, however, was neither quiet nor stealthy. The crash must have been heard streets away.

'It's the patio door!' yelled Michael to no one in particular. 'The bugger must have pushed it over.'

In fact, the bugger had not pushed it over. The bugger had—sadly for him—run straight into it. Not just into it, but straight through it.

Duggie staggered punchily across the square before regaining his composure. The sound of distant police cars added a good yard to his speed. He had taken his usual precaution of parking his car near the scene some hours before. If he could only reach it unobserved he would be in with a chance.

The last fragmented pieces of glass fell as Michael turned out of the dining-room. As he reached the now empty aluminium frame, he stopped in horror. It seemed that every bit of broken glass was blood-soaked! Although near, no supporting car had yet reached the square. Michael dithered for a moment before deciding to follow the blood trail that was crystal clear even in the street light. It led across the square and into Oxbury Walk, a crescent-shaped alley that opened into the neighbouring street.

Supple though he was, Duggie Frobisher now realized he was not the fittest of people. Although aware of this fact he was still surprised just how unfit he had become. He had only run across the square and down the alley, yet he could not have felt more restricted if his legs had been tied. Not only that but he was wet. In fact, not just wet but soaking. Where, he wondered, had all that water come from? Just ahead of him was his car. A few yards more and he would be able to snatch a breather. It was as he ran between his car and an old parked van that he felt himself falling. It was a strange fall, it seemed to take so long. The whole of the tumble seemed to be in slow-motion. Slowly, oh so slowly, the street came up to meet him. He could never remember being so tired. He felt that he must have a sleep. Yes, that was it, just a little sleep.

At first Michael thought he had lost him. The blood trail had petered out some distance back and he could no longer hear footsteps. It was the heel of the shoe that still rested on the kerbstone that first caught his eye. Michael slowed his pace to a walk and approached the dormant figure with an air of nonchalance. Balancing one foot on the kerb, he rested the other in the small of Duggie's back. 'Come on then, sunshine, you're nicked. That'll teach you to be lippy to the local sheriff. You can report *that* to your "pro-bay-shun officer" if you like.'

Duggie made no response.

'Come on. It's no good hiding down there, you've been sussed out.' Michael bent down and turned over the inert youngster. He suddenly caught his breath. Even in that light he had never seen such a white face. If the face was white, it was in direct contrast to everything else—that was red. And such a red! It was everywhere, the clothing absolutely soused. Michael needed no doctor to pronounce life extinct. Duggie Frobisher was not so much dead as empty. It looked like every drop of blood had drained from his body.

Inspector Wilson thought the world was against him. What with Patterson, the assault on Helen and now a dead prisoner he was beginning to wonder just what God he had offended. He had been at Cabul Lane for five years now, each of them totally miserable. He knew he had never been meant to police such an unsuitable area. Unsuitable for his particular talents, that is. Sometimes he wondered what D5 branch at Scotland Yard were up to. If he had been posted to Hampstead or Teddington, for example, he considered he would be at least a chief inspector by now, but five years in this God-forsaken hole was like a life sentence to a man of his background and sensitivity. It was all very well for inspectors such as Ted Dunn—Dunn was never going any higher and he knew it. He was therefore well suited to such an area. There were times he believed the man actually *liked* the damn place! But then he never had been able to understand Dunn. Ernest Wilson believed that supervising officers should always lead from the rear. He had absolutely no desire to be the 'Sheriff of Dodge'. Instead he saw himself as something of a diplomat, but to be a diplomat one needed to work in a 'diplomatic' area. Now whatever the gifts needed to police Cabul Lane, diplomacy was certainly not one of them. Oh for that administrator's desk at Scotland Yard! It would come soon though, he was sure of it. The only problem was, would he keep his sanity long enough to enjoy it?

Now if Ernest Wilson deluded himself as to his value to the force, he was nothing short of perverse about his standing with his men. He considered that he radiated an air of respectful, icy detachment; they thought he was a wally—and a timorous one at that. Take his nickname, for example. No matter in what context the men spoke of him; no matter how urgent the story; no matter how short the time; he was *never* referred to solely as 'Ernest'. No, it was always the full, grandiose title—'Going-the-other-way-Ernest' or, occasionally, 'Ernest-the-rabbit'. This related to his habit of concluding every Walter Mitty crime story he ever told—and there were many, God but there were many!—with the same dozen words: 'If I hadn't been going the other way, I'd have nicked him.'

Ernest Benjamin Wilson then was not only unloved and misunderstood but also paranoic. In fact, on first hearing of the downfall of PC Preacher Patterson he was almost suicidal. Since the time of that assault though it did seem he had adjusted. The dead Douglas Frobisher, however, had just put him neatly back to square one.

'Why does this consistently happen to me? Go on, tell me why!' he screamed at quiet, pipe-smoking Jack Baker, one of his two uniformed sergeants. 'It's a plot, y'know,' he continued, nodding his head violently. 'It's a plot to stop me getting away from this place. I tell you, I won't stand for it! Take Patterson for instance. The man was a religious nutter! Never should have been in the job in the first place. But will they sort out the fools who let him through the interview board? Will they hell! They're fire-proof. It's poor sods like me who wind up carrying the can. God, I'll be here forever now! I'll never get away. How the bloody

116

hell could I be expected to know that the maniac liked to rip the knickers from plonks and nurses? Go on, tell me that!' His eyes then narrowed and his voice trailed almost to a whisper. 'I don't know why the fool thought he needed to do it in the first place. It's my opinion that half of these girls don't even wear knickers. I've seen what goes on here, I'm not blind, y' know!'

In response the sergeant gave just the slightest of nods. This was to indicate that yes, he did realize that the inspector was not blind. Baker's nods were the equivalent to four minutes of conversation from anybody else.

'And how about that lunatic, Butler? The man's obviously not suited for the job, anyone can see that. Not satisfied with punching a sergeant on his first day here, he now kills a damn prisoner! There's going to be changes, y'know, Sergeant. Oh, there's going to be changes all right. That lot don't know what "close supervision" is. But they are going to, I tell you, they are going to.'

The sergeant momentarily toyed with the idea of mentioning that in order to carry out some close supervision, one would need to spend some time on the streets, a location that Wilson was particularly averse to. Instead he just raised one eyebrow slightly.

The personal radio suddenly crackled into life. '832, 832, from 421, receiving—over.'

'421, 421, from 832, go ahead—over.'

'Carole, can you give me your location—over.'

'Myatt's Street—over.'

'Good. Can you meet me at the junction of Sparrow's Lane and Lamp's Alley in say about . . . five minutes —over.'

'Will do. 832 out.'

'Y'see! Y'see!' cried Wilson triumphantly. 'What did I say? Didn't I tell you? What are those two monkeys up to at five in the morning at that location? It's one of the darkest and most secluded places on the whole manor. He's a married man with two kids and she's a single girl half his age. Tell me that, uh?'

The sergeant gave the question fair consideration, then,

having reached no firm conclusion, raised his other eyebrow in indifference.

'Right! Book the "general-purpose" car out, Sarge. If I'm going to start tightening up on discipline, then there's no time like the present. We've had enough trouble for one night and I'm going to take a stand.'

Some minutes later, with the ignition switched off and the lights extinguished, the car rolled silently up to a point some sixty yards from the end of Sparrow's Lane. A fleeting glimpse of uniform was seen disappearing into the alley that ran at the side of White's warehouse.

'There they go,' observed Wilson. 'We'll leave the car here, Sergeant, and follow on foot.'

Lamp's Alley was dark and littered with all manner of hazards. These ranged from brick rubble and old mattresses to stagnant puddles and dog's excrement. To anyone without a torch or knowledge of its layout, the alley was a veritable minefield. Inspector Wilson was neither familiar with its layout, nor did he possess a torch. His first misplaced step positioned him directly on a dog-turd of unparalleled length. Meanwhile Baker sensibly tiptoed quietly along behind him.

'Blast! Sometimes I wonder what they feed these animals on!' Wilson glanced disgustedly down. 'Yuk! It's nigh over my ankle!' He wiped the shoe frantically on a disembowelled mattress.

Resuming his quest, he had almost reached the end of the alley when he noticed a bright light coming from the flat roofs above some lock-up garages in the next street. The alley turned sharp right, then left, before leading straight to the rear of these premises. Some adjacent shops had proved extremely vulnerable to break-ins and a light had been installed as a deterrent some weeks previously. A fire escape led up to these roofs and there, exactly in the centre and clearly illuminated for anyone to see, were the two uniformed officers locked in an embrace and whistling 'Begin the Beguine' rather loudly!

'I think my whole bloody shift has gone sex-mad and barmy!' exclaimed the inspector, still scraping his foot.

Cupping his hands he called loudly up to the now swaying couple. 'Anderson! Campbell!' George Anderson and Carole Campbell instantly released their passionate holds and looked aghast as the supervising pair ascended the iron staircase.

'Just what the hell do you think you are playing at?' demanded Wilson. 'Don't you think I have enough bloody problems with Patterson and that lunatic, Butler, without you two having a floodlit orgy in full uniform whilst on duty? People like you disgust me, Anderson, do you know that? I think it's wicked to play on a young girl's emotions like this. You a married man and father too! What sort of example is this? You should be able to control your base instincts. It should be a requirement of the force. People outside this job look up to you, Anderson, don't you realize that? I don't suppose you care though, you're not the type. You let us all down by your behaviour, not just me but Sergeant Baker here and the rest of your colleagues. In fact, you let down everyone from the Commissioner to the youngest cadet.' The inspector took a quick breath as he really warmed to his subject. Sergeant Baker gave a pained wince.

'It's not right though, Anderson, and I am going to do something about it. This young girl has been placed in my charge and I will protect her, of that you can be sure. Even in spite of herself I will. Do you know what you have lost in these last few minutes, Anderson? I'll tell you. You have lost something really precious. You have lost my trust and your own good name. I need men under me that I can rely on, Anderson, and that just seems to rule you out, wouldn't you say?'

Not once during these series of questions did he pause long enough for the PC to reply. Undaunted, Wilson then turned to the girl. 'And as for you, Campbell, I should think your mother would be appalled. I know I would be if you were *my* daughter.'

Carole Campbell was one of four sisters. Necessity had taught her that one did not wait for verbal opportunities, one just cut straight in. 'My mother, sir?' she asked in genuine puzzlement. 'What's my mother got to do with it?'

'Oh, I don't know I'm sure,' said the inspector loftily. 'I suppose my problem is that I credit other people with my own moral standard. It is just that I assume even nowadays there are some mothers of young girls who are not over-happy when their daughters throw themselves at married men. You know that, at the very least, one of you will now have to be transferred, I suppose?'

'But we're practising, sir,' explained George Anderson.

'What for—a public orgy?'

'No, sir, the Newington Formation Dance team, sir. Carole and I are partners. You see, this floodlit flat roof is perfect for practising and usually, sir—well, usually there's no one about. We only do it for ten minutes or so and only then if the manor is quiet. We were on the television last week in "Come Dancing",' he added proudly.

'Excuse me, sir,' cut in the girl politely. 'You've got something on the side of your shoe.'

Wilson stared open-mouthed at the pair. 'Sergeant Baker, am I hearing right or have I finally cracked? Are these two fools telling me that whenever they think it is quiet on the manor, they come ballroom dancing in full uniform on a bloody roof? Is that what they're saying? Is it, Sergeant?'

Sergeant Baker rubbed his chin thoughtfully for almost a full minute. His late-day facial stubble almost rustled. He finally spoke. 'I think that's about the size of it, sir, yes. That plus you've got something on your shoe.'

Wilson clapped both of his hands to the sides of his head and held them there, scraping his shoe once again as he did so. 'Go! Go! Get out of here! I'll see you two in my office as soon as we start duty tomorrow night—that's providing I don't have a breakdown beforehand. Now just get out of here, will you?' George Anderson opened his mouth to speak as Wilson swiftly pointed a threatening finger directly at him. 'If you don't get out of here . . .'

The two dancers began to scuttle down the iron staircase.

'It's the entire relief's day off tomorrow night, sir,' said Sergeant Baker helpfully. 'And the day after that—'

George Anderson paused halfway down the stairs. 'That was what I was going to—'

'WILL-YOU-GET-OUT-OF-HERE-ANDERSON!' yelled Wilson.

As the two uniforms faded into the surrounding darkness, Wilson looked desperately at his sergeant. 'What the hell do I do about this? You can just imagine what the chief superintendent will say about it, can't you? He'll go bloody berserk.'

'Might make an interesting change of direction for him though, guv'.'

'In what respect?'

'Well, instead of teacups being responsible for the demise of the force, he could blame those poofy ballroom dancers. It'd make a nice change that, sir.'

'Seriously, Sergeant,' said Wilson, shaking his head as they moved off towards the alley. 'What am I going to do about those two?'

Baker sniffed. 'Mind if I light me pipe, guv'?'

The inspector gave an airy wave. 'You can set yourself on fire if you wish. No, on second thoughts, do that when you are *off* duty. I don't think I could stand another disaster.'

'W-e-l-l,' drawled the sergeant, puffing out the first billowing cloud. 'If I were you, I wouldn't do anything. I don't think there's much danger of those two waltzing around the rooftops any more, and what would you gain if you did take action? It would be bound to come out that they had been up here many times before and where would that leave you? With forty yards of pink tulle and dog-shit on your shoe, so to speak. Incidentally, that still bloody stinks. No, guv', I think the most sensible move you can make is to chew the bollocks off the pair of them—well, him at least—then quietly forget the whole thing. After all, sir,' said the sergeant, pointing at the inspector's shoe. 'One more mishap on your relief and you're a dead cert for permanent night-duty on the Isle of Dogs.' Baker paused as if to let his words sink in before continuing in similar tone. 'As for young Butler, guv', well, I think you're worrying yourself unnecessarily there. I mean, the "prisoner" wasn't actually a prisoner at all, was he? He was dead by the time that Butler reached him. I know he's a bit impetuous and all that but not even Butler can arrest a dead man. It's a straightforward "accidental death" or misadventure at the most. Nothing to do with the Old Bill at all.

This uncharacteristically helpful approach from the sergeant was not without a selfish motive. Like most others at Cabul Lane, he considered that five neurotic years of Inspector Ernest Wilson was more than enough. Anything that might help speed him safely off the streets and into his dream Shangri-la at Scotland Yard, could only be looked upon as an investment.

'I suppose you're right, Sergeant. I have enough problems as it is without creating a whole new set. I think I'll take heed of your advice on this one, thank you.'

'Sensible decision if I may say so, sir,' nodded Baker as he gave an extra long draw on his briar and puffed out a slow, rolling fog. 'Y'know,' he said thoughtfully. 'I wouldn't mind seeing that young Carole in her sequins and tango frock. She's got a great arse on her that girl, a really great arse.'

CHAPTER NINE

In the two months that Preacher lay in intensive care, his condition hardly altered. He certainly *looked* better but then it would have been difficult to have looked worse. This cosmetic improvement was due entirely to the subsidence of much of his swelling. His injuries, however, had not improved and in addition he was suffering greatly from shock. Detective Inspector Bromley had hardly been able to restrain his frustration. In spite of numerous requests, the doctor in charge of treatment had consistently refused him access. The fact that a search had revealed a considerable amount of ladies' underclothing in Preacher's bedroom cupboards, merely increased this frustration.

The mood of Cabul Lane Police Station was one of total disbelief. There were, of course, the usual know-alls who, with hindsight, claimed they had suspected Preacher all along. After all, they pointed out, there was something really weird about the bloke and they never had liked him. But then Preacher had *never* been popular and had always been something of a loner. Yet there is a world of difference between being a 'loner' and being a 'lurker' who smacks young girls over the head with blunt instruments. Not to mention slicing off their undergarments with Stanley knives.

The one fortunate aspect was that the story had not broken publicly. The fact that a serving PC had been all but left for dead in the back of his own car, would have been news enough. For that same officer to have been the prime suspect for a series of sexual assaults, would have been headline material. Before Bromley could charge Preacher, he had many loose ends to knit together. Therefore, the very last thing he wanted was for the media to be clambering all over the manor. He realized the story was eventually bound to break, and this left him with a dilemma. The longer he concealed the crime, the more chance he had to solve it. Yet if he did not solve it, the delay would be disastrous for his career. Bromley was never a man to take risks with so important a commodity and in copper's parlance 'his bottle was going'. One thing was sure. Sooner or later some mercenary sod would leak the story to the press. Where would he be then?

During these same two months, the four recruits had begun to acquire a real taste for the force. Helen had recovered physically if not emotionally and was now at work, whilst Angela's somewhat dizzy attitude ensured a degree of popularity out of all proportion to her service. Of the boys, David had begun to use his eager talents in the district rugby and football teams, and Michael was considered to be the keenest recruit to arrive at the station for years.

This keenness, plus his recognized appreciation for the opposite sex, caused him to be elaborately set up by several members of his relief. At the end of his sixth week of service, he was taken quietly aside by Sergeant Tomlinson. 'I have a highly confidential job for you, 171. D'you think you're up to it yet?'

'A confidential job, Sarge?' marvelled Michael. 'Yes, not half! I'll have a go at anything,' he responded proudly.

'Well, how would you like to keep a very important and extremely secret observation for us?'

'You bet!'

'We are quite concerned about an address in Joinery Row, we think it's being used as a spieler.'

'Sergeant?'

'Spieler, lad, spieler. An illegal gaming-house to you. Anyway, there is a probability that we will raid it this afternoon. It's early-closing day in the area so there are bound to be a few punters in there. All I need is for you to watch the place. You simply sit opposite and count the amount of people coming and going. Any figures that you provide would be absolutely essential to the evidence. Do you think you could do that?'

124

'Sure, Sarge, sure. But where do I do the observation from? I mean, I haven't got to know anyone who lives around here yet. Wouldn't I need somewhere really concealed?'

'Don't worry, son, that's all fixed. You just go around to the back of 32 Joinery Row—you can get there from the alley in Dugdale Street—knock at the door and ask for Mrs Beryl Tozer. Just say that you've been sent round by a few friends of hers down at the nick. Ask her if you can use her front upstairs window to keep observation on number 45. It's dead opposite her place, so you wouldn't miss a thing.'

'Will that be all right, Sarge? I mean, isn't this sort of thing supposed to be confidential and all that?'

'Confidential?' echoed Tomlinson. 'You'll never find anyone more confidential than Beryl—er, Mrs Tozer, son. She's as good as gold is our Mrs Tozer. We've used her place many times before, she'll know all you need to know. All you have to do is to tell her we've sent you and leave yourself in her good hands. Oh, one last thing. Don't go mentioning any of this to Inspector Wilson. You know what he's like, he doesn't mind all this unofficial stuff just as long as he doesn't *officially* know about it.' The old sergeant then gave a knowing wink to the young constable. 'What the eye don't see, y'know . . .'

'Shall I put my civvies on, Sarge, or perhaps some old clothes?'

'Oh, er—no. No, keep your uniform on, it's really quite important. Mrs Tozer much prefers a uniform in these situations, she thinks it makes it more official-like. Besides, it also impresses the courts, makes them feel that we're not being too sneaky about it so to speak. Okay, do you know exactly what you've got to do?'

'Yes, Sarge, I'm to ask Mrs Tozer at number 32 if I can use her upstairs window to keep a count of who goes in and out of number 45.'

'Good lad! But don't forget you'll need to keep a "time-count" as well. Just a little graph will do. You know the sort of thing: 3 p.m. till 3.15 p.m. equals four adult males and one adult female. 3.15 p.m. till 3.30 p.m. equals six adult males and so on. Now I can't stress how important this count is. It's the numbers that you are going to provide that will make up most of our evidence, got it?'

'Got it, Sarge!'

'Okay then, off you go. I'll expect you back here at six o'clock with a precise count. By the way, you won't need your bat-phone because Mrs Tozer objects to the noise —neighbours, you know.'

Joinery Row and Dugdale Street were the last pair of back-to-back streets to survive both the last war and the grim redevelopment that followed. The two roads ran parallel, each with an alley at the rear. Number 32 was neatly central. The back of the house lay in the shade of the late winter sunshine and once into the long shadows, Michael thought the place seemed quite gloomy. The approach to the house was guarded by a high, white wooden fence. This had a latch-gate that swung invitingly open at fingertip touch.

His first impressions were really quite good. The curtains appeared fresh and clean and the paintwork gleamed. Catching sight of his reflection in the spotless kitchen window, the young constable smoothed down his uniform with his hands and straightened his helmet and tie. Appearing satisfied with these minor adjustments, he then knocked officially on the brass-knockered door.

Michael had really given little thought to the occupier of number 32. Beryl Tozer was not a name that fired him, although he imagined Inspector Dunn would have been ecstatic. All he was seeking to do was impress the occupants of the house as a smart young officer who was undertaking a particularly important task. Yes, all things considered, he thought, Mrs Beryl Tozer was about to be impressed.

A spicy, sweet smell pervaded his nostrils but other than that nothing else stirred. It took a second knock, even more official than the first, to achieve a response.

'Who is it?' enquired a muted female voice.

'Police,' announced Michael proudly, as he drew himself up to his full six feet two inches.

'Just a minute.'

The door swung open and the short passageway that led from it displayed the most exotic of décor. Short spears, ritual masks and tribal fly-whisks festooned the walls and ceiling. Brightly coloured rush mats littered the floor, yet this exoticism was as nothing in comparison to the woman who had opened the door. She must have been every inch as tall as Michael but if anything appeared taller. She wore a silk leopard-skin-patterned robe that was slashed almost to her navel. The small, tight curls that covered her perfectly shaped head were in direct contrast to the large, round earrings that dangled so sensuously from her lobes. Her square, white teeth were framed by wide, full lips and finally there was her skin—such a skin! Although technically brown, it was a brown that Michael had never seen before. It was a deep, dark, rich brown that sheened like velvet.

Michael's first reaction was a thirty-second gape.

'What can I do for you?' enquired a deep, yet soft voice.

'I, er, I . . . I want to speak to Mrs Beryl Tozer, please.'

'You have that pleasure.'

'You? You are Mrs Beryl Tozer?' asked the incredulous Michael.

'Don't you believe me?' An amused curve played around the woman's lips.

'Well, you don't look like a—' Michael was about to say Beryl but changed his mind. What the hell does a Beryl look like anyway, he thought. 'Well, I just thought that a Mrs Beryl Tozer would be, well, I thought she would be—' He broke off once again feeling that he was slipping deeper and deeper into confusion.

'I have been Mrs Beryl Tozer ever since I married Mr Tozer. It happens all the time, you know—people marrying and changing their names, I mean. So what is it that Mrs Beryl Tozer can do for you?'

The young man glanced nervously about him. 'Er, well, it's confidential really.'

'Oh, I see. Do come in then.' She led him down the passageway and then through the door of a rather luxurious, if somewhat ostentatious room. A huge white leather three-piece suite dominated, whilst a large white onyx coffee table rested upon an oval-shaped carpet of tumbling white yak hair. A huge mock-Edwardian telephone perched precariously upon a cluttered bar-top and the whole scene was crowned by a brass and glass candelabrum that hung disproportionately down from the ceiling. The big difficulty Michael experienced during this short journey was tearing his eyes from the rhythmical pivoting of the woman's hips.

'Won't you sit down?' she asked as she waved him towards the settee.

'Er, thanks,' he mumbled as he took up a position at the far end of the settee.

'Once more, what can I do for you?' she repeated as she perched herself provocatively on the chair arm opposite him.

'Well, I've been sent here from Cabul Lane and—'

'Oh, I see! I am so sorry, I forgot. Sergeant Tomlinson told me something about it yesterday. You want to use my bedroom, I understand. Is that correct?'

Michael made no answer but just stared.

'Well, is it?' she repeated.

The reason for Michael's inattention was easy to behold. If he had been fascinated by her rear then her front was now causing his eyes to fall out. The robe had parted widely and a goodly portion of her breasts was revealed. This included all of the valley and three-quarters of the mountains on either side, and mountains they certainly were. She may have been well over six feet in height but every inch of it was perfectly proportioned. The display did not end there. The left thigh, which was crossed so elegantly over the right, was also free of any concealment. In addition, there must have been half a dozen photographs around the walls all featuring the same subject, namely a nubile Beryl Tozer clad solely in a necklace and two ankle bracelets. In most of them she stood full-frontal, head back, feet apart, swallowing a flaming torch. Mrs Beryl Tozer, it appeared, was a naked fire-eater!

Perhaps it was the thought of the flames that caused the sudden rise in Michael's temperature. On the other hand it could just have been the body beneath them. Whatever the reason, perspiration was gathering in abundance on his normally immaculate forehead.

'Can I get you a drink before you start your observations?' Mrs Tozer asked. 'Perhaps tea or a beer?'

Michael's 'observations' had, in fact, already begun. They had commenced the second that Beryl had opened the door. In fact, it would be safe to say that he had never been so observant in his life. He was now *so* observant that he was worried sick in case he missed something! 'Yes, yes, a beer would be lovely, please.'

The woman rose to her feet and adjusted her robe. The exposed thigh now vanished but what seemed like an acre of breast took its place. It was a trade-in that delighted the observer. As she disappeared into the kitchen, the young man took the opportunity for a close study of the framed photographs. They appeared to have been taken in a nightclub, an expensive one at that.

It was during the course of these photographic studies that Michael discovered that the young lady's talents were not solely confined to fire-eating. According to one eight-by-ten-inch print, she was also a sword-swallower!

'Hope you don't mind lager, it's all I seem to have in the fridge.' He turned towards the door in time to see Beryl's entry. She was clutching two glasses in one hand and two cans in the other. 'I think I'll join you,' she said. 'Come and sit here with me.' She nodded once more to the settee.

Michael did as he was bid and after bounding into position, she leaned forward to offer him a can. Yet again both the gown and Michael gaped. She smiled as she followed the direction of his stare.

'You must excuse my attire but I work in a club and rarely arrive home until after three in the morning. I'm

129

afraid I haven't long been up. Now, you tell me what it is that you want.'

'Well—er,' stammered the young man, 'I just need a position where I can watch the door of number 45 opposite.'

'If that's all you want then there's no problem, except that the only vantage point is my bedroom. Perhaps when you've finished your drink I'll show you the way?'

Michael could not understand his inability to converse. His talent to amuse had long caused envy amongst his male colleagues and he was considered to be something of a 'smooth operator'. At that precise moment, though, he was neither smooth nor was he operating. For the first time in any relationship with a female, he did not feel in charge of the situation. It was a very worrying experience.

'Have you been a policeman very long?' she asked, the slightly amused look still playing around her face. Briefly, and not without difficulty, Michael recited his career to date. 'I see – and now you want to use my bedroom?'

'Well . . . er . . . I mean, if it's awkward or anything, I'll call back.' As he heard his words he could barely believe it was him speaking them. 'I, er, mean, perhaps your husband might not approve. You know, him not being here and so on.'

'I don't have a husband. Didn't you know?'

'N. . .no.'

'I thought Sergeant Tomlinson would have told you. It's no secret, half your station knows it. I "bought" my marriage five years ago, when I was eighteen. I paid two hundred pounds to an English sailor in Nigeria to marry me and bring me here. I haven't seen him since the wedding. Donald Rodney Tozer was his name. Mine was Princess Agboluaje. He thought Beryl was a better match for Tozer than Princess, so we changed it.'

'You're a princess?' asked the astonished Michael.

'Good heavens no! That was just my Christian name. It's not uncommon in my part of the world. I still use it in cabaret though. "Princess Swabe" I'm billed as. "The only *royal* fire-eater, snake-charmer and sword-swallower in the business".'

'Don't you mean the only royal *six-feet-two-inch nude* fire-eater, snake-charmer and sword-swallower in the business?' corrected Michael, stringing together his longest sentence since his arrival.

She threw back her head and roared with laughter. 'Well, it all helps of course.'

'How does a person start? You know, becoming a fire-eater and such like?' he asked.

'My father used to do it in hotels in Lagos, to entertain the tourists. I suppose I must have learnt it from him. There's nothing special about fire-eaters, you know, so one needs to be a little different. Clubs only became interested when I called myself a princess.'

'And took your clothes off,' pointed out the young man, now becoming more confident by the minute.

'*And* took my clothes off,' she agreed. 'You see, you've proved my point. You were as shy as a choirboy when you first arrived here. But now, within the space of one minute, you've mentioned my nudity twice! It just goes to prove that it pays to be a little different.'

'No!' cut in Michael quickly. 'It could also mean I have a thing about tall nude women!'

She appeared thoughtful for a moment. 'Y. . .e. . .s,' she murmured slowly, almost to herself. 'I was told about you. At first I thought I'd been misled but it appears you might be coming out of your shell after all.' She nodded as she looked him straight in the eyes. 'We shall see, we shall see.'

Having drained the last of his lager, Michael made a laboured point of looking at his watch. 'Heavens! Is that the time? I'm already late. When can I begin my observation?'

'Whenever you wish, I'll show you the way.' She too drained her glass and stood up. 'Follow me.'

'It's a pleasure!' responded the increasingly daring constable.

She paused at the door and glanced seductively back

131

over her shoulder. 'Well, come on then, it's your big moment. You're going to accompany a lady to her bedroom.'

As Michael followed those swaying hips up the stairs, he experienced his first niggling doubts. Things were never this easy. Twenty minutes before he had been an honest, reliable lad intent on nothing but the job he was paid to do. Yet, following the first sight of the statuesque Beryl, he had sunk a can of her beer, fallen ecstatically for her all too obvious charms and was now following her up to her bedroom. The lady could not have been more blatant if she had battered him with a club and dragged him in by his hair. Could it be a trap? Was some outraged husband about to leap out on him brandishing a machete?

These misgivings, however, were only to be fleeting. Whatever Michael's shortcomings, modesty was not amongst them. It was fairly obvious that she had been smitten. After all, why shouldn't she be? It was a case of pure and simple chemistry. He had known it before and would doubtless know it again. There was now no doubt in his mind that he was about to make a conquest. Why complicate it then? Get on and both enjoy it was the thing to do. He felt like congratulating the girl on her luck.

The bedroom was rather sumptuous. Again, white was the predominant colour. The bright walls, ceiling, bedcover and carpet, contrasted starkly with the deep plum-red of the heavy velvet curtains. White fitted units ran the length of one wall and Michael was rather pleased to see that a good half of this unit was made up of mirrors. There was, after all, a great deal of Mrs Tozer and the added bonus of a mirror would enable him to see most of it.

'You can use that chair by the window. If you care to make yourself comfortable, I'll fetch you up another lager.' Her slight gesture had caused a sudden falter from the expectant Michael. An unusually penetrating ray from the late winter sun had struck her left hand. The resultant sharp sparkle indicated a diamond of true quality.

'Is that an engagement ring?' he asked.

She fluttered her hand. 'Yes indeed and a rather expensive one too,' she admitted proudly.

This latest admission threw an instant strain on Michael's rather obscure principles. He had never been averse to playing around with married women—but an engaged woman? It somehow seemed immoral. His recently found composure began to dissolve rapidly. 'Er . . . er . . .' he bleated.

'Yes?'

'Well, er, where is he? Who is he? What is he? It's very off-putting you know.'

'Why is it off-putting?' she asked. 'And what exactly is it "putting you off"? What has been going on in that tiny mind of yours, young man? I'm surprised at you, you a policeman and all. Just because you've been invited to a lady's bedroom, you know, doesn't mean that . . .' She let the sentence trail away and shook her head in mock sorrow.

Michael was now totally perplexed. Perhaps this was it? Perhaps he was to be tormented by this woman until Sergeant Tomlinson burst in and discovered him in her bedroom. No, that was nonsense. Hadn't Tomlinson himself arranged it? There was no way that he could be blamed for actually being in the bedroom. It was all very bewildering.

'Look,' said Beryl soothingly. 'Sit yourself down and don't worry. I'm engaged to an Arab gentleman I met in the club. He is back in Kuwait until the end of the year and then I'm going to join him there. So you can relax. He is not going to come bursting in and chop off your hand or something. So there's nothing for you to worry about. Now, do you want a lager or don't you?'

'Please,' nodded the young constable.

She glided from the room and left him alone with his confused thoughts. Finally pulling himself together, he took a piece of paper from his tunic pocket and began to draw a time graph. He listed the afternoon in fifteen-minute intervals and promptly realized he was twenty minutes late in starting. He had to admit he was in an excellent position for the observation. The frilly net curtains that were draped between the velvet and the windows gave clear visibility of the street beyond but retained complete privacy in the bedroom.

The quick tattoo of feet indicated not only that Beryl was returning up the staircase but that she was doing so at some speed. He looked enquiringly towards the door but there was no indication that anything was amiss. Her smile was as wide as ever and her gown was even more revealing. Probably because of the glasses and cans in her hands she had been unable to adjust it. He was not sure just how much of this he could stand. His ordeal, however, had not yet begun—although it was about to.

'There!' she said, placing the two glasses and one of the cans on the white bedside locker. 'I haven't been long, have I?' With one hand she held the remaining can towards him and with the other she reached for the ring-pull top.

'No!' he began—but he was too late. What seemed like every droplet of lager burst from the can with an intensity that struck him in the mouth and cascaded down his neck, soaking his shirt and tunic and quickly spreading down as far as his trousers and shoes. He could not believe that one small can of lager could contain so much liquid. Some of it even ricocheted from his chin and back on to the front of Beryl's robe.

She recoiled with an exaggerated intake of breath and clapped her left hand over her mouth with what appeared to Michael to be mock horror. 'Oh, you poor love! What have I done? What have I done?' she repeated. 'Quick, take everything off before it stains. I'll help you.'

Almost before he knew what was happening, Beryl was unfastening the first of his buttons. 'D'you mind?' he said angrily as he pushed her roughly away.

'I was only trying to help. Here, you're not embarrassed at the idea of taking your clothes off in front of me, are you? My, my. Who would have guessed it!' The smile that had consistently played around the corners of her mouth now gave way to an enormously wide, sensuous grin. 'Look, if it helps you feel better, I'll take mine off first.' She gave what appeared to be a smoothly rehearsed shrug and her robe dropped easily and silently at her feet.

Michael felt like a drunk in a brewery. There was so much to see he did not know where to look first. After all, six feet two inches of naked Nigerian femininity does take a little absorbing.

'Well, now you know how it's done, how about a little co-operation, sweetie?' asked the woman.

For a moment Michael neither moved nor spoke—he just stared at her astonishing body. Suddenly four hands joined together in a button-loosening flurry. Shirt, trousers, pants and socks, all were removed with an eager zest. Within seconds they faced each other eye to eye without as much as a handkerchief between them. They kissed, nibbled and bit each other's faces. Slowly, oh so slowly, Michael eased the towering woman back towards the bed, the wide, white-satined bed. Just when he thought he had succeeded and was preparing to give the final push that would place her yieldingly on her back, she spoke.

'Uh-uh, this is *my* game.' She swung him around with consummate ease and reversed roles by pushing him down, backwards on to the bed. He made a token gesture of resistance but soon opened his arms to welcome her on to him. To his surprise she did not move but just stood smiling down. 'Relax, lover, relax,' she ordered. 'You are not going to believe it, but this is *discussion* time.'

'Discussion time!' he echoed. 'What the hell is there to discuss?' He began to raise himself up from the bed.

'Oh, there's a great deal to discuss, baby, a great deal,' she responded, pushing him back down again. Once more he attempted to rise. This time she climbed on to the bed and mounted him, although rather too high up his body for maximum compatibility. With her knees planted on the bed at either side of his chest, she knelt up and across him.

'Okay,' he said as he revelled in the view. 'Let's discuss.'

'It won't take very long, lover. I just need you to understand one small detail.'

'Fine, what is it?'

'Well, I just hope you don't expect sexual intercourse, that's all.' With that, she placed her hands behind her head and leaned provocatively backward.

'Don't expect sexual intercourse?' he exploded. 'Well, what on earth are we doing here?'

'Well, I know what I'm doing here, lover—I'm enjoying it. Perhaps you should tell me what *you're* doing here.'

'I'm enjoying it too, of course,' he hastily assured her. 'Particularly the view. But I must admit that I did have this little hope that sexual intercourse would take place. It may have something to do with the fact that you've been flashing various parts at me ever since I arrived. Yes, I think you would be quite justified in assuming that intercourse was not too far from my mind,' he added tartly.

'According to the reflection that I see,' she said, nodding towards the mirror, 'it's more than your mind that's interested. Anyway, I am about to give you an explanation. Are you ready to listen, or are you going to lie there and sulk?'

'I'm listening! I'm listening! But can I *touch* while I'm listening?'

'Touching is definitely allowed but only for those that listen,' she agreed, leaning forward to enable her swinging breasts to meet his reaching hands.

'You like?' she asked proudly.

'I like,' he agreed readily.

'Good. If they are going to keep you quiet for a while then perhaps we can now have a serious discussion. You know that I'm engaged—yes?'

'So you said,' he replied, without removing his attention from the manipulation of her nipples.

'Very well,' she began, but was interrupted by her own involuntary quiver.

'Oh, that's nice. Where was I?'

'You were being both serious and engaged,' he reminded.

'Ah yes, so I was. Well, it was made perfectly clear to me on my engagement that I was expected to be a virgin on my wedding day.'

136

'But you were once married.'

'Yes, but only for a day,' she answered, slowly and emphatically. I met Ravi—that's his name—soon after I arrived here when he was a young student. We never had full sex because of his religious beliefs. Now be fair, if I'm not going to have sex with my long-term fiancé, I can hardly be expected to have it with some randy copper who is just using my bedroom for a couple of hours' observation, can I?'

Michael stared at her in complete disbelief. 'I've never heard the like of it! Look at you, you're a big, highly sexed, worked-up woman. You've got knockout tits and nipples like teapot lids. You're stark naked, practically sitting on my face and now you're telling me I can't have it off?'

'Not, "having it off" as you so inelegantly call it, is not the be-all and end-all of a relationship, you know. There *are* other things.'

'Such as?'

She smiled and removed his persistent hands from her breasts. Very slowly she then began to gyrate them. 'As a special treat for a special feller—I can do "tricks" if you wish.'

'Tricks?'

'Yes, tricks. I'm really quite good at them. In order to preserve my virginity I suppose you could say I've needed to be. One thing I can assure you—you won't be disappointed. What do you say—is it tricks?'

'Tricks it is then,' he agreed magnanimously. She bent forward and paused with her lips just an inch from his face.

'Do you have any preference?' she whispered, slipping her hand behind her.

'None—Oh, that's nice! Perhaps a little slower there though? I'll just take things as they come—if you'll pardon the expression.' He lay back and closed his eyes in anticipation. This was going to be a very interesting observation indeed.

One has to give credit where it's due, thought Michael. Until he had met this woman he was smugly convinced that he knew all there was to know about sexual relationships. Yet within the space of three short hours she had taught him a whole new curriculum. Physically he may have been lying on a bed, but mentally he was floating three feet above it. He felt a relaxed, euphoric glow that he had never known before. He decided that, on balance, he quite liked tricks. After all, the whole pleasure went on so much longer. Nearby St Mark's clock had just struck seven and he was still at it. Seven o'clock! Bloody hell! He was supposed to be back at the station at six—and with a carefully detailed count! He opened his eyes fully for the first time for almost ninety minutes. At first glance and starting with her legs, he could see every particle of Beryl except her head. Where the hell was it?

'Beryl, quick! I was supposed to be back at the station an hour ago. Where are you? Good heavens, you must be double-jointed to do that!'

Tumbling out of bed he scrambled around for his clothes. At first he was so exhausted he almost fell over. Quickly regaining his balance, he reached for his trousers. While poised delicately on one foot, he noticed his reflection in the large mirror. 'Beryl! Whatever is the matter with me?' He stared, aghast.

'Nothing's wrong with you, lover,' assured Beryl. 'I've given you a little bite here and a little bite there but it's nothing that won't heal up.'

'A little bite!' he echoed. 'Is that what it is? I'm going to look really great when I get back to the nick. I've got no observation details, I'm an hour and a half late reporting, and my neck's been savaged by Dracula! Sergeant Tomlinson's going to be over the moon with me!'

'You should be thankful it's only your neck he'll see, lover.' She lay face down on the bed with her chin on her hands, watching him hop. 'You should on no account share a shower.' The idea seemed to amuse her for she suddenly burst into laughter.

It was an indication of Michael's concern that he dressed himself quicker than he had undressed.

'Wait, lover. I'll give you something for your tea back at

138

the station.' Beryl slid off the bed and reached for her robe. The sight of her stretching into the garment caused some indecision in Michael. The necessity to return to Cabul Lane in record time no longer seemed to have the same urgency.

'Now, now,' she murmured, evading his renewed attentions. 'You'd better make haste back to your station before half of it comes up here looking for you. Come on, I'll give you one final treat. You'll be able to take this one back with you.'

She eased him out of the bedroom and down the stairs by a series of fingertip prods. Occasionally he turned and raised a hopeful hand towards her loose-tied robe. 'Uh-uh!' she would rebuff with a shake of the head. 'Your time is up and you're out of bounds. Sergeant Tomlinson beckons.'

'A kiss! A kiss! You can't turn me out without a kiss, surely?' he begged.

'A kiss, then, it is,' she agreed. 'But that's all, mind you. No crafty feels allowed.' She slipped easily into his arms, the smooth silk of her robe proving a perfect foil to the rough, tough serge of his uniform. He found her as sensuous at that moment as he had when she had first stood naked in the bedroom.

'Sure you won't change your mind?' he whispered, not without difficulty as he negotiated the pleasures of an open-mouthed kiss.

'Quite sure, lover—on your way,' she replied with equal difficulty.

'Do I see you again?' he persisted.

'Perhaps, if the sergeant gives you another observation . . . ?'

'I don't mean that. I mean can I take you out for a meal or something?'

She shook her head vehemently. 'I'm engaged, lover. I'm a committed woman. Don't get me wrong now, it's nothing against you but I know exactly where I'm going and I'm determined to get there.'

139

She looked into his puzzled face and the smile that had rarely been far from her lips broke wide once more. 'You're wondering what makes me tick, aren't you?' He nodded. 'Look, I've always adored policemen but I don't form long-term relationships. You can accept me as I am from time to time if you wish—but only from time to time and no more than that. In fact, I think I might prefer it if we did not even meet again.'

'I just don't understand you. I thought—'

A look of anger swept over her face. 'Don't you?' she interrupted. 'Are you sure? Just because I happen to be a female edition of yourself, you seem to think that's wrong. I suppose it's all right for a man to hang scalps from his belt but not a woman, eh?'

'I didn't *say* that,' he protested.

'But you *implied* it. Listen, did you have a good time this afternoon?'

'Never had a better one!'

'Very well, leave it at that. It was an experience and you learnt something. That can't be bad. In addition, I would like to point out that you also got paid for it! Whether you'll still have a job when you get back though is another matter.' She kissed him lightly on the tip of his nose. 'Just get it into perspective, eh?' Giving a little pout, she tilted her head girlishly to one side. 'Friends?'

'Friends,' he confirmed.

'Right, run along then and get your excuses ready for the sergeant. Oh, I almost forgot, wait a moment.' She disappeared into the kitchen. The sweet, spicy smell he had noticed when he first arrived was now even more pronounced. She soon emerged with a small tin-foiled package. 'Be careful, it's still hot.'

'What is it?' he asked.

'Nigerian apple-cake, you can have it for your tea.'

'I didn't know you had apples in Nigeria.'

She drew herself up to her full height and thrust out her breasts almost into his face. 'There was a lot that you didn't know about Nigeria, lover, wasn't there?'

'There was indeed,' he agreed. 'There was indeed.'

*

140

'And just where the bloody hell have you been, 171? I've almost alerted Interpol! You should have been back here an hour and a half ago.'

'Oh, er, I got delayed, Sergeant. I ran into a disturbance on the way back. I couldn't let you know because I didn't have my bat-phone.'

'I see,' nodded Tomlinson. 'This disturbance, serious was it?'

'No, not really, Sarge. Verbal mainly. Husband and wife thing, y'know. I straightened it all out there and then. They seemed quite happy when I left so I didn't think it was worth reporting. Er, there is just one other thing, Sarge.'

'Oh yes, what's that?'

'Well . . . I don't quite know how to say this.'

'Try.'

'Well, while I was dealing with this disturbance, Sarge . . .'

'Yes?'

'Well, while I was dealing with the disturbance . . .'

'You've said that.'

'Yes, well, while I was dealing with the disturbance I seem to have lost my count graph. I did look everywhere for it, Sarge, but I couldn't find it no how.'

'Well, well, that is a surprise, 171. Tut-bloody-tut, who would've thought it?' He stared expectantly at the young constable for some time before continuing. 'So really we could say that the whole afternoon was a total waste of time, eh?'

'It looks like it, Sarge, doesn't it?' agreed Michael.

'It does indeed,' nodded the sergeant. 'Interesting though, ain't it? You see, we have a dozen prisoners in the charge-room at the moment and they are now going to sue us for unlawful arrest. And do you know why, 171? Do you?'

'N-no, Sarge, why?'

'BECAUSE YOU'VE LOST THE BLEEDIN' EVIDENCE, YOU DOZY PRAT, THAT'S WHY! I just hope that you've got a lot of money in your piggy-bank, son, because this is going to cost you a packet! Speaking of packets, what've you got in that one?' He pointed down at the tin-foiled parcel.

'It's just a cake for my tea, Sarge.'

'And where'd you get it?'

'Bought it, Sarge.'

Tomlinson glanced up at the station clock. 'You found a bakers open at half past seven at night?'

'Er, no. I bought it on my way out this afternoon.'

'Did you indeed? Marvellous stuff that tin-foil, ain't it? It still feels hot. Funny you should lose your count graph and not lose your cake though, don't you think? What sort of cake is it? Wouldn't be Nigerian apple-cake by any chance?'

'I, er, I don't know what it's called, Sarge. The lady in the bakers didn't say.'

'Oh, I see! Well, that explains your ignorance,' said Tomlinson. 'Anyway, you can take it from me, lad, that it *is* Nigerian apple-cake. You can always tell Nigerian apple-cake because it has a most peculiar side-effect. You don't even have to eat it to become afflicted.'

'Sergeant?'

Tomlinson reached up to the young man's collar and tugged it down an inch or so. 'Look in the mirror and you'll see what I mean. It fetches you out in blotches. I bet if you was to look right now you'd find them all over your body. It's amazing stuff that cake, son, absolutely bloody amazing. Right, go and have your grub break and work out your finances, although you'll probably find it cheaper to resign. I'll see you back here in forty-five minutes. Oh, and don't be late this time, eh?'

Michael wandered dolefully into the canteen and sat down. At first he had the place to himself, the rest of 'C' relief had long finished their meal break. As he unwrapped the tin-foil, his thoughts were interrupted by the arrival of Bert Bones the 'C' relief van driver.

'What ho, boy, you're late, ain'tcha? Wassamatter, been busy?'

142

'Not really, I just forgot the time.'

Bert nodded. 'It can happen I s'pose, although I wouldn't make a habit of it if I was you. The guv'nors don't like it, particularly when the manor's quiet.'

'What do you mean?' asked Michael.

'Well, when it's quiet they suddenly realize they've got a bunch of blokes to supervise. They then start charging all over the bloody place playing barons and serfs.'

'Here, wait a minute! I thought there were a dozen prisoners in the station?'

'Dunno where you got that from, boy. I'm the van driver and I've only fetched a dog in all afternoon and that was dead.'

'Do you mean to say there are no prisoners in the building?'

'S'right. There ain't been one down the pokey since the prison bus collected them for court at eight o'clock this morning.'

'Are you positive?'

'A'course I am. I ought to know, it's the van driver's job to feed 'em. Hello, what've you got there?'

'Oh,' said Michael, slowly realizing that Tomlinson had well conned him. 'Just some cake.'

'Been to see Trixie then, 'ave you?' asked the old driver with a nostalgic gleam in his eye.

'Trixie?'

'You can always tell a bloke who's been to see Trixie. She never fails to work on him with that bloody awful Nigerian apple-cake. God knows why she calls it apple-cake, it tastes more like camel shit. In any case, there ain't any apples in Nigeria.'

'It's a bit short on camels, too,' said Michael curtly. 'Anyway, who is this Trixie?'

'Well, if you've got your cake then you must'a seen Trixie.' Placing his left hand on his waist, he walked slowly towards Michael swaying both hips and shoulders alternately. Then, dropping his gaze in mock modesty, he mimicked, 'Ah do tricks, lover—do you have any preference?'

Michael raised his hands in surrender. 'Oh yes,' he nodded. 'I've got it now. You mean Beryl. Still, I suppose Trixie is a more appropriate name.'

'She must'a thought highly of you, boy,' said the old driver admiringly.

'Why's that?'

'Well, look at the size of the cake you've got. I'm sure it's a mark of ability, you know. If you do well she gives you a really large lump. Bloody hell, boy, she must'a been pleased with you!'

Michael took a big breath and bit deep into the cake. He chewed slowly for a moment before his jaws came gradually to a standstill. He sat with a full mouth and a thoughtful expression, like a shy winetaster with a dubious vintage.

'Well, boy?' asked the driver curiously.

'You're right. It *is* camel shit,' agreed Michael. 'And I think I've bought a ton of it.'

CHAPTER TEN

The rattling trolley cut into Reggie Patterson's meditations like the bell of doom. His impending transfer from the intensive-care unit depressed him deeply. He had lain in that unit for exactly two months and for much of the time he had been not just conscious, but also fully aware of just how and why he was there. At no time, except for those first few hours, had he even been in the slightest distress. Oh yes, he was ill right enough. Once or twice he had even thought he might die, yet he had never felt anything other than tranquil. The unit had been a haven. There he had felt safe from everyone. He thought it must have been like living in a womb. He felt warm, comfortable and protected, with all his needs attended to. He was required to make no effort for himself. He had enjoyed that, it had been a good feeling. In the unit he had felt so removed from life that he had not even spoken. Of course he could have, of that he was sure, but somehow he felt safer not speaking. He would speak to no one, not to doctors, psychiatrists, nurses or detectives. Particularly he would not speak to detectives. There had been a detective standing in the corner for a whole week, immobile, silent, just staring at him, waiting for him to crack and say something. Well, he was not going to speak because as soon as he did so they would take him away. He could remember his mother's words from all those years ago. She had warned him about strangers. 'Never speak to them,' she had said. 'They'll take you away if you do, Reggie.' She was right, of course, but then mother had always been right.

There had been vulnerable times when he had needed to be particularly on his guard. These were usually when he was in the process of waking. It was then that they would ask their questions. Trap questions all of them. 'How do

145

you feel?' questions. 'Can you hear what I'm saying?' questions. 'Are you in any pain?' questions. Sometimes it had been very difficult not to answer. On at least two occasions words had almost formed in his mouth, but so far he had held out. By not talking he had learnt quite a lot. They assumed that because he did not speak, he did not hear. But he did hear! What he heard indicated that mother was right. Every one of these strangers wanted to take him away. That detective—the one that stood silently for hours in the corner—he was the one who most wanted him to speak. But he must not speak, he knew that. One single word and he would be in their clutches. They would then take him from this warm, sleepy sanctuary to somewhere evil and wicked. Somewhere where they would do terrible things to him, just like mother had said they would.

What Reggie could not understand was *why* they were moving him. After all, he had not spoken, had he? In his mind he had drawn up the rules of the game. These rules clearly stated that if you did not speak then they could not move you. Well, he hadn't spoken and they *were* moving him. Cheats, cheats all of them and none more so than that silent fool in the corner.

The trolley's route from the unit would be via the wide door at the end of the room. In order to negotiate this exit, the porter would need to push the trolley very close to the silent detective. Reggie decided to let the officer know that in spite of everything that had happened, he wasn't beaten. He would not do this with words, of course, for that could be fatal. No, he would smile at the man. Even better—a wink! Yes, that's it—a wink! As the trolley carried him past, he would turn his head and wink very slowly and deliberately at the detective. What a fool the man would feel! Reggie could barely suppress a laugh as the thought went through his mind. What a crusher! What an absolute crusher! To have been watching dutifully for a whole week and to have obtained nothing but a wink! He would like to see the man explain that on his overtime sheet!

The trolley rattled its way across the polished unit floor

and the door came ever closer. Now that should be the time. With a supreme effort, Reggie gave the biggest move he had made for two months as he turned sharply towards the unrelenting watcher. Every bruise, cut and fracture in his body tightened. The torment was unspeakable. A dozen piercing stilettos seemed to gouge his pain-racked torso. With gritted teeth and agonized clenched palms, he finally made it. 'It'll be worth it,' he told himself. 'It'll be worth it.' Reggie then gave the slowest wink of his life and opened his eyes fully to assess the impact he had made. The dark, sturdy oxygen cylinder that had stood impassively in the corner, responded neither to the wink nor to the tearful sobs that followed, as Reggie passed gratefully into oblivion.

Dr Robinson sat at his desk finishing his latest entry to PC Patterson's medical notes. After a quick read through he sat back and tipped his reading glasses up on to his forehead. 'I'm sorry, Inspector, but the patient is still too ill to be interviewed.'

'But it has been two months now, Doctor, and he was transferred to a general ward this morning. Surely I can have a few minutes with him?'

'Once again, I'm sorry but no. In any case, he hasn't been transferred to a general ward as you put it. He is separated from the ward by a glass partition. In fact, there is more than a possibility that he may be back in intensive care very soon. He tried to retard his recovery this morning by throwing himself from the trolley as he was being moved. He is not yet mentally fit to be questioned.'

'Has he ever been mentally fit? Was he right mentally to do what he did to those young girls—most of them nurses, I might add? Also, I need to discover just how he sustained his own injuries. I need to question him soon whilst he still remembers something about it.'

'As to whether he has ever been right mentally, you had better take that up with the police that employed him in the first place. In my opinion he has *never* been right mentally. There is a flaw in his character that should have been obvious for all to see.'

'Don't blame me for the actions of police selection boards, Doctor,' snapped Bromley. 'Police selection boards are classic examples of there being "more out than in". I accept no responsibility for their action whatsoever. I have long given up wondering about the logic of some of their choices. All I am concerned with is squaring up this crime. I have got half a dozen serious assaults in my crime-book and three of them could just as easily have been murders. You have my number-one suspect tucked up safely in bed and I can't get at him. At this rate he could string us along for months.'

'Why do you say, "string us along"?'

'Well, isn't that what he's doing? Has Patterson sustained any injury that should have impaired his speech, or even his understanding?'

'Well, there is shock, of course. That can manifest itself in all sorts of peculiar ways.'

'You mean the shock of copping a ten-year stretch, I assume?'

'I mean the shock of being brutally beaten up. I have rarely seen such dreadful facial injuries. But the most worrying aspect is the injuries to his kidneys. I am afraid he will need renal dialysis for some time. It's quite possible he may even be permanently damaged. I do think you are being less than fair, Inspector.'

Bromley sighed wearily. 'Oh, I suppose you're right. It's just that it is so frustrating to think that a thirty-minute interview could clear up so many diabolical attacks.' He rose to his feet and stretched out his hand. 'You'll let me know immediately I can interview Patterson?'

'Of course.'

'Oh, by the way, I take it I can leave an escort in the ward? It will have to be a twenty-four-hour one, I'm afraid. I mean, all I need now is to come in here one morning and find he's legged it during the night. I think if that was to happen I'd take over his bed in intensive care.'

'Will the escort be in uniform?'

'Probably not, although I don't think I can spare any CID

officers for the job. I'll use uniformed officers with civilian coats. That suit you?'

'You can use the Commissioner in a pink frock if you wish. It's just that I would sooner not have a uniform around the ward all day.'

'Why is that?' asked Bromley, turning at the door.

'Nurses, Inspector. Student nurses to be precise. Put a young man in uniform in a hospital ward and those young ladies will find a million excuses to visit him. Somehow the situation never seems so bad if he is in plain clothes. For my part I don't give a damn. It's just that nursing officers do get so worked up if they see a uniformed copper flirting with their fledglings.'

'Point taken, Doctor, point taken. I can clearly remember one Christmas morning in St Thomas's Casualty some eighteen years ago . . .' For a moment Bromley stared nostalgically into space. 'Y'know, Doctor, I never did meet a copper who didn't love nurses. Strange thing that, must be all those black stockings and rustling petticoats. Anyway, if he has to be in uniform, I'll make sure it's no one under fifty. Cheerio, Doctor.'

'Inspector! Before you go I would like to make a suggestion.' Bromley, who was almost out of the room by this time, sensed an urgency and hurried back to his seat by the desk. 'When you said just now that Patterson was stringing us along, I don't think you were far from the truth. Now whether he is doing it deliberately or whether it is a genuine subconscious defence, I'm not sure. Therefore, what I would suggest is this. When you pick your escort-cum-guard, why don't you pick someone who knows the patient well? Someone he can trust. A friend of his, say. Someone who may just be able to draw him out. This is not just for your convenience but also for mine and mainly for the patient himself, of course. Otherwise, at the rate he is going he will soon be another Miss Haversham.'

'Miss who?' asked a bewildered Bromley.

'Haversham,' repeated the doctor. 'You know, the recluse in *Great Expectations*?'

'Oh, I see, *that* Miss Haversham! For one awful moment I thought you were talking about a sex-change! That would be all I needed!'

'Well, there it is, Mr Bromley. It's only a suggestion but it's all we have.'

'The problem that I can see straight away, Doctor, is that to the best of my knowledge Patterson has not got a friend in the world. And that has nothing to do with recent events. He has always been a loner. I think it will be difficult enough to find anyone to volunteer for the job, let alone hold a cosy conversation with him. Anyway, like you say, it's all we have at the moment. I'll see what I can do. Goodbye, Doctor—and thanks.'

'It would seem, PC Butler,' said Sergeant Tomlinson as the early-turn parade lined up before him, 'that, for a young recruit, you are very much in demand. The detective inspector wants to see you as soon as possible. I dare say he needs your advice over a particularly difficult crime. Wait a minute! Wait a minute! Where the hell are you going?'

Michael paused at the door and gave a puzzled look at the sergeant. 'You said the DI wanted to see me as soon as possible, Sergeant.'

'I know, lad, I know, but "as soon as possible" for members of the Criminal Investigation Department means either nine in the morning, or after the pubs shut in the afternoon. It's only berks like you and me who start work before the sun is up. Detective inspectors must never arrive until the streets are properly aired.' He shook his head in perplexity. 'It'd throw the whole force into confusion if they did.'

'Well, Butler—I can't keep calling you Butler—' said the DI. 'What's your Christian name?'

'Michael, sir.'

'Well, Mike, I want you to do something for me. No. No, you're all right this time,' assured Bromley. 'There's no Nigerian apple-cake on the menu. What I want you to do is

150

"sit" with PC Patterson in the Royal Friary Hospital and just talk to him. Even more importantly, get him to talk to you. I don't want you to ask him about the assaults—well, not just yet anyway—all I want you to do is to relax him. Get him to open up. Talk about anything you like, the weather, sport, girls, absolutely anything, but just get him to talk. I want you to build a relationship with him—understand?'

'But why me, sir? I can't stand the bastard. I saw what happened to that young nurse and as far as I'm concerned he got all that was coming to him.'

'I've picked you simply because you were the last person he actually conversed with, or even spent any time with. Patterson was a loner and would suspect a trap if anyone else at the nick got the job. You, being such a new recruit, may just get away with it. You simply tell him that because nobody else volunteered, you decided to be particularly noble and step forward. If you use your loaf you'll have him eating out of your hand in no time.'

'How long am I to be there?'

'Twelve hours a day—to begin with, that is. I'll review the situation after three or four days.'

'Twelve—' began the dismayed young man.

'Don't worry, don't worry. You'll get your overtime. You will be relieved by two others who will be under strict instructions not to talk. This will hopefully endear you to him. For the purposes of this exercise you are Mr Nice Guy.' Bromley then pointed a warning finger at Michael's head. 'But under no circumstances are you to let him know you hate his guts—and equally important—don't show it! D'you understand me?'

Michael nodded dejectedly.

'Okay. I'll square everything with your sergeant. All you have to do is to sit down in a warm, comfortable hospital for a few days just chatting and listening. For that you can claim four hours a day overtime! Money for old rope, I reckon. Oh, and while I think of it—' His voice took on a note of severity. 'No nurses! Absolutely no nurses! You are

151

not being let loose in that ward to get your leg over, you are there solely for police work. If you've got that straight you can put on your civvy jacket and make tracks. I shall pop down round about lunchtime to see how you're making out.'

To say that Michael was not in favour of his special task was an understatement to say the least. His attitude was not helped by a meeting with Helen as he left the station. Like the rest of the early-turn shift, she was anxious to hear just what it was about the young man that the DI found so compelling.

'So what's the mystery, Mickey?' she laughed. 'Not another assignation with the tall Trixie, surely?'

Once he told her of his task, however, her mood changed instantly and she became very quiet. Suddenly full of remorse for the way in which he broke the news, Michael took her quickly by the arm. 'I'm sorry, Helen, love, are you okay?'

She gave just the faintest of shudders before smiling once more at him. 'I'm fine now, Mick, honest. It was just that for a moment . . . well, I felt that someone had walked over my grave. It's funny, you know. I've never been able to accept that it was a copper who attacked me. The fact that you are just off to sit with him has made him feel very close again.' She gave a little wry laugh. 'Just when I thought I'd got over it, too.'

He stood for several seconds on the front steps of the station still clutching the girl's arm, indifferent to his colleagues and members of the public who were toing and froing past them. He had always felt an instinctive warmth towards the girl, but suddenly, and for the first time, he wanted to take her in his arms and just hold her, to reassure her and perhaps kiss away a few of her fears. He opened his mouth but no words came forth. Her dark eyes looked quizzically up at him.

'If you are going to hold my arm all afternoon, Mickey Butler, people will start talking,' she chided.

'Helen.'

152

'Y. . .e. . .s.'

'Helen,' he repeated, his composure returning. 'You're beautiful and if you play your cards right, well, you could just be lucky enough to have my body.' He gave her arm a final squeeze and strode off down the steps three at a time.

Reggie Patterson lay in the small glass-partitioned room next to the sister's office in Cavell Ward, on the third floor of the Royal Friary. Paul-the-Painter from 'B' relief had been used as a stop-gap escort until the arrival of Michael. He should have been off-duty some three and a half hours previously. He had punctuated this time at twenty-minute intervals by calling the station on his personal radio and enquiring as to the whereabouts of his successor. Paul Ford was not happy.

'Where the bloody hell have you been, mate?' he asked irritably. 'I've promised to spray the wing of my mate's Granada before I go to bed. I've been here for twelve bloody hours now and I'm screaming bored. No one to talk to, sod-all on the telly and nothing to read. I've got the right hump, I can tell you. If it wasn't for those nurses walking up and down I would have gone barmy. Anyway,' he said, buttoning up his coat. 'If you spend some time on that big Irish staff nurse you might get a blanket-bath. Ta-ta and be good. But if you can't be good, be magnificent.'

Preacher lay quietly in a sunny corner of the room propped up on a mass of pillows. Injuries apart, he seemed to have changed a great deal since Michael had last seen him. There was an air of tranquillity, almost serenity, about him now. Although his face was back to its normal proportion, the scars were still red and angry. In addition, there was an inch gap on the left of his mouth where once four teeth had been.

'Afternoon, Reggie,' sang out Michael. 'You certainly look much better. How d'you feel?'

Reggie Patterson made no response, except with his eyes. These remained staring at Michael for a few seconds before closing in a deliberate gesture of indifference.

'They asked for volunteers to sit with you, Reggie. As it was me and Dave Ducker that found you, I thought I would like to be the one to look after you—now that you're on the mend, so to speak.'

At these words of concern, the patient opened his eyes momentarily and gave a brief, disbelieving smile before closing them again.

'It's true, Reg,' insisted Michael. 'You've got me here for the next few days so you'll have to make the best of it, I'm afraid. How are they treating you? Well, I hope.'

After asking such a banal question, Michael decided he was just not cut out for polite small talk. If Preacher did not want him to speak then that was just fine. He had no desire to converse with the man anyway. With two books and a newspaper, he was more than happy to slump in the chair and just read. He gave only a passing thought to the 'big Irish staff nurse' and a blanket-bath before spreading his *Daily Mirror* over the foot of Preacher's bed.

'Will you be after takin' the newspaper off the bed now? The print comes off on the sheets an' we have more things to do than to keep changin' the linen.'

Michael did not need to look up to realize who had appeared. Raising his head he had practically chimed, 'Good morning, Nurse,' before he had set eyes on her.

Staff Nurse Ryan was a sturdy dyed-blonde, with hand-wrestling forearms and Guinness-bottle legs. Michael made two instant resolutions. The first one was never to upset her and so was the second. A blanket-bath from this lady, he thought, would have the gentility of a rugby scrum.

'Ah, yes, I'm sorry, Nurse. I'll clear away at once.' His anxiety to please was so great that he had screwed up the paper and deposited it in the bin before he remembered he had not read it. Straightening his tie, he gave a nervous smile and sat up tidily in his chair. 'No nurses,' Bromley had said. 'You are not there to get your leg over,' the detective had warned. Well, thought Michael, at least the man has a sense of humour. Any bloke rash enough to throw his leg over the redoubtable Nurse Ryan, would probably have it thrown straight back at him—detached!

The staff nurse hit Cavell Ward like a typhoon. With commands here and glowers there, most patients lay stiffly at attention in their beds. As she finally stormed her way through the ward, Michael emitted a great sigh of relief and rummaged around in the waste-bag for the remains of his newspaper.

'She put the fear of Christ up you, didn't she?'

He froze. That was clearly Preacher's voice! As far as the young policeman knew, those were the first words the man had uttered for at least two months. Apart from hearing the words, Michael was also experiencing the first sign of panic. What was he to do? Should he pretend he had not heard and hopefully draw a repeat from the taciturn patient? Or perhaps he should act as if nothing unusual had taken place and just slip into a normal conversation? He elected for the latter.

'Phew!' exclaimed the nervous young escort, making a great play of wiping his brow. 'She's got hairs on her chest that one.'

'Yes,' agreed Patterson calmly. 'I bet it would be difficult to remove *her* knickers without a struggle.'

'I suppose you're right,' responded Michael. 'Still, looking at it from that angle, I should imagine it would be difficult to remove *anyone's* knickers without a struggle. Presuming they don't want to take them off, that is,' he added hastily.

'Quite,' nodded Patterson.

'Is there, um, is there anything I can get you, Reg? A drink maybe?'

'No, I'm fine. Tell me, did you *really* volunteer for this job?'

'Of course! I heard that you were quite bad at one time and I just felt that I should be here. I appreciate that I haven't known you very long but, er,' he paused as he searched desperately for a suitable lie. 'But, well, we got on excellently for the little time that I did know you. Like I

155

said, Dave and I were very keen to come. Finally Tomlinson relented.'

'I'm very grateful,' said Preacher. 'Very grateful indeed. You see, he is going to try to roast me. I'm to be offered up like a sacrifice.' His calm words suddenly broke off and he replaced them with a chilling cackle. 'He won't succeed though. I'll always be a step ahead of him.'

'Who are you talking about, Reg?'

'That slick sod Bromley, of course—who else? Although he's never going to get me on the sheet. Intellectually I'm a mile above him. He not only knows it but he knows why—that's what infuriates him more than anything else.'

'Why is that, Reg? Why do you think he's after you so strong?'

'I don't just *THINK*, I *KNOW*!' shrilled Patterson, his voice rising.

'Of course. Of course you do, Reg,' soothed Michael. 'It's just that *I* don't know, do I? I mean, you can't expect me to know, can you? After all, beside the likes of you, I'm still a boy in the job,' he added modestly.

'Yes, you're right, I'm sorry. I shouldn't have shouted at you like that,' apologized Patterson.

'This "reason", the one that Bromley is after you for—What is it?'

'Jealousy!'

'Jealousy? What is he jealous of for heaven's sake?'

'Background—he hasn't got any. The man has no class, you see. Never will have, of course.'

'And you think that's the reason, Reg?'

'I'm *sure* it's the reason. You see, it's not important in your case—you have no pretensions. With all due respect to you, Michael, you are what you are and that's what you will always be. But Bromley!' He shook his head violently. 'A different kettle of fish altogether. He knows that at the end of the day he has to nail me to the cross, just like they did to Jesus. How can he possibly relax in his position as detective inspector when he knows that PC 698 Patterson is intellectually his master? Tell me that, eh? You can't, can you?' He continued, without waiting for an answer, 'Bromley has been out to destroy me ever since he discovered my background.'

'But how do you know this, Reg? After all, I understand that he's only been at the station a short time himself.'

'The Lord told me.'

'Oh, I see,' answered Michael, not knowing what else to say. He was now feeling well out of his depth. Bromley had said he would be here around lunchtime and it was nearly that now, in fact the lunch trolley was approaching the ward. He glanced quickly beyond the entrance but there was no sign of the detective inspector.

After his initial outburst, Preacher appeared to be lapsing into silence again. Michael decided that whatever the course he was to adopt, it had to be one that encouraged conversation. The main problem was that Preacher's last remark had been religious. Now when it came to religion, Michael was not a star student. He swallowed hard and made a try. 'Er—the Lord . . . Does he speak to you often, Reggie?' he asked weakly.

'Frequently.'

'I see. Er—is it always about Bromley or does he talk to you about anything else?'

'Sometimes he speaks about girls.'

Michael pricked his ears. He may not have been very good on the religious swings but he was more than passable on the female roundabouts.

'That's handy!' he said brightly. 'I could do with a conversation with him myself. What does he tell you about these . . . er, these girls?'

Preacher shrugged and for a moment appeared to be searching for words. Finally he spoke. 'He tells me about the wicked ones.'

'Which ones are they, Reggie? I've been trying to find them all my life!'

'You know the ones! You've seen them! They're everywhere!' He shook his head in disgust. 'Prostitutes, all of them. The Lord wanted chastisement.' He shrugged once more. 'So they were chastised.'

Please, please, Mr Bromley, thought Michael. I'm sure I'm getting a confession here and I haven't a clue what to do with it. Please hurry up!

'Mr Patterson! It's time for your tablets.'

Michael's meditations were interrupted by the return of Staff Nurse Ryan. What the young man had first assumed was the lunch trolley proved to be the drug trolley. She pushed the wheeled container to the foot of the bed and glanced at the notes that hung from the patient's bedrail. Returning to the trolley she counted out three small capsules. Before these could be dispensed, a stomach-turning groan rent the air. This was followed by a series of crashes. All three looked quickly down the ward to where a huge fat man hung grotesquely from a bed. Blood had spurted from his mouth and spread treacle-like on the floor. His drip lay at a drunken angle and had smashed a glass fruit-bowl. Even as Michael and the nurse raced out of the door towards him, the volume of blood receded and was replaced by a steady stream of popping bubbles. Screams and muffled cries came from nearby patients and a black student nurse ran in from the far end of the ward. As quick as this newcomer was, both Michael and Nurse Ryan preceded her. To even Michael's inexpert eye the man was already dead. He assisted the two nurses to pull the huge body back on to the bed but the weight was enormous, it made their feet slip on the tacky floor. Once the body was righted, Michael saw the face clearly for the first time. 'Ugh! What's that poking from his mouth?' He winced.

Staff Nurse Ryan answered his question with one of her own. 'Do you smoke?'

'No,' said Michael.

'You're very lucky,' she said matter of factly. 'That is his lung.' With a quick flurry she threw the curtains around the bed-space with one practised hand.

'Okay, thank you very much for your help, Constable. We can cope quite well now by ourselves,' said the staff nurse. Assistance had indeed arrived in the shape of two more nurses and a sister. 'If I was you though, I would take off those shoes and wash them in the sluice-room. You'll find it at the far end of the ward,' she added.

Michael crouched and unfastened his laces before stepping out on to the dry part of the floor. He was now feeling quite nauseous. Holding his shoes at arm's length, he tiptoed away in his socks. Just before entering the corridor he gave a searching glance towards Preacher, but the excitement appeared to have exhausted that gentleman and he was either sleeping quite soundly or carrying out his usual pretence.

To clean the shoes took far longer than he had imagined. The blood seemed to have seeped into every hole and crack. He was also becoming concerned lest the DI should appear in the ward and find Preacher unguarded. The way events had developed lately made that seem more than a probability. Satisfying himself about his footwear, he dried the shoes on a large paper towel and hastened back to the ward. He was in time to see the white-faced and stocking-footed Nurse Ryan staring into her drug trolley. She did not need to say a word, her expression said everything. He glanced quickly towards Preacher's bed, and although the man still appeared asleep, Michael was instantly aware that something was very wrong.

The pair raced to the bedside and the nurse wrenched back the blankets. A blood-stained catheter that had caught up in the bedclothes clattered to the floor.

'Sister! Quick!' called the nurse.

The curtains around the fat, dead patient parted and the sister looked anxiously across the ward. She too kicked off her shoes and scuttled quickly over the floor. Michael began to wonder what disaster would happen next.

'I think he's taken a tubful of pills,' said the nurse calmly.

'Which?' asked Sister curtly.

'Potassium supplements,' came the quiet reply.

'Out!' snapped the sister, pushing Michael in the chest and curtaining off the second bed-space in less than ten seconds. 'Nurse Jenkins! Nurse Robertson! Leave that patient and come here—quickly now!' Kicking off their shoes, the two named nurses skidded across the ward.

Michael's total knowledge of medicines terminated at aspirins for headaches. As far as he was concerned, potassium supplements was something one spread over compost heaps. Yet in spite of this ignorance, he had already gathered that potassium was incompatible with Preacher's physical condition. He would have been even more worried if he had known just *how* incompatible. Bells rang, buzzers buzzed and a whole motley crew of white-coated people dashed hither and thither. A stretcher-trolley appeared and Preacher was wheeled quickly away.

It was now fairly obvious that there was to be no quick, easy recovery for the unconscious policeman. Michael had reluctantly come to the conclusion that he would now have to tell Bromley. The only problem was, exactly *what* was he to tell him? With all the turmoil in the ward, no one remained still long enough to speak to him. As if the situation was not already confused at the height of the drama, the meal trolley had arrived! He was then not only barred from Preacher's bed-space but also from the whole of the ward! What was it, he wondered, that was so damn secret about a dozen sick people eating boiled hake for lunch?

Summoning up all of his courage, Michael called the station on his personal radio. Mr Bromley, it appeared, had left his office five minutes previously. He was apparently on his way to the Royal Friary Hospital. The young man sighed. It might just have been a little easier to have broken the news over the bat-phone. He could at least have claimed bad reception once he had told him the worst. Ten minutes later, the sound of the detective inspector's steel-tipped heels could be heard clip-clopping down the corridor. Michael rose nervously to his feet.

'Why aren't you with Patterson?' demanded the detective inspector almost before he was close enough to speak. 'You are supposed to be alongside his bed until you are relieved.'

'Er—well, sir, you see . . . Preach—er, PC Patterson, is back in intensive care, sir. He's had a bit of a relapse.'

'A relapse! What sort of relapse?'

A white-coated figure had also been hurrying along the corridor, although with less obvious footwear. This figure now spoke. 'An unfortunately fatal relapse, Inspector. I'm afraid Mr Patterson is now dead.' Bromley tilted back his head and closed his eyes. 'Perhaps you would like to come into my office? You'll find it marginally more comfortable than this corridor.'

A few minutes later, the doctor and the two policemen crowded into a small ante-room at one end of the ward.

'But how did he get the drugs?' asked the incredulous Bromley. 'And what the hell were you doing, lad? You were there to prevent just this situation arising!'

'It was, I agree, totally unfortunate,' smoothed the doctor. 'And we will of course hold an inquiry. The staff nurse who was responsible for the drugs was called away to a dying patient. I gather she was assisted in her efforts by this young man. Nevertheless she must still be held responsible. PC Patterson then climbed from his bed —heaven only knows how, he should have been too ill to even sit up—ripped out the catheter and seized the first tubful of pills he could lay his hands on. These were unfortunately water pills for a patient further down the ward; in other words, potassium supplements. Just about the worst possible medicine for a patient on renal dialysis.'

'These pills, they could kill him as quickly as that?'

'You have to remember, Inspector, that Mr Patterson was also an extremely sick man. Apart from the sheer physical effort of covering that distance to the drug trolley, there was also the problem of the catheter. To have ripped it out like that must have been agonizing. It may be that the physical strain alone would have killed him. The pills just assisted in the task—it's the potassium, you see. He could have got the same result with bananas.'

'Bananas!' snapped Bromley. 'Yes, I think you're bloody right there! I think this whole damn hospital is bananas! How the hell can—'

Further conversation was cut short by a curt message over Michael's personal radio: 'Is DI Bromley with you, 171?'

'Yes, Sarge,' answered the young man.

'Get him to telephone me here as soon as possible. It is very urgent. Over.'

The doctor had gestured towards the telephone before Bromley had even phrased the request.

'Yes . . . yes . . . yes . . .' repeated Bromley into the handset. 'Where? . . . I don't believe it! Are you sure? . . . Okay, I'll be there in five minutes.' He replaced the receiver and, with his hand still resting upon it, stared vacantly at it for a few seconds. He eventually lifted his gaze to the room's two other occupants. 'There has been another attack on a WPC,' he murmured hoarsely. 'This time he's killed her.'

CHAPTER ELEVEN

The distance from the hospital to the murder site was little more than a mile. The detective inspector's mind raced as he negotiated the mass of little side streets. Yet it raced to no purpose: it was like a sports car on blocks. The revs were at maximum and the wheels were a blur but the car did not move. He had been convinced that Patterson had been his man. Perhaps he still was? Perhaps this was just a carbon-copy murder, the work of some weak-minded nutter who had suddenly taken to the idea of battering plonks. After all, it had happened before. Just one crime that is a little out of the ordinary, is often enough to trigger off a whole host of replicas. The alternative to this theory was too alarming to behold. It meant, in effect, that the last eight weeks had been wasted. It was even more than that. In an effort to obtain an admission from Patterson, the whole matter had been kept from the media and doubtless the trail of Patterson's own assailant had gone cold. So what now? Bromley felt he would be an extremely fortunate man to emerge unscathed from this situation.

It was the white tape that first caught his eye. It ran in a long curving loop across the pavement and part of the road along the front of the White Stone Park hostel. Three panda cars and two white Rovers were parked untidily at the kerbside. Typical, thought Bromley. He had hardly known a murder scene where the uniformed coppers hadn't stomped all over the place prior to the arrival of the Scenes of Crime Officer. He saw straight away that this was to be no exception.

Detective Sergeant Mary Keegan had taken a quiet but firm control since her arrival fifteen minutes previously. The immediate area around the corpse had been partitioned with chairs from the hostel and even the crew of the first car on the scene had been dispatched some thirty yards. Those two officers, together with some dozen or so other uniformed constables, now stood in a shocked group by the main gates of the hostel.

'Hello, guv',' she greeted. 'The detective superintendent's on his way. I don't think he's very pleased, he had some rather big plans about lunch.'

'What've we got?' asked Bromley curtly.

'It's young June Southword, from Cabul Lane . . . or rather it was. It would appear that she was about to hang a few bits and bobs on the washing line when she was clobbered. We're still waiting for the divisional surgeon but I would guess she was killed instantly. The side of her head above her left ear is practically stove in.'

'Has she any other injuries?'

'None that are obvious. We think he may have been interrupted. The area car wasn't called here, it arrived quite by chance. As it drove in one side of the hostel, the suspect must have run out of the other.'

'By chance?' asked Bromley. 'What *chance*? Just why should the area car arrive at that precise moment?'

'Well, a late call came from Tower Bridge Magistrates' Court. They wanted June to give evidence in a dangerous-driving case that was due on at two o'clock this afternoon. It was the girl's weekly leave day, so the car crew drove up to tell her.'

'I see. Where's the crew?'

Mary nodded to the group of uniformed officers huddled at the gate. 'There are two of them and they are amongst that bunch. There is Tubby Osbourne, the driver and the r/t operator Steven Collins. Er—Stevie had been going out with June quite a bit lately and I'm afraid he's not taken it very well. In fact, it was a couple of his sweaters that she was hanging up.'

Bromley nodded and walked towards the body. He stopped some two yards short and, for a minute or so, just stood staring down at it. It looked for all the world like a badly broken doll. 'It must have taken a pretty ferocious

164

whack to have inflicted that sort of injury,' he said. 'The skull's cracked like a boiled egg. Do we have a weapon?'

'Not yet.'

'Well, while we are waiting, you can put those lads to work searching for it. Meantime I'll have a chat with young Collins. I had better not speak to him in sight of the body, so I'll take him in the hostel. If the detective superintendent arrives perhaps you'll tell him where I am?'

'Do you want a sweep-search done at this stage, guv'?'

'Yes, and I want it done systematically. If you think you need reinforcements then contact the nick, but I want this weapon found. There are several old derelict houses in the next street and most of them back on to the hostel. It may be a good idea to start there.'

Some thirty minutes later, the entire early-turn relief, plus a sprinkling of CID officers, began a painstaking search of the house and grounds of the three old buildings that backed on to the hostel. These semi-mansions lay on the north side of the slope that led down from the murder spot. Each of them was a crumbling, neglected heap that provided shelter for an assortment of rats, cats and vagrants.

If the houses had been neglected, then the gardens were a veritable rain-forest. They were a maze of twisted, creeping brambles and tangled bushes and trees. The only way through was to batter down the clinging branches. Yet this action could easily hide the very object they were seeking to uncover. Helen had confiscated a broom from the cleaning cupboard of the hostel and laid into the branches with a vengeance, almost hatred. It was not so much that she *discovered* the weapon, it was more that the object laid claim to her. As she had moved her foot forward, the heavy iron bar had clipped her unprotected ankle a sickening blow. The blood and scalp hairs that now lay smeared across her instep, however, were not hers, but those of a far more unfortunate young lady. With the discovery of the weapon, the uniform activity in the murder decreased. An incident-room was set up in Cabul Lane and

165

a dozen CID officers, six of them experienced detectives and six of them trainees, began the legwork on the case.

The girls residing in the hostel had become understandably agitated and a permanent male guard was posted to the front door. Hostels are impersonal places by definition but White Stone Park was now like a morgue. It was in an effort to provide some relief to this atmosphere, that Michael suggested the four friends should spend a social evening together and discuss a party to celebrate Angela's approaching birthday. It was several days before their respective shifts enabled them to be collectively off-duty and, acting on a suggestion of Angela's, it had been agreed that they would not talk shop. Even the slightest mention of the job was declared taboo and the first to break this rule was to pay for the dinner wine. It was doubtless this reason that caused David to talk, if somewhat uncharacteristically, of his private life. By the time they had left the restaurant and adjourned to the Red Lion pub, he was almost garrulous. He began to speak more and more of Brenda. Each of the three had been aware of his relationship with her but not of the extent of his intensity.

'I've decided to marry her,' he announced with drink-rimmed eyes.

None of them spoke, in fact not one set of eyes was raised from the table-top. 'Yes,' he continued, 'I thought we could manage it next year. She'll still be young enough to have a baby and I'll have a chance to save a few bob by then. I thought perhaps we could get married on my twenty-first birthday. After all, we won't need very much, perhaps just enough for a good honeymoon. She already has a nice home.'

'Oh, she has a nice home all right,' agreed Michael. 'She also has a nice daughter. How d'you think she is going to take it?'

'I . . . I don't see any problems,' faltered David.

'You don't?' enquired Michael acidly. 'A lusty, busty twenty-year-old, who fancied you rotten from the start, bouncing about all over the house and *you* don't see any problems? What are you planning—a harem?'

David reddened. 'It's not like that at all!' he snapped. 'Why do you have to cheapen everything? It's always got to be sex with you, hasn't it? I happen to love Brenda and that really gets up your nose because you've never been able to really love anyone in your whole life. I fully realize there's an age gap between us but it won't make any difference, I assure you.'

'An age gap?' exploded Michael. 'She's twenty-one years older than you! That's not a "gap" that's a bloody great prairie!' He shook his head repeatedly. 'Look, Dave, your Brenda is a fine-looking woman, I'll grant you that much and there is no doubt that you seem to be very good for each other. But you can't *marry* her, Dave, you can't! It would be a disaster!' Michael turned in frustration to the two girls. 'Speak to him you two for Chrissake! He beds a woman for the first time in his life and straight away he wants to start a sodding dynasty!'

Angela moved her chair and sat close against David. She took his hand and looked directly into his face. 'Dave,' she said softly. 'Have you spoken to Brenda about this?'

'Well, no, not really. But she'll agree, I know she will.'

'I'm sure your Brenda is an attractive woman, Dave,' continued the girl, 'but you really must think this out. Have you worked out how old she will be when you are forty, for example?'

'Why is everyone so obsessed about age for God's sake! Of course I've worked it out! She'll be sixty-one and that doesn't matter a damn to me. In my relationship with that woman, her age simply doesn't come into it. Now will you three please get that into your thick heads?'

'But we're not criticizing you for *sleeping* with an older woman,' interrupted Michael. 'What I'm having a go at you about is marrying her! You can sleep with the entire Newington Old Ladies' home if that turns you on—all I'm saying is don't marry any of 'em.'

'Just why are you so bloody pious, Mickey?' asked

167

David. 'It seems you can do whatever you want to a girl but when I want to treat one just a little bit decent, you become really offensive.'

'Look, Dave, make no mistake, I happen to believe that sleeping with a girl *is* "treating her decent". After all, sex is a two-way thing, or at least it should be. She's no fool that Brenda, she wouldn't do anything unless she wanted to. If you are lucky enough to be kipping with an older woman —fine, I've done it myself, it's magic. But just remember the golden rule—never get married and spoil it.'

David made no response to this latest advice. Instead he stared sullenly down into his glass. Helen, deciding it was time to take a little of the weight from his shoulders, made her first entry into the current conversation. She began it with a dig at Michael.

'You know what that indicates, don't you?' she asked him.

'No, what?' he replied with only mild interest.

'All those Freudian fantasies you seem to have about older women simply mean you have a mother fixation.'

'What the hell's a "mother fixation"?'

'Well, in basic terms it means you have this subconscious desire to sleep with your mother.'

'That's crap!'

'It's an undisputed Freudian theory,' she announced pompously.

'It's still crap! What's more I'll prove it to you. See that barmaid? The one in the next bar?' He pointed along the semicircular bar to where a large blonde woman was pulling firmly on a brass-topped beer pump. 'Do you know who that is?'

'No,' answered Helen. 'Should I?'

'Her name is Jeannie McDavitt, she's twelve and a half stone if she's an ounce. She's the epitome of all barmaids. If I owned a pub I wouldn't employ any barmaid who didn't look like Jeannie McDavitt. Look at her! Everything about that girl is big. Sergeant Tomlinson reckons she's even got big hair!'

Helen stared across the bar and could see instantly how the sergeant arrived at that conclusion. Absolutely everything about Jeannie was indeed big. He was also right about the hair, it was the biggest hair Helen had ever seen. This impression was given by the style of it. Great waves rose and fell around her face like sea round a rock. Huge tumbling curls bounced generously down to her shoulders —big shoulders, of course—where the bright chestnut glint reflected every light in the Red Lion.

'All barmaids should look like Jeannie,' said Michael philosophically. 'I reckon a bloke can trust a fat barmaid—and that's more than you can say for some of the beanpoles you get in poofy wine bars. Look at her,' he instructed admiringly. 'I could fall in love with just one of her legs! Never mind about a campaign for "real ale", let's have a campaign for real barmaids. That girl is the Boadicea of every drinking man.'

'Okay,' said Helen testily. 'So we've had the big tour of Jeannie McDavitt. Just what does that prove?'

'How old do you think she is?'

Helen shrugged. 'Forty . . . forty-two maybe?'

'Not bad! Forty-four to be precise.'

'Well, isn't that just ducky? So she's a big girl and she's forty-four. Congratulate her for me, will you? Now if you don't mind I would like to get into a subject just a little less wearing.'

'You started this, Helen, with all your crap about a mother fixation, so hear me out, there's a good girl. Two weeks ago, I spent one whole night and a half of the next day in bed with Mrs McDavitt. Quite frankly it was superb. Between midnight Wednesday and two o'clock Thursday afternoon, I was in love with Jeannie McDavitt and doubtless she was in love with me. Okay, it was of short duration and a shallow love I grant you, but love it was. Now, according to your theory, Helen, I bedded Jeanie—or perhaps she bedded me, I'm still not sure which—because I had this hang-up about sleeping with my own mother. Well, for your information, young lady, I

169

have wanted to lay a fat blonde barmaid ever since I was nine years old. Oh, and incidentally, she really is blonde. I can safely vouch for that. My mother on the other hand is a seven-and-a-half-stone midget with dark hair. And I'll also tell you this, the spanks I occasionally got from my mum were nowhere near the fun they were from Big Jeannie. Fit *that* into your Freudian theory, Miss Rogers!'

Both the girls and David found their gaze now involuntarily drawn to the barmaid. It seemed that she could feel their eyes because she looked up from pulling yet another pint and gave the staring trio a friendly smile. It was while they smiled weakly back that she made her next gesture. This was a generous lip-puckering kiss, directly and unmistakably towards Michael.

'Mickey,' said Angela wearily, 'I swear you are the biggest liar I've ever met but will you please tell me one thing straight?'

'For you, sweetie, anything.'

'How the hell does any of this help Davy?'

'It's a warning, of course, sweetie. Can't you see it? If he was to spend less time and energy on those fresh-air-racked football pitches and more time in healthy, smoky bars, he wouldn't have to marry the first good woman that came along. He could fall in love with Jeannie McDavitt once a week, or even twice on her day off. Who knows, if he was to play his cards right he could even make it with you.'

Angela blushed instantly.

'Angie! You're blushing! You who bared all in the training-school fishpond! It certainly looks as if I struck a spot there, doesn't it?' He turned to David for confirmation but David had problems of his own. 'Davy! You too! You're as red as she is! Well, well, Helen, what d'you think we have here then—a romance?'

'Mickey,' began Helen. 'There are times when I think you are the nicest bloke I've ever met. Then there are other times when I think you're the biggest shit.'

'Sounds like I've got the balance just about right then, doesn't it?'

'Look, I hope no one feels I'm anti-social,' said David. 'But I'm tired. I've also had enough of this conversation and I'm early-turn in the morning. I think I'll make a move.'

'Me too,' agreed Angela.

Michael seemed quite disappointed. He opened his arms and turned his palms imploringly upwards. 'Doesn't anyone fancy going on anywhere else? Surely you do, Helen?' he added hopefully.

Helen shook her head. 'No, I've had enough to drink for one night. On the other hand, I don't feel like going back to that hostel yet either.'

'Well, I'll walk you back,' offered Michael. 'It'll take an hour or so and it might just tire you out.'

'But if I take the van, how are you going to get back to the section-house?' interrupted David.

'Walk, son, walk! You athletes don't have the monopoly on energy you know. If I can spend fourteen hours in big Jeannie's bed, I can walk the five miles back to the section-house on one bloody foot.'

'Yes, thanks, Mickey, that's a good idea. I think I'd quite like a walk,' agreed Helen.

David shrugged. 'Come on then, Angie. G'night you two.'

Angela also bade her good-nights and had all but reached the door before Michael called her back. He leaned his head confidentially towards her and the girl bent forward to meet him halfway. 'Don't be too put out by all this talk about plump, mature women, kid. I can still fall in love with a pretty girl.'

'One for the road then, Helen?' asked Michael as they listened to the old van's spluttering exhaust fade into the distance.

'Okay, just one. But that will almost certainly take me over my personal limit. I shall probably become very emotional, I warn you.'

'Me too,' he agreed. 'In fact, one more pint and I shall probably be anybody's. You will be gentle with me, won't you?'

Helen watched with increasing interest as Michael placed

171

his order at the bar. Jeannie McDavitt had undoubtedly made a point of moving her position in order to serve him. The pair of them certainly seemed to share far more conversation than was strictly necessary for a pint of bitter and a vodka and tonic. Michael had obviously made some remark that amused the barmaid greatly, for she threw back her head and her wide, full lips parted in an unashamed gale of laughter. There was, Helen grudgingly admitted to herself, a certain sensuality about the woman. Surprised though she was at this discovery, she was dismayed to experience just a first twinge of jealousy. She then began to wonder not just *if* the pair had made love, but *how* they had. Would Jeannie have been nude or partially dressed? Would it have been with the light on, or would it have been in the dark? Do twelve-and-a-half-stone ladies parade round bedrooms scantily dressed? Blast the woman—and blast Michael too for even mentioning it.

'Here y'are, lovely,' he said cheerily as he slid the glass across the small table. 'You can now become emotional with my blessing.'

'Mickey, do you take *anything* seriously?'

His face changed instantly. 'As a matter of fact I do.'

'What, for example?'

'*You*, for example. You and Dave to be precise. You are both just throwing away your lives. The most maddening thing is that deep down the pair of you know it. You, Helen, have less excuse of course because you are not only more experienced, you're more bloody sensible. Or at least you are in most things. As for him, if he has to lose his marbles about an older woman I can't understand why he can't do it about you. If nothing else it would halve my worries about the pair of you!'

'As it happens I'm really fond of Dave. He's just not my type, that's all. Life is not as simple as that.'

'What do you mean "not your type"? Do you mean he wouldn't treat you like dirt and walk all over you, is that what you mean? No, I don't suppose he would, the silly sod. He'd probably put you on a pedestal and worship you. He'd knock

172

out three kids in three years and bore the rest of us silly showing us photographs of you holding the babies. We would all have to say how nice they were. He'd be talking about the kids and we'd have to pretend we weren't admiring your tits. One day when that boy emerges from his trance he's going to make some girl a smashing husband.'

'You're a strange lad, Mickey. I think beneath that sweeping, cavalier exterior, lurks a potentially caring little suburban spouse.'

'Who, me? No bloody fear! I'm not shopping at Sainsbury's for any woman.'

'What, not even for Big Jeannie, or perhaps even for—dare I say it—Trixie? Tut-tut-tut, shame on you, you chauvinist,' she mocked.

'No, not for Big Jeannie, Big Trixie, or Big-anyone-else.' He moved forward slightly and whispered, 'In fact, not even for a truly beautiful woman like you.' There was silence for a second then he laughed. 'And that's the third blushing face I've caused in fifteen minutes! Drink up and I'll walk you home. All this psychoanalysis is making me tired.'

There was a distinct chill in the air as they left the warmth of the saloon bar and stepped bravely out into the dark, windy street.

'If we walk quickly we should do it in forty minutes or so,' said Michael, thrusting his hands deep into his pockets. 'If we walk fast enough you may even keep warm.'

Helen shivered and, slipping her arm through his, nuzzled her head briefly against his shoulder. They spoke little as they strode the windswept pavements. In fact, Helen quite enjoyed the silence, it somehow seemed more intimate. It was exactly forty-five minutes before they turned into the hostel. Michael nodded briefly to the watching uniformed sentinel as he accompanied Helen into the building. 'Would you like a cup of coffee, John?' Michael asked the huddled policeman. 'I'll fetch you one down if you want.'

John Hamilton shook his head nervously. 'No thanks, mate, the stuff's coming out of my ears. I thought this would be a nice little number tonight. You know, looking

173

after all these WPCs on my own. Instead of which there are as many blokes in the bloody hostel as there are plonks and they are all doling me out coffee to placate their bloody consciences.'

'Is . . . er, is Davy Ducker still here? He should have fetched young Angela Helms back about an hour or so ago.'

The PC shook his head. 'No. He was here but he's about the only one who didn't stay. He was in and out in a minute.'

'Are you sure?'

'Positive! I ought to know because he was the only poor bugger who didn't offer me a coffee!'

'Sod!' muttered Michael. 'I had great hopes for that relationship.'

Michael sat on the edge of the bed browsing through an underwear catalogue whilst Helen busied herself with a boiling kettle in the communal kitchen.

'Here you are.' She thrust an over-filled coffee mug at him. 'So that's how you keep up to date.' She nodded towards the catalogue.

'As it happens, I've never been keen on pictures of unclad young women. They used to say in the Army that it was a bit like eating chocolate with the paper on. I once knew a bloke—'

'Michael, I'm leaving.' She stood staring at him with tear-filled eyes. 'And it's not the vodka either.' She forced a fleeting tight smile.

He balanced his mug on the bedside locker and rose to his feet. He moved towards the girl but she held her equally filled mug in front of her like a weapon of defence. 'No, hear me out, Mickey, please.' He returned to the bed and she sat on the chair opposite. 'Just too much has happened since I've come to this place and I realize I can't cope.' She shrugged. 'I suppose I was silly to even think that I could. I thought I would be able to leave all my previous life behind and, of course, I found that I couldn't. I wear the uniform but I'm still the same person underneath. The attack

174

frightened me far more than anyone realized, even me. That was bad enough but since poor June's murder I've hardly stopped shaking. Mickey, my nerve has totally gone—I'm a mess.'

'You'll get over—'

'Mickey, I *won't* get over it! I've examined this from all angles and although I honestly don't wish to be rude to you, I simply *don't* need your advice. And I certainly don't need meaningless platitudes such as "You'll get over it". I want to *talk*, Mickey. I've listened enough and you are the only one that I can talk to. Will you listen to me? Will you listen to me without interrupting? Will you just be the best goddamned friend I ever had—will you, Mick, will you?'

''Course,' he whispered hoarsely.

'The mess I am in is entirely of my own making—I know that. It doesn't make it any easier to bear though. You see, apart from the obvious things that you already know about, there is one more. I'm pregnant. That in itself would present a problem for any girl in my position. I mean, if the chief superintendent can get so worked up over teacups, I dread to think what he'll say about one of his plonks in the family way. But, you see, the situation is made far worse by the fact that I actually *want* the baby. Oh, I know it's stupid and completely impractical and never in a million years would I deliberately set out to have a child. Yet the fact remains that now I *am* pregnant I want this baby more than anything else that I've wanted in my life. It suddenly seems to have given me a whole new meaning. For the first time someone is really going to need *me*. So you see, I have no choice. I daren't risk a situation where the child could be harmed. A miscarriage now, Mick, would kill me, it really would.'

'Can I ask you a question?'

She smiled. 'You don't have to, I know what it is. I not only know the question but I know the supplement. It's "A"—Who is the father? and "B"—Does he know? Correct?'

He nodded.

175

'I am two and a half months' pregnant with the child of a bloody carpet salesman and he is most certainly not aware of it. Does that answer your question?'

Michael closed his eyes and slowly shook his head in disbelief. 'So what are you going to do?' he murmured so softly that he was scarcely audible.

'I have an aunt who has been particularly kind in the past, and as my uncle has recently died she's insisted I go there. I don't think it would work out in the long term but I don't really have a choice.'

'Helen.'

'Yes?'

He did not answer for several seconds. 'Helen . . . I think I admire you more than any other woman I've known in my life and—'

'No, Mick. No!'

'You don't know what I'm going to say yet!' he protested.

'I know *exactly* what you are going to say. I nearly always do—and it's NO!' She leaned forward and took his hand. 'Look, Mickey, you and I get on very well. Let's leave it at that, eh? You're not the type of man that helps girls in my situation, you're more the type that puts them there in the first place. No, I'm sorry, that was unkind. What I think I meant was that the worst thing you could possibly do to yourself, to me and also to my baby, would be to become terribly noble and give the child what used to be called a "name". You just stick to being an "uncle", Mickey, it's safer.'

'I don't know what to say, Helen. I think the world of you and yet I feel so bloody helpless. I suppose I should say, "If there's anything I can do for you" . . . etcetera. But what can I do? Nothing, it seems.'

'Actually there is one thing you could do for me, Mickey. Although with your track record I'm not sure if you are capable.'

'Try me.'

'Very well, but I must warn you, you are almost certain to get it wrong.'

'Helen, for God's sake! What is it?'

She stood up and looked intently down at him. 'Mickey, would you stay the night and just let me cry on you for hours and hours? I don't want to carry on with this pretence of being brave any more. Just for once I want to spend a whole night—a whole night, mark you, not just a fleeting hour of passion—with a friendly arm around me. I don't want sex, Michael. All I suppose I really want is a big man's cuddle. There are no strings to this request except that we don't make love. If we did that I'd be straight back to square one and I couldn't take all that again.'

Michael stood up and seemed to tower over her even more than usual. He took a step across the threadbare carpet and rested his hands lightly upon the hips of her neatly tailored skirt. 'Let me get this perfectly straight, Miss Rogers. You are asking me to take you—you, one of the best-looking birds I've met in my life—to bed and not even touch you? Is that what you're asking?'

'No, I'm not asking you to *take* me anywhere. I'm asking you to *accompany* me. And I *do* want you to touch me, that is exactly what I want. In fact, I want you to hold me tight all night. I want to be fussed, spoilt and cuddled. Then tomorrow I'll face reality, whatever that is.'

Michael gave a wry smile. 'It seems I've entered an era of bedding good-looking girls who spurn my body! You're not about to inflict some bloody awful apple-cake on me, are you?'

She gave a tearful shake of the head.

'Providing you don't mind me leaving at the crack of dawn for early-turn, then come on! This is a quick clean-of-the-teeth-and-straight-into-bed job, I think. Will you lend me a brush?'

'You agree?' she asked. There was some surprise in her tone.

'Of course I agree. Now come on, find me a brush.'

She stretched up and kissed him lightly on the chin. 'I

177

won't be long. If you'd care to go and warm up the bed I'll just have a quick bath.' She turned and took one pace towards the door but he pulled her back roughly.

'Helen,' he said, his voice suddenly much harder. 'I think the world of you and I do understand how you feel. I have absolutely no desire to upset or distress you any further. *BUT* you are a very attractive girl. If you come out of that bathroom all soft, pink and womanly then I would probably be on you before you were halfway across the room. I'm not made of stone, you know. The night is going to be difficult enough for me as it is without you honeymooning it. We either get into that bed with smoke in your hair, dust on your face and cold bums and feet, or we don't get in at all!'

She smiled with moist eyes. 'I suppose I would be allowed a pee?'

'You'd be allowed a period, it might be safer.' The words were out before he realized their implication. 'Oh, I'm sorry, Helen, that wasn't very tactful, was it?'

The girl shrugged. 'Tactful it wasn't—sensible it probably was. Now, will you please warm up that bed?'

A few minutes later Michael braved the chill sheets and slipped into the modestly sized bed. His six feet two inches were a problem in most beds but Helen's was little more than a generous single. The bathroom door opened and Helen moved briskly across the room in a brilliant-white towelling robe. On reaching the bedside she shrugged it smoothly off and for the first time Michael saw her completely nude. She shivered as she pulled back the covers.

'Just a minute!' he commanded.

'What's the matter?' She looked up anxiously.

He shook his head. 'Nothing, I just wanted to have a good look at you first so I can see just exactly how bloody noble I'm going to be.' He pursed his lips in admiration. 'Okay, you can get in now.'

She turned off the bedside lamp and slipped quickly between the sheets.

'Christ, Helen, your bum's freezing!'

'You wait till you get to my feet!' she warned. To an accompaniment of agonized complaints from Michael, she buried herself in him. 'How are you so warm?' she marvelled.

'How are you so bloody cold?' he echoed. 'Even your tits are perishing! No wonder Eskimos only rub noses. I can understand now!' Her hair, which was usually tightened into a bun, flowed freely into his face. 'Do you know I can smell cigars in your hair?'

'Good,' she whispered. 'It'll stop you getting excited.'

In an effort to gain as much space as possible, he lay on his back diagonally across the bed. Helen had turned into him with her arms around his waist. His powerful right arm was wrapped heavily around her smooth but cold shoulders. 'Oh, but you feel good,' she sighed contentedly. 'But you should have let me bath though, it would have got rid of the cigar smoke.'

'Don't worry about it. If I become too excited I can pretend I'm in the saloon bar.'

'Michael.'

'Yes, kid?'

'Thank you.'

He kissed the top of her head. 'That's all right, think nothing of it. Some people rescue princesses from dragons. But me? I just sleep with 'em. God, I feel noble!'

The room was particularly dark and Michael could hear the distant swish of the occasional passing car. At least we beat the rain, he thought. By now Helen was so quiet that he assumed she was asleep. The bed had now warmed considerably and other than a few minor adjustments, he found the position quite comfortable. Soon his eyes began to close yet he was by no means asleep. His thoughts were particularly active. He was finding it difficult to believe he had made it into Helen's bed for such an unusual purpose. Perhaps it wasn't unusual though. After all, not everyone had the same sexual appetite. He was still pondering this point when he realized that his right shoulder, which had been particularly warm, had now chilled rapidly. At first this puzzled him but he soon realized why—it was soaked with tears. Helen was not asleep at all, she was, in fact, very much awake. She was not just awake but quietly crying her eyes out!

Finally the dam broke. Great quivering sobs came up first from her lungs, then her whole body shook. He tightened his grip on her and pushed his lips even harder into her cigar-scented hair.

'It's all right, kid, it's all right,' he soothed.

'Oh, Mickey, fuss me, fuss me,' she sobbed as she curled up tight like a small child. 'I'm so frightened, Mickey. Please cuddle me tight.'

He moved his left arm across to her and embraced her with an intensity that made her gasp. This seemed to have an effect that his soothing words had been unable to produce. She gave a little laugh through her tears. 'This is all new to you, isn't it?'

'What is?' he asked, puzzled by her sudden change of mood.

'This "soothing friend" bit.'

'I suppose it is really—how am I doing?'

'You're marvellous, but you don't have to crack my ribs to prove it. Just hold me, Mickey, just hold me.' She settled down into him once more but this time the crying had stopped. Her breathing soon became deep and rhythmic. Although they had been naked and entwined for almost an hour, it was only then that Michael's body began to make its first reaction to the girl's presence. She was right, he thought, it *was* all new to him. A bloody great erection, a naked girl beside him and there he was thinking desperately of Sergeant Tomlinson! This was a futile effort to take his mind off those firm breasts that were currently being crushed against his rib cage.

'Mickey,' she suddenly whispered in a voice barely audible.

'Yes, kid?' he asked optimistically.

'It might be less frustrating for both of us if you took your hand off my bum—it's quite warm now, thank you. G'night.'

'Good-night, kid.'

'Mickey?'

'Eh?'

'Did you really sleep with Big Jeannie?'

'Would I lie to you?'

'Only three-quarters of the time. Good-night.'

'Good-night.'

As a distant clock struck twelve, yet another hopeful young man presented a coffee to the watching constable downstairs—his ninth of the night.

It was almost 6 a.m. as Michael descended the hostel staircase. John Hamilton, in spite of the coffee, had finally fallen asleep. The weather had blown up into a real south-westerly and as he tiptoed past the slumbering sentinel, Michael raised the hood of his anorak. Leaving the main door his pace quickened, yet in spite of the gusting wind, he distinctly heard running footsteps behind him. Turning, he was just in time to see the approaching blow. For a brief moment he was dazed, then a second thud caused him to drop slowly to the wet gravel.

CHAPTER TWELVE

The soothing hiss of the gas fire contrasted greatly with the gusting, window-shaking April wind. 'Sounds very unfriendly out there, Davy,' murmured Brenda as she lay dozily against him on the settee. 'I bet you're pleased your football match was cancelled today?'

David made no reply. Primarily because he hated lying to anyone but particularly so to Brenda. The match had not been cancelled at all and now, on some bleak, muddy sports ground some twelve miles distant, the name David Ducker was a dirty word. Cabul Lane's third-round cup tie against the local bus garage was not a game to treat lightly. In spite of this, their powerful midfield player, whose deep runs were such a feature, was currently curled up on a sofa with what the team captain disparagingly called 'some big old mum'. It was a measure of David's feelings for Brenda that he had undertaken such a deceit. With eight goals in six matches he had become something of the team star. Yet the woman's warm, ample charms had, not for the first time, seduced him away from his mud-splattered, sweating colleagues. The words, 'Good goal, Davy!' 'Well played, Davy!' and 'Magic, Davy!' did not somehow compare with, 'Love me again, Davy.' However, he had planned more for the afternoon than that. This was the day he was going to propose. He was sure she would agree. As the weeks had slipped by she had become so warm and responsive, all her original doubts seemed to have vanished. It was true they had not made love that afternoon but she had said her period was imminent and she felt slightly out of sorts. Even that made him feel good. Six weeks ago he was not even sure what a 'period' was, but now a woman—a beautiful woman—trusted him enough to confide.

He had no idea how first to broach the subject, his only

knowledge had come from films and television. He dismissed the idea of dropping to one knee, it seemed a bit silly and, short of a seance, so was the idea of asking her father—he had been dead twenty years. Usually Brenda appreciated plain-speaking. Very well, he thought, that's how he would do it. Straightforward and no messing.

'Brenda, I have something important to say,' he announced. He took a deep breath—so far so good.

'And so have I,' came the surprising response. 'But I'm getting mine in first.'

'Oh . . . er, all right then, what is it?' faltered the young man, his speech flow now destroyed.

'We have a problem.'

'What sort of "problem"?'

'A big problem. In fact, we have a very big problem. To be precise we have a "Sandra" problem. My daughter believes I am taking the bread out of her mouth, or rather the man out of her life. You see the difficulty.'

'But that's nonsense! I've never given her the slightest encouragement. How did she find out about us anyway?'

'I told her. We couldn't keep it a secret for ever, you know. After all, you always seemed to be around when Danny came home from school. Besides, she couldn't but help notice the change in me. She's given me an ultimatum. It's you or her.'

'But that's selfish!'

'Of course it's not, Dave. This is her home, this is all she has. I can't take that away from her, can I? Be fair.'

'Be fair? But I was going to ask you to marry me!'

'That's a joke now, isn't it? That idea was never a starter, Dave.' She sighed. 'I did tell you this would happen, didn't I?' She tilted her head and kissed him. 'Look, Dave, in just over two months you have given me more real happiness than I've known in the rest of my adult life. That's not wasted, Davy, that's treasured! I'm going to put all that in my little heart bank and pull it out on bad days. I shall probably bore all the other old crones to death when I'm in the old folks' home.'

'But, Brenda, don't you understand? I love you and I want to marry you. Surely your Sandra couldn't object to that?'

'Look, my Sandra is a very intense young lady. When someone else comes along she will forget you within minutes. Unfortunately, no one yet has come along. It's an unpleasant fact of life, Davy, but you and I must now finish.'

'Is that why we haven't made love? You haven't got a period at all, have you?'

She shook her head.

For Davy this last gesture seemed the greatest betrayal of all. 'I can't believe it. One minute you are so close and loving, the next you are acting as if I never existed.'

'Oh, you exist right enough and for your information—your ego, too, if you like—I probably love you in a way that no other woman in the rest of your life will love you. I love you because I also appreciate every second you've given me. You see, you've turned my world upside-down. I asked you not to even speak to me about love and here you are proposing! And do you know what? I could cry with happiness about even being asked! That's what you've done to me, Davy Ducker. Now, when my Sandra comes home this evening, I will courageously tell her you are back in play once more. There will at least be no competition from her mother.'

David's bewilderment finally gave way to anger. 'Okay! If that's the way you want it—fine!' He pushed her away and reached for his coat. 'I'll not grovel any more. I can't do very much about being in love with you, unfortunately that seems to be something I just can't help. But you don't have to worry, I'll not bother you again.' He turned as he reached the door. 'Oh, by the way, in case your daughter *does* find herself a bloke—poor sod, whoever he may be—then drop me a line. I'll keep a spot nice and warm for you. In that way we won't upset the sad little bitch.' The door crashed behind him.

Brenda remained immobile on the settee, her glazed

eyes staring without actually seeing. 'Oh, Davy,' she mouthed. 'Am I going to miss you . . . !'

The weights in the basement section-house gym bounced heavily on the rubberized mat. Three times the lifter had managed to raise them above his head and three times he had just failed to hold them there. In sheer temper he snatched once more at the bar and this time, with only the slightest of quivers, reached up and held the heavy steel bar in place. He marked this achievement, not by bouncing them down on to the well-marked cushion, but by hurling them with a lung-busting grunt just as far as he could. The vibration shook not only the gym but the first two floors of the building.

Michael Butler had entered the room at the exact moment of impact. 'Well! Well! Aren't we in a little paddy then! Who's upset you? I know, don't tell me. Brenda's either got an early period or she's lost your best vest in the laundry. I'm right, aren't I?' He nodded wisely. 'I can always tell, you know.'

The sweating, panting David advanced two paces towards the newcomer and pointed a very thick finger at the tip of his nose. The five or six inches difference in their heights suddenly seemed to vanish. The smaller, stockier man seemed infinitely more intimidating.

'Don't you wind me up, Mickey Butler, because I am not in the mood for it. So you can shut up or sod off. Understand?'

'Now, now! Is that the way to treat a friend with your welfare at heart? I ask you!'

'Yes, you're very good on welfare, aren't you, Mickey?' said David tartly. 'Your own bloody welfare. Now will you piss off?'

It was rare for David to use so many expletives in so few words and Michael wisely decided to moderate his brashness. 'All I've come for, Davy, is to invite you to a party on Saturday week. Now surely that can't upset you, can it?'

David picked up a towel and began to dab at his soaked brow. 'I'm not in a party mood. What's the occasion anyway?'

'It's a double do. There is Angie's birthday party and Helen's leaving party. You can please yourself which will be your reason to attend.'

David shook his head and sat down on the floor with his back against the vaulting-box and the towel draped loosely around his neck. 'Yes, I'm really sorry about Helen, I'll miss her a lot.'

'You knew?' asked an astonished Michael.

'Of course I knew. It was only a matter of time really, any fool could see that.'

'Well, I didn't.'

'Quite! Any fool with *feeling*, I meant.'

'Thanks a bunch. Anyway, does this mean you'll be coming to the party?' The sitting figure nodded wearily. 'Good, because I've volunteered you for a job. I told the duty sergeant that you'd like to cover the Arsenal versus Leeds match on that day. There's a dozen of us going from the nick, including Angie. I think this is the safest thing to do. This way we're all certain to finish at six o'clock at the latest. It'll give us a couple of hours to get to the party. Will you fetch Brenda? It could be a good opportunity to show her off to the lads.'

David made no reply at first but climbed to his feet and made his way to the dark-leathered punchbag that hung motionless from the ceiling. After four or five powerful short jabs he spoke. 'Brenda won't be coming.'

'Oh . . . Things a bit difficult with you two, are they?'

'Things are *finished* with us two—that is, unless I can get you to take an interest in her daughter Sandra,' he replied bitterly.

'Her Sandra? What, that big-eyed raver in the short leather skirt? Not half!'

David tore into the punchbag once more in a brief frenzy. 'You just do and I'll break your effing neck,' he grunted.

'Tut-tut, Davy Ducker, but you really are a very difficult man to please.'

For the second time in as many minutes, David advanced on the chattering Michael. This time he stopped just short of him. His eyes narrowed as he looked enquiringly at the side of his friend's head. 'What on earth have you done to your face? You've got a black eye that stretches nearly to your earhole!'

'Oh-ho!' exclaimed Michael sarcastically. 'So *I* have no feeling, eh? Well, how about you, sunshine? Here I am, a poor wounded policeman, and you not only don't even notice it but you also threaten me with violence! Not once—but twice, I might add!'

'Come on, don't sod me about, Mickey. What have you done? That's going to be one hell of a bruise before the day is out!'

'I was jumped on and attacked at the girls' hostel.'

'What! Do you mean that—'

'No! Nothing as dramatic as that. I wasn't attacked by the usual mysterious pervert. At least, not the one that you're thinking about. Oh no, I was attacked by some bloody nutter from the crime squad who thought he was going to capture the murderer single-handed. I tiptoed past that dozy sod Hamilton because I didn't want to wake him up, when suddenly some idiot belts me twice on the side of my face!'

'What was the crime squad doing there at that time of the morning?'

'Well, I've found out now that they're every-bloody-where! Apparently they've had two of them in the grounds all night keeping observation. I hope they've not kept too comprehensive a record—half the blokes at the nick must have crept in and out of that place in the last twenty-four hours.'

'So how do you feel?' asked David anxiously.

'Oh, I feel just wonderful! How do you think I feel? I get jumped on by some prat who wouldn't know Jack the Ripper from a brown hat. I then get sent to hospital for stitches and I'm placed sick at work. I've got the king and queen of all headaches so I come to see you for a bit of sympathy—and what do I get from you? The threat of another bloody duffing! Oh, I've had a great day, I have. Absolutely magic! magic!'

'Mickey,' said David, as he resumed his seat against the vaulting-box. 'Do you sometimes get the feeling that everything is a bloody mess?'

'Well, poor Helen certainly is.'

'When is she leaving by the way?'

Michael joined his friend against the box. 'Today. In effect, you could say she's already left.'

'But surely she has to give a month's notice?'

'Usually yes, but that girl is one step away from a complete breakdown. Anyway, she's coming back for the party so you can see her then.'

'You know,' said David thoughtfully. 'All of the time we were at training school, I used to look around the class and wonder how we would all cope out there on the streets. I thought we were all so young that I found it difficult to see how any of us could do the job.' He shook his head ruefully. 'The job's turned out a piece of cake. It's our private lives that're the problem!'

Within a few days Michael's countenance had resumed its usual good features and he was back at work. He had been reluctant to take the time off in the first place: it had been his dignity that had suffered not his health. However, the force is never very happy about its constables wandering around with black eyes, particularly when they were as impressive as Michael's.

His return to work had coincided with the arrival of the final details for the Arsenal match. Nine PCs and Angela, together with an inspector and a sergeant, were to parade at Cabul Lane at 10.30 a.m. where they were to be picked up by a Transit and conveyed to the ground.

It was a cold dry Saturday and after a quick snack, two hundred officers from all parts of London assembled in the

188

Arsenal indoor training area to hear their postings. At twelve noon David and Angela were allocated the west touchline, whilst Michael was to be positioned in the crowd on the north bank. Having been suitably fed and watered, the rank and file were instructed to take up their positions in the crowd. The drawback was that as yet there was no crowd, nor would there be for another two hours. There was still a full thirty minutes before the gates even opened! Soon after 2.30 p.m., however, the police were in business and by 3.30 p.m. a steady stream of youngsters were either arrested or ejected.

'Beats me why they get so excited,' said Angela. 'I know I don't appreciate the finer points of football but I don't think it's very good.'

'Well, I *do* understand the finer points,' replied David emphatically, 'and you can take it from me it's bloody awful.'

The standard of play in the second half did improve but only to the point of mediocrity. Then, at twenty minutes to five, the referee put twenty-nine thousand people out of their misery by blowing a much-needed whistle on a 0–0 draw.

'Perfect result!' Michael sang out happily as he made his way down to his two friends on the touchline.

'Was it?' asked the puzzled Angela. 'I'm pleased I'm not a football fan then because I thought it was dreadful.'

'Oh, it was, sweetie, it was! It was absolutely abysmal. But it was the best possible result for the Old Bill. If either team had nicked a late winner we would have been bound to have had crowd trouble. But as it is, a nil–nil draw means they're so bloody bored all they want to do is go home. We'll be away from here in another ten minutes and you'll be back at the hostel by six-thirty at the latest.'

Angela gave a smile of delight. 'Mickey, you don't know how relieved I am to hear you say that. This has been such a worrying week for me. Helen has done all the preparation for the party and I've been terrified that we would become caught up here in some drama.'

189

'I told you there was nothing to worry about, didn't I? You just trust your old pal Mickey and you won't go far wrong. Ain't that right, Dave?'

David, who hated to count anything before he had hatched it, spent it or worn it, was noncommittal. 'We're not back yet, are we? I would never bet on any of your ideas. They invariably wind up with some poor sod getting the sack.'

'Okay, lads! That's all. Back in the training area!' called an inspector across the now empty terraces.

'Well, I was never one to say I told you so. But . . .' said Michael, raising two fingers to his doubting friend.

The hubbub of conversation amongst the assembled constables was firstly due to sheer relief that the match had ended, and secondly to the bonus of a comparatively early dismissal.

'Are all your groups present?' asked the chief superintendent to the assembled inspectors.

To a man they assured him they were—even inspectors need to go home.

'Right then, pay attention everyone. I have some good news and some bad news. The good news is that as from this minute you are all on overtime. And the bad news, I'm afraid, is that you are all now bound for Brixton, where, apparently, World War Three has just broken out.' He raised his hands to forestall any question. 'I know what you're going to say and I can't answer it, *any* of it, so don't ask me. There are to be *no* exceptions. If your mother-in-law is on the turn, or your kids have measles—hard cheese. It won't do you a bit of good because everyone is going— and that includes you girls. Right, get to your transport and tell the driver to put his foot down. That last bulletin I heard said we were losing it. Good luck, ladies and gentlemen.'

'"Just trust your old pal Mickey and you won't go far wrong",' mimicked David as they queued for the Transit. 'Won't go far wrong? Tell me, Mick, have you *ever* been bloody right?'

Michael slipped an arm around the shoulders of each of his two friends. 'Now the thing to do is to look on the bright side. After all, you're now on overtime,' he pointed out cheerily.

'Mickey,' said Angela, as she lifted his embracing arm from her shoulder. 'Sod off.'

CHAPTER THIRTEEN

Brixton was unbelievable. Unbelievable, that is, in its transition from an orderly urban shopping centre to a smoking, chaotic battlefield. Great billowing clouds rose from an assortment of burning vehicles, whilst ashes and charred paper flaked down like black snow. A continuous procession of casualties streamed back into the station. They walked, staggered or were carried in unconscious. Ambulances fought a losing battle as they ferried an ever-increasing number of burnt and battered coppers to the distant hospital. Perhaps the most ominous sign of all was a chief inspector drawing a line of men across the road in a last-ditch stand to keep the mob from the police station.

'What the hell has happened?' Michael asked a bandaged and blood-stained WPC.

'I honestly don't know,' replied the girl tearfully. 'There was some sort of eruption at Railton Road this afternoon and now there are hundreds of blacks and whites burning and looting everywhere. It's pandemonium out there.' She waved her arm vaguely towards the centre of Brixton. 'No one seems to know what's going on.'

A smoky-eyed chief inspector hastened towards the group and ordered them back on the Transit. 'Right! Up to Barnwell Road as quick as you can. We have a unit cut off there.'

'Where's Barnwell Road?' came back the obvious response.

The newcomer swore vehemently and ran to the end of the uniformed cordon, returning with a tubby middle-aged policeman. 'He'll show you the way—but step on it! Oh, and driver, on no account leave your vehicle unattended—Got it?'

'Got it, guv',' replied the worried-looking civilian.

As the Transit raced through the shopping centre, Michael soon noticed a large group looting an electrical shop. Several of the looters were already carrying away televisions and stereo units.

'Hang on!' he called sharply.

'Don't worry about it,' dismissed their guide. 'Half of the manor's being either looted or burnt and there's nothing we can do about it. If we stop for every shop-breaking we'll never get there.'

Barnwell Road was, ordinarily, a quiet little Victorian side street of small terraced houses. The north end of it ran into Railton Road which had been the core of the entire unrest. The driver regularly had to manoeuvre the Transit around burning cars and barriers. Each time he slowed to do so, a volley of stones and bottles would crash against the sides of the vehicle. Miraculously the windows remained intact. The distance from the police station was some half-mile and could usually be accomplished in a few minutes. That evening, however, it had taken over half an hour and seemed a million miles away. Street after street was strewn with burning wrecks and time and again the Transit was forced into a detour.

'Well, this is it,' frowned the PC as he peered through the stained windscreen. 'There doesn't seem to be any of our lot here though.'

Inspector Wilson, who had been in a state of silent stupor ever since leaving the football stadium, was now required to make a decision. A dozen faces looked expectantly towards him—nothing came back. Sergeant Baker removed his pipe from his mouth and tapped it on the heel of his shoe. 'Come on then, guv',' he said to the inspector. 'Let's me and you go for a look-see. Stay on the coach, everyone, but keep that bloody engine running.'

As the dazed Wilson followed the sergeant out of the Transit, David moved over to their guide. 'What's brought this lot on for heaven's sake—is it a revolution?'

'Revolution?' The older man gave a cynical laugh. 'I very much doubt that. They certainly aren't revolutionaries who have been nicked here this afternoon, more like opportunists. Of the first seventy nicked, sixty-one had previous convictions. Within an hour of the first trouble erupting, every mugger, housebreaker and pusher was on the street ready for business. Brixton had just become the world's biggest takeaway. If it's in a shop window and you fancy it, then just take it away.'

'But things can't blow up as quickly as that, surely?'

'Can't they? Well, you're about to discover they can. Law and order's broken down out there, mate, and at the moment it's nothing but a bloody great jungle. But if you think it's bad today, you just wait till tomorrow.'

'What's happening tomorrow?' asked Angela anxiously.

'Tomorrow the politicians will arrive, and do you know who'll get the blame for this lot?'

'No,' said the puzzled girl.

'You will. Or rather, you, me, him and one or two others.' He pointed generally around the Transit. 'It certainly won't be the bloke who set fire to Woolworths or poured flaming petrol on my two mates.'

The group listened to these observations in respectful silence, but the return of Sergeant Baker and Inspector Wilson cut short any further lecture.

'Right, listen carefully,' said Jack Baker. 'Apparently there were four PCs here and they were chased into the flats in the next street by a gang of some forty or so. We don't know what happened to them and all this took place about an hour ago. Unfortunately it's all we have to go on. What I, er, what Inspector Wilson proposes to do, is to split you into pairs and search the estate. We will search it section by section, and as we have no personal radios, at no time do I want any of you more than a hundred yards or two minutes from the Transit. Is that clear?' A murmur of assent rumbled around the vehicle. 'Right, here are your pairings.'

The news that he was to be paired with the old copper pleased David immensely. That Angela was to be paired with Michael pleased him not at all.

'I don't know what you're worrying about. I really don't,' said Michael irritably. 'She'll be quite safe with me.'

'I'm worried because you're such an irresponsible bugger. You know yourself what you're like. You are just as liable to do some lunatic thing and sod off without her.'

'Just what do you take me—'

'Will you two stop arguing and get on with the search?' yelled Sergeant Baker uncharacteristically. 'There's enough aggravation going on out there as it is without you pair starting your own.'

'It's all right, Davy, I'm a big girl now, I'll be okay,' assured Angela. 'But thanks for your concern.'

'Well, all right,' he mumbled reluctantly. Turning once more to Michael, his voice rose. 'But I'm holding you personally responsible for her safety, don't forget.'

Michael seized Angela's wrist roughly and led her away. 'He's like some bloody mother superior,' he muttered.

For the searching pairs the problems were twofold. Firstly, of course, they had no radio, and secondly, other than David's new colleague, none of them were familiar with the Brixton manor. In addition there were one or two other minor irritants, such as darkness and hunger. It was now well into the evening and most of them had eaten nothing but the hamburger and biscuit they had received on their way to the football match. In addition to these shared problems, Angela now had one of her own.

'Mickey, I need a lavatory.'

'What!' exploded Michael. 'There's a bloody civil war going on and you need—all right, all right, I'm sorry.' He gave a helpless shrug. 'But I haven't a clue where we'll find one.'

'We *could* ask,' suggested the girl.

'You know,' he said, thoughtfully, 'I don't think I've ever known a bird who, when the situation started to become interesting, didn't want to go to the lavatory.' He stared at her for a moment. 'Look, don't mind me asking, but this need of yours, well, there's numerous recesses and old cars and such like around, you know. I wondered perhaps . . .'

'Mickey, I need a *Ladies* not an "old car". Girls are different to boys, you know.'

'Yeh, so David keeps telling me. Okay, let's ask someone.'

The directions, when they came, were a little tantalizing. Yes, there was a toilet and yes, it was open. Unfortunately it was two streets away. Now these streets were quite short, no more than three minutes' walk the informant had said, but when one is in the dark, on a strange and seemingly hostile manor, two short streets can be a hell of a distance. This insecurity was not helped by the strict instructions 'not to wander'. On the other hand, no WPC in a riot situation is going to be of much use if she is preoccupied with finding a lavatory.

'Okay,' announced Michael decisively. 'We'll take a chance. But for heaven's sake don't hang about. Come on, let's step it out.'

'Mickey,' replied Angela tartly. 'It is because I need a lavatory that I am in no condition to "step it out"! I'll do my best and you'll just have to bear with me, I'm afraid.'

Giving one last visual sweep of the estate, both Michael and the girl made off towards the public toilets. Their only piece of good fortune came on their arrival at the scene. Ordinarily the place would have been closed but the earlier events of the day had caused both male and female attendants to flee—*without* securing the premises. 'Thank God,' sighed the relieved Angela. 'I don't think I've ever been so pleased to see anything.'

'Just cut the conversation and get on with the business—PLEASE!' insisted Michael.

As the girl hastened into the small brick building, Michael decided that a visit of his own would not come amiss. Two minutes later, somewhat refreshed, he stood in

196

the doorway impatiently awaiting her return. His attention was soon drawn to a group of chanting black youths, some fifty in number, who appeared en route for the general mayhem at the northern end of Railton Road. 'Let's-kill-the-Bill! Let's-kill-the-Bill!' went the repetitive verse. The group, who were running through the estate opposite, were happily separated from his immediate presence by a sturdy wire fence some twelve feet in height. The leader of this group soon displayed great vigilance by pointing out Michael's presence to his chanting colleagues. The group in turn showed instant flexibility by promptly changing direction. Their new course took them directly towards the fence with a totally new chant—'We're-going-to-kill-the-Bill! We're-going-to-kill-the-Bill!' What sympathy, if any, Michael may have had for Angela's predicament, was soon dispelled by the advancing horde. Even a twelve-foot-high fence is little deterrent to a mob whose express desire is to—'kill-the-Bill'. Diving into the Ladies he pounded on the door. 'Angie, Angie! For God's sake, quick! There are fifty sooties out here intent on hanging us!'

Whether it was his actual words, or just the urgency with which they were uttered, even Angela never knew. Throwing open the heavy green door she rushed out to join him in a rather undignified evacuation of the premises. Undignified primarily because she still had her knickers in her hand. Whether the mob actually recognized the pink wispy undergarment was debatable, but the new cry of—'Kill-the-Bill-Rape-the-Bill' indicated a certain degree of awareness. Seizing Angela once more by the wrist, Michael dragged her along the alley that ran from the rear of the lavatories. The rattle of the wire fence to their rear lent terror to their speed.

The alley soon swung sharp left and was illuminated at this point by a streetlamp. This lamp was attached to a heavy iron bracket some nine feet up on the top of the brick-walled corner. Releasing the girl's wrist, Michael drew his truncheon and raced towards this corner. When still some feet away, he leapt as high as he could, smashing the lamp into a hundred pieces. The effect was almost *too* dramatic, as the whole corner was plunged into inky blackness.

'Sod you, Mickey!' panted the girl. 'I can't see a bloody thing!'

'That's good because we're going over the wall.'

'What? I'll never get over that, it's much too high! Let's run.'

'They'll be over that fence within seconds. If we run they'll catch us—you, anyway—within a hundred yards—and you aren't wearing drawers! It's got to be the wall. With any luck they won't see us go over. Come on, put your hands as high up the wall as you can.'

As precious as the seconds were she still found time to remove her hat and stuff it, together with her knickers, into her tunic pocket. Dropping on all-fours, Michael gripped the girl's ankle and literally propelled her up the face of the wall. There was a slight pause as she reached the top, then, swinging her body sideways, she managed to hook a toehold along the edge of the wall.

'You're on your own now, kid, because I can't reach,' hissed Michael. 'Just try rolling and you'll do it.'

There was no time to check the girl's position before he too ascended the wall. The sound of running footsteps also indicated that any ascent would have to be from a standing jump, any second attempt would be far too late. He crouched for a moment and leapt up with his arms fully extended. He reached the top of the wall almost with a margin of comfort, but just as he was about to compliment himself, his helmet tumbled from his head and rolled agonizingly down his back. He too swung pendulum- like before hooking a size twelve boot over the top course of bricks.

'Shsssssh,' he hissed. 'Don't move an inch.'

The pair lay head to head along the top of the narrow wall almost fossilized in their immobility. The first of the pursuers reached the corner but did not look up and raced straight ahead. Soon a steady stream tumbled past. 'Kill-the-Bill-Rape-the-Bill!   Kill-the-Bill-Rape-the-Bill!'   The rhythm of the chant was suddenly broken by a string of oaths. Michael saw that the cause of this confusion was a roly-poly member of the group who had fallen, this in turn fetching down several of his sprinting comrades. These oaths turned to cheers as the fat fellow climbed cheerfully to his feet and adjusted Michael's now battered helmet on his head.

'Kill-the-Bill, Kill-the-Bill!' sang out one of his gang as he punched the wearer—none too lightly—in the chest. This was the signal for everyone else to join in. Suddenly a dozen or more resounding blows thudded into the unfortunate mimic. It may have started as a joke but the prankster was no longer laughing. He snatched the helmet from his own head and hurled it high into the air—over the opposite wall of the alley! The gang turned their heads upwards in a vain attempt to spot its flight before racing away after their leaders.

Neither Michael nor Angela moved for almost a full minute. Finally a long-drawn-out sigh of relief came from a particularly uncomfortable copper.

'Phew! If he had thrown that helmet over *this* wall they could hardly have missed us!'

'What do we do now?' asked Angela as she stared nervously down.

'The trouble is, I don't have a clue where we are,' admitted Michael. 'But this wall looks like it's around a vicarage of some sort. Let's drop down and have a look.' Giving a final check of the alley, Michael eased himself into the somewhat scruffy garden. 'Come on,' he called. 'Just lower yourself gently.'

Angela froze. 'I can't, it's too high.'

'What are you talking about?' he snapped irritably. 'It's not much more than a high pavement! Just swing yourself down and I'll hold you. Don't worry, you'll be fine.' Not without difficulty, the girl eased her legs over the wall and inched a descent, losing at least four buttons in the process.

'Okay, I've got your legs,' assured Michael. 'Just relax and I'll lower you to the ground.'

In spite of these assurances Angela still clung with some terror to the wall.

199

'Come on, kid, relax and let go of the wall, it's only a short drop.'

Summoning every vestige of her courage, she released her hands from the top course of bricks. This sudden change in her demeanour seemed to catch him unawares and she began to slip through his arms. He grabbed frantically at her legs before finally managing to lock his arms around the top of her thighs. Her skirt was ruffled hip-high and her firm but decidedly chilly, exposed buttocks were suddenly pressed tight against the side of his face.

'Well, well!' exclaimed Michael. 'This really is cheek to cheek! I'd recognize that face anywhere! Stockings, too! This gets better and better!'

'Please let me down,' demanded the girl angrily as she kicked out her legs.

For a moment he made no move. Then, after indulging in a friendly but somewhat impressionable bite, he began to slowly release her. As she slipped to the ground, he deliberately left his arms around her with just sufficient pressure to cause her skirt to now ride up over her waist. Even in the dark of the garden he could feel her embarrassment.

'Is that it then, Mickey? Is that your little thrill for today?'

'Tell me, love,' he said, ignoring her temper. 'Why is it that all plonks have cold bums? Yours is absolutely perishing!'

She wriggled her skirt back into position before replying. 'Mickey, I'm scared of heights and I have no knickers. I have been on top of a wall on a cold April night with half of Brixton threatening to rape me. I do honestly think I am quite entitled to have a cold bum. As I now have few secrets from you, perhaps this might be a good time to put these back on —excuse me.' She removed the panties from her pocket and, pulling them open, eased a raised foot through each half.

'What's with the stockings, though?' he asked. 'I thought all you girls wore tights?'

'Perhaps you're not as experienced as you think you are then,' she responded haughtily. 'A girl wears what a girl is comfortable in. Although I must confess that stockings aren't the cleverest things for climbing walls.' She suddenly winced and slid her hand down the back of her skirt. 'And sod you, Mickey Butler, one of your teeth is really sharp!'

'I could always kiss it better,' he offered.

'Listen, you randy bleeder, don't you think it's about time we rejoined the rest of our group? They must be wondering where on earth we are.'

'Yes, but let's check this place first, they may have a phone. I think it's a sort of rectory but I don't see any lights.'

Michael soon realized that the rectory was now a day nursery. He first made this simple discovery by cracking his shins on a seesaw. The pair stood in silence for a moment as they tried to take their bearings. It was this quiet concentration that drew their attention to the smell of burning wood that was now filling the air.

'Look at those flames, Mick. That can only be a few streets away.' Angela pointed to where a great billowing smoke-cloud topped a sea of leaping flames. 'They must be sixty feet high.'

Whichever way the couple looked seemed to be punctuated with bells, yells and screams.

'That must be a warehouse or a large shop on fire. Perhaps we should make our way there,' Michael suggested. 'It must at least be the centre of things. Even if it is a riot, we should at least meet *someone* on our side. If we carry on wandering as we are at the moment, we are just as likely to meet another bloody gang who'll want to string us up. Oh, by the way, if we are unlucky enough for that to happen, you just keep your drawers on this time. I don't want to get them all excited again.'

Events had unfolded so quickly since they had arrived in Brixton that Angela had not had time to consider her own vulnerability. That situation, however, was now beginning to dawn on her. She was a slightly built teenage girl, barely sixty-five inches in height. She was in an extremely hostile environment, she was lost, and, in keeping with every other WPC, without a single weapon of defence.

'Mickey,' she whispered. 'I'm frightened. I'm very, very

201

frightened. I don't think that mob of youngsters were kidding. We must get out of here—and quick!'

'The fire then! That's where we'll go. We'll make our way there.' For the third time that evening he took hold of her hand, but now with a great deal of tenderness. 'C'mon, kid, this time we really will step it out!'

As they began to jog towards the distant flames, their attention was drawn by the persistent hooting of a rather battered old Ford car. Other than fire engines and ambulances, the pair had hardly seen a private vehicle since they had arrived. An elderly white-haired man peered at them from the driver's seat.

'Where're you two goin'?'

'We want to get to the fire, can we get to it this way?' asked Michael.

'You'll get to it all right and you'll probably wind up *on* it! There are about two 'undred rioters and looters down there and they've just set fire to a pub.'

'But where are the police? We've been cut off and we're trying to get back.'

'Well, yer won't do it that way. As for the police—' The old man shook his head. 'Well, they're everywhere and nowhere as you might say. The nearest group to 'ere is probably in Effra Road. They at least seem to be 'oldin' their own but you'll never make it on foot, especially you, young lady.' He leaned to the opposite side of his car and, pushing the passenger seat forward, opened the door. ''Op in 'ere, I'll take yer as close as I can.'

Albert Brewster, it appeared, lived just off the Brixton Road with his wife Ada. With the firing of so many cars, he had sensibly decided to move his away from the danger area. He was driving it to his son's house at Clapham when he had spotted the two constables.

'Will you be staying with your son, Mr Brewster?' asked Angela.

'What, at Clapham? Lord luv' yer no! I can't stand bleedin' Clapham, gel. Come to think of it, I don't like

202

me son much either. No, as soon as I reach there I'm goin'
to dump me motor and come straight back.'

'Isn't that a little dangerous? I mean, you'll be on foot on
your own, won't you?'

'Miss, if 'itler couldn't move me I'm sure that lot's not
goin' to. I'm a Londoner see, miss, and I've lived 'ere all my
life.' He shook his head sadly. 'It ain't my London now
though, but I ain't leavin' for no one. So keep your 'ead
down, miss, 'cos we're off.'

Albert took a circular route and eventually negotiated
the one-way system in Effra Road quite smoothly—albeit
from the wrong end. All the signs indicated to Michael that,
riots or no riots, the old fellow never approached the
junction any other way. ''Ere we are,' he announced
confidently. 'There's a line of your blokes down near the
church. Good luck and look after that young gel,' he
instructed Michael. 'They never oughta let 'em on the
streets so young. My car's older than she is. Ta-ta.'

Throughout the old chap's conversation, Michael never
had the heart to tell him that he would be just as lost in
Effra Road as he was anywhere else on Brixton's manor. So
it was with no little delight that he recognized most of the
coppers forming a double cordon across the end of the
road. It appeared that after a six-hour delay the riot shields
had finally arrived, although in insufficient numbers. However, these shields were already proving their worth by
drawing the missiles that were hurtling in from further
down the road. Put up a line of shields, it seemed, and
people instantly felt compelled to throw bricks at them.
Very good news, of course, for coppers without shields.

It was Angela who first saw Sergeant Baker, cowering
under a rather large plastic dustbin lid. Of Wilson there was
no sign. 'Sorry we're late, Sarge,' she said. 'Ran into a bit of
trouble, I'm afraid.'

Jack Baker nodded thoughtfully as a large bottle disin-
tegrated at his feet. 'Oh dear, how tiresome for you. It's
been such fun here too.'

'Where's Inspector Wilson, Sarge?' asked Michael.

'He went to hospital some time ago. Here, where's your bleedin' helmet?'

'Lost it, Sarge. What can I do?'

'Not a lot without a helmet, son, you'll get bleedin' killed. I'll tell you what. There are three injured blokes and one injured plonk lying underneath that old market stall over there. You could stand either end and make sure no petrol bombs roll underneath, if you like. We've been waiting for an ambulance for ages and at least one of them blokes is in a bad way. Just do what you can for them. Look out!' Two flaming bottles soared through the air and spilled their burning contents over a sizeable portion of road.

Two of the three men who lay beneath the stall had rather serious leg burns and were, together with the equally burnt WPC, attending to the remaining victim. This one lay white-faced and motionless, a thin trickle of continuous blood running from his nose, ears and mouth.

'It's Davy, Mickey! It's Davy!' shrieked Angela. 'God, he looks awful!' Angela threw herself down alongside the unconscious figure and kept repeating his name.

'It's no good, love,' said the injured girl. 'He can't hear you.'

'What happened?' asked Michael.

'They hijacked a number two bus and drove it at our cordon. He was lucky really, it only knocked him over, it could just as easily have flattened him.'

'But what is wrong with him?' cried Angela.

'I should guess he's got several fractures and his jaw is definitely broken. Look at it.'

'Well, shouldn't he be in a sitting position?' demanded Angela.

'Of course he should,' snapped one of the men. 'But we have nothing to support him with.'

'I'll support him,' said Michael quietly. 'I'll sit him up as much as possible and if you hold him steady, I'll crouch behind him and you can then ease him back on to me.'

'You'll be bloody uncomfortable, mate. There's barely room to lie down, never mind crouch.'

204

'Well, let's give it a run—okay?'

The move went smoothly to plan, except that to hold the crouching position was even more agonizing than Michael had ever imagined. Relief was to hand, however. It came in the shape of two rusty six-inch sections of sharpened railings. They had been hurled with such intensity that they zipped beneath one side of the stall and out the other—opening, in rather neat parallel lines, the head of the tall, crouching constable.

CHAPTER FOURTEEN

The turmoil began at Brixton on Saturday afternoon. By Tuesday morning London's police force was hanging on by its fingertips. A by-product of this major disturbance was the spawning of a rash of localized commotions clear across the capital. These outbreaks usually took the form of raiding parties numbering anything between thirty and three hundred. These mobs would assemble in many of the great council estates, then charge up the local high street overturning cars and looting shops. As an added problem, the Easter holiday with its traditional fairs, football matches and marches, was only days away. Manpower was stretched enough on a normal Easter but with hundreds of officers injured and the necessity to police the still inflammatory and volatile Brixton, police coverage of the metropolis became a nightmare. Cabul Lane, in common with every other inner-city station, had been stripped of manpower. The twenty-four-hour policing of its miles of streets, markets and estates, fell mainly on the frail shoulders of a dozen young girls in two separate shifts.

In an effort to muster some sort of coverage, all leaves were cancelled and every officer compelled to work at least a twelve-hour shift. This effectively doubled the strength of the force, yet the idea could only ever be a short-term policy. On the other hand there were many police-officers who would have been delighted to have worked as little as a twelve-hour day. Sixteen hours was by no means unusual and eighteen not unknown.

Some were so tired that frequently they did not go home. They would sleep wherever they could lay their heads. Armchairs, snooker tables and the civilian staff's rest-room became much-sought-after places. The latter was a particularly popular abode. Its usual complement of one menstrual, pain-racked typist, gave way readily to five or six heavily booted coppers, desperately in need of clean socks.

Since that first day, when she had worked twenty-one continuous hours, Angela's world had consisted of nothing but work and sleep. By the fourth day the hours had begun to take their toll. The girls had been divided into pairs and, providing at least one of them could drive, had been allocated a panda car with an armful of outstanding emergency calls. These calls had been stacked in some attempt at priority but a two-hour delay in response to a 'call for police' did not go down very well with the public. Angela had been placed on the night-shift (7 p.m.–7 a.m.) and had been paired for the week with Jane Robins, a fiery, dark-haired Welsh girl. Although the two were compatible, the long hours definitely added a little touchiness to their relationship.

Occasionally, during those first few nights, they had called in to the Royal Friary Hospital where both David and Michael languished. Michael, with some forty stitches and a zipped scar either side of his head, was making easily the best progress. David, on the other hand, was giving cause for concern. His eyes were open and he appeared conscious but his words were indecipherable and he recognized no one. In addition, he would sporadically rip off his clothes and hurl himself from his bed. It was this tendency that caused his transfer to a high-sided steel cot. Though lacking the intelligence to scale the cot sides, he would, in sheer frustration, stand ape-like on his pillow and rock the whole apparatus violently from side to side. It was this action that caused Angela so much distress. During a late-evening visit on Tuesday, fatigue finally caught up with her and she ran hysterically from the ward. Her recovery was swift, however; a few kind words and an arm around the shoulder can often work wonders, and Jane Robins provided both to perfection.

In addition to David and Michael, there were at least twenty other Cabul Lane officers incarcerated in the

Friary, including Inspector Ted Dunn and Paul-the-Painter Ford. It was Paul who was first to be discharged. His burns and ankle fracture had both responded well to treatment. The girls had collected him in the panda car and driven him home to his live-in girlfriend 'Topsy' Johnson.

Topsy was a rather diminutive WPC at a neighbouring station and she too had sustained several injuries. These were caused as she had dealt with a local wife-beating. The husband, tired of slapping his wife around, had varied his interest by pummelling Topsy. The twenty-five minutes she had lain waiting for assistance, and that from two other almost equally fragile WPCs, had done nothing to quieten the rage of her drunken assailant.

By Wednesday, a steady stream of police casualties were being discharged from the Friary. This was to peak on Thursday when only four Cabul Lane officers remained in the wards. One of the last to leave had been Michael, who, all things considered, looked remarkably well. His new haircut seemed his only concern. The twin lacerations he had sustained were both high on the sides of his head. He knew very well that he had been particularly fortunate with their point of impact. An inch or two closer and they would have removed both his eyes. A fraction lower and they would have parted his face. Instead, he had a splitting headache and the world's worst haircut. To his utter disgust, an enthusiastic, razor-wielding nurse had raced around his cranium, leaving him just a palm-sized tuft of jet-black curls. The overall effect was that of a haircut on some mad medieval monk.

'Well, that should curb your romantic aspirations for a while, lover,' observed Angela. 'I don't wish to be unkind but you now look totally ridiculous.'

The release of Michael also coincided with an improvement in David. Now far less aggressive, he had been transferred to a general ward where he at least managed to retain his nightshirt. Although he appeared to be fully conscious, he still did not recognize anyone. 'Not to worry,' said the doctor. 'Everything will come back gradually now, just show a little patience.'

Patience, however, seemed to be the one commodity that Angela was unable to dispense. If she wasn't telephoning then she would be calling at the ward. Time and time again, she would sit at David's bedside just holding his hand until Jane hastened into the ward with yet another emergency call.

It was Friday before Brenda Flynn's anxiety overcame her strong Catholic pride. Having read of the enormous police casualties, she had telephoned Cabul Lane in order to assure herself that all was well with David. In addition, she also had some news for him, important news at that. The telephone operator had been particularly unhelpful to say the least. 'Sorry, my dear, I am forbidden to give this sort of information over the telephone. If you want to know, you must call in person.'

'But I just want to know if he is all right and where he is. Surely you can tell me that?'

The telephonist was polite but unhelpful. Already too many police-officers had been visited by their wives *and* their girlfriends. Each unaware of the other's existence.

'Don't worry, Mum,' said Sandra as she slipped her hand into that of her tall boyfriend. 'Tony and me will pop down the station for you—won't we, Tone?' 'Tone' concurred.

Brenda watched the young couple leave, with mixed feelings. She did so want the girl to be happy but there were no half measures with Sandra; she would give everything for her man and expect everything back in return. Men, thought Brenda, didn't work like that. Girls like Sandra would always get hurt. They seemed to be born for men to let them down. She sighed. Well, at least David would be happy that the girl was now courting. But would he be prepared to call round again? Brenda prayed he would.

'Well, who are you?' asked the station officer. 'Are you his immediate family?'

'No, we're just sort of friends of his, I suppose,' answered Sandra.

'I see,' murmured the sergeant. 'Well, I'm afraid I can't

tell you where he is, but if you leave your name and address I'll tell him you called, or at least I will when he comes round. No doubt he'll then phone you.'

'You mean he's in hospital?'

'I'm sorry, I thought you knew. Yes, he's been knocked about a bit and he's suffering from a little amnesia but he's expected to recover soon.'

'But why can't you tell me where he is?'

'As I said, I can only give that information to his immediate family. But don't worry, I will tell him you called.'

Sandra's news did nothing to reassure Brenda. 'But surely they told you more than that!'

'No, Mum, he told me nothing. But there are only four hospitals he can be in. Guy's, St Thomas's, King's College and the Friary. We could try them all, couldn't we?'

Brenda was reaching for her coat almost before the girl had finished the sentence.

In the general trend of street disturbances, the Cabul Lane manor had been rather fortunate. It was barely a mile from Brixton and had at first appeared to have escaped the wanton looting that was the lot of many of London's other small shopping centres. No one believed this could last, however, the potential pickings were far too great. Every copper knew that there was an element who, sooner or later, would have to hit the Cabul Road shops. The problem was, when? It would be dark, of course, which would place it after nine o'clock. It would also need at least thirty men to combat it. Yet how can any station that is being policed by a dozen girls, spare thirty men for what, after all, was only a potential threat?

It was the bravado of a pimply necked fifteen-year-old that finally solved the problem. Having been captured removing an outsized cardigan from the 'reduced' counter of a gents' outfitters, he was asked if his plan had been to grow into it. 'Oh, yer,' he sneered at the shop owner. 'You won't feel so bleedin' clever on Saturday night, I bet.'

'What's happening Saturday, son?' asked the owner casually.

Realizing he had already said too much, the boy became unusually reticent. 'You wait, you'll see,' he muttered. It was the sort of veiled threat that pimply faced fifteen-year-olds will mutter every time they are captured, but this time old Ben Weisenthal decided to mention it to Chief Inspector Ron Hill, who had been placed in charge of operations. The result was that instead of being seconded to Brixton on Saturday evening, forty men were kept on reserve in Cabul Lane Station. This was very much a brave decision by Hill but it was one he felt he had to take. If Brixton erupted and Cabul Lane manor remained tranquil, he would have forty men in the wrong place at the wrong time. Just the sort of calamity that could hold back the promotion of a chief inspector for years. It would have been far easier to have sent the men to Brixton and ask for them back should a local emergency arise. It would have been far easier—but also too late. Hill reasoned that if he could win this local battle he could well win the local war.

It had been a typical Easter Saturday, dry cold and with a biting wind. At 6.45 p.m. forty constables, four sergeants, and two inspectors reported for duty at Cabul Lane prior to their departure for Brixton. It was a drill they were now familiar with: an assembly in the canteen, a two-minute chat from the chief inspector, then outside in the street to the four Transits that had almost been their home for a week. The lack of sleep showed clearly in most faces now; the dark-circled eyes and hollowing cheeks had become almost a trademark. The 'two-minute chat' that evening, however, was a little different to anything they had heard to date.

'You will certainly be going to Brixton, lads, but not until later. First we have some business of our own to settle,' explained Hill. He then proceeded to outline his plan of campaign. An integral part of this were the two constables —the youngest and scruffiest pair he could find—who were sent out in plain clothes to reconnoitre the two huge housing estates that lay either end of the Cabul Road shops. 'The four Transits will be kept in the yard out of sight. This will hopefully give the impression that we have already left for Brixton. Once we know their raid is definitely on, you will each climb aboard your vehicles as fast as you can and make for these four locations.' He tapped his fingers repeatedly on the map. 'If this raid on the shops goes according to pattern, they will break every window in sight regardless of contents. They will then carry away as much as possible and, if they are not interrupted, will repeat the trip again and again until the premises are either cleared or you arrive. They will then store the property in garages, pram sheds and bedrooms—Yes, what is it?' He pointed to a raised hand.

'How do we know that a raid is coming?'

'Oh, it's coming all right. If you walk the streets you can feel it. The only thing I am not sure about is *when*! I hope it's tonight because we are prepared for them. But if they hit the manor when we are absent then they will certainly succeed, and if they succeed they will keep at it every night until they've stripped each shop on the manor. Any other questions?'

'Prisoners, sir. What arrangements have been made for getting them back to the nick?'

The chief inspector gave a long, deep sigh and looked slowly around the canteen. 'Yes . . . prisoners,' he announced, almost to himself. 'This is going to be a somewhat delicate item for me to talk about, I'm afraid.' He paused as if to let his words sink in. 'If there are as many as I think there could be, then every one of you could easily wind up with a prisoner. If you do that then Brixton will be short of forty men on the first Saturday night since the riots began. It will most certainly be busy there tonight, gentlemen, I can assure you of that. We will need every man we can get. So just remember, if you nick a body in Cabul Road, then you will be leaving the rest of your colleagues short at Brixton. Do I make myself clear?'

A puzzled young recruit raised a wavering arm. 'So what do I do, sir . . . If I arrest a shopbreaker, I mean?'

Bert Bones reached up and eased the youngster's still

extended arm back to his side. 'Just stay with me, son, just stay with me.'

Mary, the civilian switchboard operator, entered the canteen and, without a word, handed Hill a piece of paper. He dropped his head in study for a moment before looking up with the faintest of smiles. 'At ten-thirty tonight, the Farrier's Lane estate mob is going to hit the southern end of Cabul Road. At the same time, the Rockton Gardens estate lot are going to try their luck at the northern end. Just for good measure, several of them are joining forces for the precinct shops in the centre. You have nearly three hours before kick-off, gentlemen. I suggest you make yourselves as comfortable as possible.'

Of the station's total of a dozen WPCs, half had completed their stint, while the remainder were about to start. There was the briefest of overlap as they exchanged some tired pleasantries. Hill chose that very moment to call them all together. 'I know it's been a long day, girls,' he began.

'You mean a long *week*, sir?' suggested Jane Robins.

He smiled and raised a hand in acknowledgement. 'A long *week* then, Miss Robins,' he corrected. 'Anyway, to get to the point, I want you day girls to stay on for at least another five hours. I fully realize that will then be seventeen hours you will have completed and I also realize that you are due back at seven in the morning. Now, before I explain further, how do you feel about it?'

At twenty-seven years of age, Betty Wilson was the oldest WPC in the station; nearly three months pregnant, she was also the tiredest. 'What's our choice, sir?'

'We have a little something on around ten-thirty tonight. I would like you six girls to stay, firstly to provide numbers and secondly to assist in case we have a rush of female prisoners. Hopefully we will have none, but on the other hand we may well have a couple of dozen. How do you feel about it?'

'Can we put our feet up till then, sir?' asked Betty.

'You can stand on your head as long as you're around the place till midnight,' answered the grateful chief inspector.

'I'll just settle for taking off me shoes if you don't mind, sir—thanks all the same though.'

Jane Robins reversed the panda car across the yard and out into Cabul Lane. 'I don't know why we've got those four bloody great Transits here. There's little enough room as it is,' she complained.

'It's part of Ron Hill's master plan to fool the revolutionaries,' said Angela. 'That's why we're due back in at ten o'clock. You and me are going to be in the forefront of the goodies versus the baddies. Your reversing doesn't get any better, does it?'

'What have we got?' asked Jane, nodding towards the pile of papers on the clipboard.

Angela thumbed quickly through the sheets as they threaded their way into the early-evening traffic. 'Four break- ins, one missing person, a dispute between neighbours, and a drunk in the Old Kent Road. What do you want to deal with first?'

Instead of answering, Jane slammed hard on the brakes. 'Did you see who just went into The Feathers?'

Angela swung around in time to see the saloon door closing. 'No, who?'

'The Weasel.' She shook her head sadly. 'That's bloody awkward, that is.'

'Why?'

'Well, whenever the Weasel's on the manor it's a good policy to alert the rest of the units. It's just so if they receive a call there they will be prepared—he's always aggravation, that one.'

'So what's the problem?' persisted Angela.

'Well, the problem is,' said Jane tersely, 'that I don't feel I can blurt out that particular information on the bat-phone when it's his father who's running the show tonight! We'll just have to mention it quietly as and when we see the other two pandas. Right, come on, let's pull this drunk out of the Old Kent Road.'

It was shortly after nine-fifty that the two girls returned

214

to Cabul Lane. They handed in the results of their calls to the communications officer and poured themselves a coffee.

'How's things out there?' asked Sergeant Tomlinson.

'It's really strange, Sarge,' frowned Jane. 'Within the last half-hour the manor's gone completely dead. I know it's a cold night and all that but there's hardly a soul about.'

'Well, that's a good sign, ain't it, love?' called Mary, the switchboard girl.

'Oh no, it's not!' said Jane, shaking her head vehemently. 'Whatever it is, it's not a *good* sign. There's an atmosphere out there you could cut with a knife. I don't know what it is because I've never known anything like it before. But I'll tell you one thing—it's scary, it's really bloody scary!'

Together with the rest of the girls, Angela and Jane attended the final briefing in the canteen. They passed the knowledge of the Weasel's whereabouts to everyone within whispering distance.

'Okay, pay attention now!' called Chief Inspector Hill. 'Our two intrepid spies have just reported that there are around one hundred and fifty yobs assembled in Farrier's Lane estate and nearly the same number in Rockton Gardens. This is slightly more than I anticipated, so I have asked for the assistance of a couple of dog vans. This will give us four dogs, two at each end of the road. Now make no mistake, this is going to be a trial of strength and we must *not* lose it. It's going to be dark out there and they will most certainly not be playing to the Queensberry rules. Remember, I want no heroes. You will be no good to me or to yourself or your colleagues if you are stretchered off in some ambulance. There will only be three rules out there tonight. One—get in first. Two—let 'em know you're the guv'nor. And three—stay in touch. I want no one wandering off on their own. Oh, and by the way, I don't want any of you girls anywhere near the trouble, is that clear?' Each girl nodded briefly. 'You will stay in the station and go out only to deal with emergency calls that are nothing whatever to do with our particular disturbance.

Understand?' Again they nodded. 'Okay, well, if you're fed and watered you can get your Transits. We'll be on our way within a couple of minutes.'

The two large groups of youths that were now fully assembled in the estates, had arrived there by word of mouth. Many had come miles. This was impressive up to a point. For that many people to gather at that time of night did show a certain common purpose. The big flaw in the plan, however, was that there was really *no* plan. There was not only no plan, there were no leaders. The call had gone out and they had simply assembled. They were now off to loot the Cabul Road shops and cart away the goodies. The Old Bill were all at Brixton so it would be easy. The first two or three began to move off towards those glittering windows and the rest simply followed. None were really sure what was expected on such an excursion. Should they sing? Perhaps they should chant? How about their football teams? Yes, that was it, they would exalt their football teams! The only trouble was that there were four different teams represented: West Ham, Chelsea, Millwall and Arsenal. They still hadn't got it right when the police arrived.

The mob's organization may have been lacking but the determination was certainly there. They charged straight at the police lines. It was then they discovered that they had an additional problem—the police were not playing to the usual rules. Within fifteen minutes it was all over. No one was arrested but scores were thumped. Some slightly, some badly, a few even bitten. One hundred and fifty were splintered into twenties and thirties, then to fives and tens, and finally to twos and threes. By eleven o'clock they had all gone home and not an arrest was made. Eight windows had been broken, two cars had been scratched, a jellied-eel stall overturned, and a second-hand dress shop looted. Police casualties consisted of an inspector with a black eye and a handler who was bitten by his own dog. Forty-seven men were therefore sent off to police Brixton, and five young girls and one mum-to-be looked forward to their beds.

With customers not appearing until twenty minutes before

closing time, and just six WPCs to cover the whole manor, many publicans understandably decided to grant themselves a little extension. The girls' only complaint about this violation of the licensing laws was that they were on duty and couldn't enjoy it.

'There's just one little niggle that's bothering me now, Angie,' murmured Jane as she drove down Cabul Road.

'—And that is?' asked her questioning friend.

'The Weasel. He's been in The Feathers for four hours now and that's always bad news.'

'D'you think we should have a look?'

'I suppose it wouldn't do any harm. He'll probably be helping himself to those jellied eels. It was the stall in The Feathers' car-park that got turned over.'

Showing sensible discretion—and no little apprehension—Jane eased the panda into the kerbside on the opposite side of the road to The Feathers.

'Good heavens! They don't hang about, do they?' marvelled Angela.

'Who don't?'

'The boarding-up people. Look over there at the side of the pub. There's a bloke already fixing the roof of the eel stall.' She pointed to where a small van stood with opened doors and a white-coated workman was hammering in nails. 'I hear they've been making a right killing during these disturbances. They've apparently been charging up to three hundred quid just to shore up a window!'

'Well, I don't think that one's going to do much. Look at him—poor sod, he can hardly walk.'

Before Angela had so much as set eyes on the workman, the saloon-bar door was thrown open and several struggling figures could be seen illuminated in the doorway.

'Oh, Christ, no!' exclaimed Jane. 'Quick, call for assistance. It's the Weasel and he's fighting drunk!'

The response to their call could have been greater. Panda two did not appear to have heard at all, and panda three already had a disturbance of its own. The station officer at Cabul Lane suddenly cut in sharply. 'Panda three, I don't care if you've got the gunpowder plot! Drop everything and get down to The Feathers as soon as possible! And panda one, are you still receiving?'

'Yes, Sarge.'

'You two girls just be bloody careful. Stay out of his reach until we can get some sort of assistance down to you. D'you understand me?'

'Yes, Sarge.'

The struggles at the public-house doorway had temporarily ceased with the eventual ejection of the Weasel. True to form, however, he picked up a large steel bracket from the wreckage of the jellied-eel stall and drew back his arm.

'Drop that, Peter!' snapped Jane as she strode briskly across the road.

'Says who?' sneered the youth, with his arm still in the throwing position.

'I say so, Peter. Drop it—please.'

He rolled back his head in a brief snort of humour, then rocketed his arm forward. The nine-inch bracket smashed the ornate glass window into a thousand pieces. Both girls reached him simultaneously.

'You're nicked!' announced Jane as she seized his throwing arm. Angela was but a fraction behind as she took hold of the other arm. With a quick twist of his body he threw the older girl to the ground with surprising ease. 'You make me laugh, you prats, you really make me laugh.' As he finished the sentence he thudded a powerful kick into the face of the kneeling Jane. Now roaring drunk, he turned his full attention to Angela who, terrified, still clung grimly to his left arm. Making a powerful fist he drew back his right arm. 'You're a fucking copper—well, cop this!' Before he could make the next move the girl swung a desperate foot deep into his crotch. For a moment he bent double. As this appeared to be the most effective method of restraint tried so far, she repeated the treatment. Unfortunately, she still remained clinging to his arm. While this proximity was helpful for kicking crotches, it was singularly unsuitable for escaping retribution. With a roar, he wrestled his arm free and curled it around the girl's neck.

By this time the bar staff and several customers had emerged from the public house. One of the crowd seemed to know him. 'Let her go, Peter, my son,' he implored. 'She's only a kid, look at her. I bet she ain't twenty.'

By way of an answer, the Weasel swung the girl across the front of his body and held her, shield-like, facing the crowd. He tugged her head back with his left hand causing her to arch up on to her toes.

A moan came up from the dazed Jane.

'Only a kid? Is that what you think? I'll tell you what this "kid" is, shall I? This kid, as you call her, is a whore. That's what this *kid* is. So I'm going to do to her what I did to all those other whores!' With that he rummaged briefly into his jacket pocket and slid out a pocket-sized industrial knife—a Stanley knife.

CHAPTER FIFTEEN

Paul-the-Painter Ford had always considered he was an unlucky person. It wasn't that he was unenterprising —quite the reverse—it was simply that whenever he had a good idea, something always went wrong and spoilt it. Take that delivery service, for example; that had been typical. Being in the force, the shift work suited him and together with an equally entrepreneurial constable from Peckham, he had bought an old van. Being on different shifts, he considered they could offer a twenty-four-hour delivery service anywhere in the Home Counties. He thought it was an idea that could not go wrong. But the very first load that was carried by his partner went wrong all right. Coming straight off night-duty, the idiot fell asleep at the wheel and drove smoothly into the Grand Union Canal. Well, now it had happened again. Just as things seemed to be working out, he was faced with another disaster. The burns he had suffered at Brixton were healing nicely and although the plaster of Paris on his ankle was a little restricting—he could not change gear, for example—it did not hurt. He would certainly be off sick from the force for some weeks, so it was obviously an excellent time to hire a little automatic van and take advantage of the mayhem. A bit of hardboard here and a pane of glass there, was worth fifty quid of anyone's money. He had actually been driving down Cabul Road to another looting when the eel stall was tipped over. An immediate cash deal of thirty pounds to fix the roof had been excellent business. Or it would have been, if these two daft cows hadn't got themselves involved with the Weasel.

Paul reluctantly picked up the four-by-four-inch joist that had earlier been wrenched from the roof of the stall and tried it for weight and balance. Seemingly satisfied, he fetched it down smartly across the neck of the knife-brandishing drunk.

'Paul!' exclaimed Angela, staring first down at the sprawling drunk then up at the frustrated carpenter. 'Am I glad to see you!'

'Well, that's more than I can say for you! You've ruined my business. Look, get this straight before help arrives. I did not assist you or help you in any way. In fact, you've never even seen me. If the guv'nors find out I've been fixing roofs whilst I'm off sick with a fractured ankle, they'll go crackers. Now, look after her—' He nodded down to the groggy Jane. 'And if he moves again, belt him with this joist. In fact, it might be a good idea to belt him *before* he moves. I must go now. It looks like panda three in the distance.' Sliding into his van, he pulled an old cap from his pocket and tugged it down hard over his head. 'And don't forget,' he called. 'Keep your bloody fingerprints off that knife!'

'Right, young lady,' said Sergeant Tomlinson. 'We've got the detective inspector out of his bed and he's on his way in, so let me have the story first. You're going to be sick of telling it before this night is out, I can assure you.'

Angela recited the events exactly as they had unfolded—that is, until she reached the point where the Weasel was poleaxed. 'Then this bloke comes along, Sarge, and—'

'What *"bloke"* and where did he come *from*?'

'I dunno *what* bloke, Sarge. He was just a bloke. I'd never seen him before. Little fellow he was—er, wispy sort of beard he had. Oh, and specs—he was wearing specs, too. Anyway, he picks up this bit of wood and belts the prisoner with it.'

'And where did the piece of wood come from?'

'It was just lying around, Sarge. There was a stack of the stuff. Most of it had come from the jellied-eel stall.'

'What did he say?'

'The Weasel?'

'No, this shining knight with the wispy beard.'

'Oh, well, he didn't say anything other than that he had to go because he had an urgent appointment.'

'Mr Bromley will no doubt tell you that you should have detained him. He's a material witness, young lady.'

'I couldn't, Sarge, could I? I mean, Jane was out cold and there was only me to deal with the prisoner. If a bloke saves my life I can hardly arrest him, now can I? Be fair.'

'True,' the sergeant agreed. 'But, you see, this isn't really an area for shining knights. Particularly with wispy beards and specs.'

The communications officer joined them in the charge-room. 'I've sent the message to Brixton control, Sarge. Mr Hill is in the thick of it somewhere in Railton Road. As soon as they find him they are going to swift him back.'

Tomlinson shook his head sadly. 'I'd prefer not to be here when he arrives.'

'What will happen to him, Sarge?' asked Angela. 'Mr Hill, I mean.'

'I honestly don't know, girl, except it won't be good. It's one thing to be a chief inspector and have a son who's an arsehole. But it's quite another to have one who's a murderer. He'll be transferred straight away, of course, but if I know Ron Hill he'll leave the job.'

'Will that affect his pension, Sarge?' asked the communications officer, who with twenty-three years' service was very much into pensions.

'Yes I'm afraid it will, Joe,' sighed the sergeant. 'It'll cost him a bloody fortune in the long run, poor bugger.'

Mary, the telephone operator, had sat silent during the conversations. She finally looked up from her knitting. 'I do hope that no one takes offence at this but—' She paused for a moment. 'Well, I'm afraid it's *all* your faults. You've been covering up for that lad for years because of his father being such a smashing bloke. Now what've you got? The bastard's not only a murderer but he's killed one of your own girls, *and* his father will still be a broken man. It hasn't worked, Sarge, has it?'

The sergeant did not answer.

Jane Robins sat rigid as the last of a dozen stitches was inserted into the side of her mouth.

'There you are, young lady,' said the doctor finally. 'Another couple of weeks and you'll be as pretty as ever. Most of the stitches are inside your mouth. There are only two at the most that may show.'

A few minutes later, Jane and Angela sat in the back of panda three as it weaved its way back to Cabul Lane.

'This is all I seem to have done lately,' said Angela ruefully. 'Collect sick coppers from Royal Friary Hospital.'

Jane mumbled a response that was unintelligible because of the swelling to her mouth.

'If it's any consolation to you, Jane, the Weasel completely cracked in the charge-room—probably because he was drunk. Anyway, DI Bromley couldn't get it down quick enough. It may not have been quite ethical but it sure was effective! Mr Bromley reckons he did it all because he hates his father. I reckon that's crap. I think he cut up girls because he simply *liked* cutting up girls.'

Under Bromley's watchful eye the girls made their written statements. It had long been obvious to Angela that Jane knew no more about the Weasel's downfall than did the detective inspector. She had, after all, been knocked to the ground before Paul Ford had struck.

'So you say, Miss Helms, that this saviour of yours clobbered young Hill and then had it away in a van. Is that correct?'

'That's correct, sir.'

'Hmmm, pity. He would have rounded off the evidence nicely. Do you think anyone from the pub may have known him?'

'Not unless they took the van's number, sir. And because it was dark and parked at an angle, I doubt if they could have seen it. I certainly couldn't.'

'Did PC Patterson know about the Weasel, sir?' asked Angela, desperately trying to change the drift of the conversation.

'Yes, Hill first met Patterson when Preacher helped out

at the children's Christmas party at his previous station. They must have been birds of a feather in many respects because they became quite friendly in spite of the difference in ages. Sometimes Hill would give him the victims' underclothing just to "prove God's will was being done". Ironically enough, he had never intended to harm any nurses. He was simply unable to differentiate between nurses and plonks when they were off-duty. As for Patterson, he was so far gone at the end he thought Hill was actually a messenger direct from God. Are you absolutely sure you never saw even part of the number on that van?'

'Yes, sir.'

'Well, anyway, whatever Hill said, Preacher would always believe. Ironically we had a situation where a serving copper knew everything there was to know about an operational psychopath, but was too bloody barmy to separate it from his own religious fantasies! How about the make of this van? Don't you even know that?'

The breaking of a difficult murder case—or any other prolonged case for that matter—is usually the excuse for a celebration drink in most CID offices. A compulsory weekly levy is usually fixed on each member of the department to pay for this. A couple of trainee detectives are then dispatched to the local off-licence, and the uniform branch, in the shape of the three or four most senior officers, invited to the drink out of courtesy. This time-honoured drill was hardly prudent in current circumstances. Firstly, one could hardly invite the chief inspector when it was his son who was about to be charged. Secondly, no one in their right mind would have dreamt of inviting the current chief superintendent. If he was unpopular and obsessed by teacups, he was pathological about whisky glasses. Finally, it was three in the morning and, leaving out the inaccessibility of off-licences, plain-clothes detectives would be as rare as midday bats. Any celebrations, therefore, would have to wait for a more civilized time.

'Okay, Miss Helms,' said Bromley as he studied the completed statement. 'Well done, and if you find yourself in the vicinity of the CID office on Monday afternoon, pop in for a glass of something. In the meantime, give the description of that van some thought, will you?'

Any further pleasantries were interrupted by the arrival at the office door of Sergeant Tomlinson.

'Have you finished with Miss Helms, guv'?'

'Help yourself,' gestured Bromley magnanimously.

'Angie, I've got a bit of a problem at the enquiry counter and I think you may be able to assist.'

'Sarge?' queried the puzzled girl.

'It concerns a friend of yours—Dave Ducker?'

The colour drained instantly from her face. 'He's . . . he's all right, isn't he? He was getting on so well this afternoon.'

'He's okay! He's okay! Well, at least I think he is,' said Tomlinson, slipping a reassuring hand on her arm. 'It's just that I have a rather tearful female at the counter who claims she is his girlfriend and wants to see him. The problem is, I'm reluctant to tell her anything because I'm sure she's not telling the truth. She must be at least forty and young Ducker's not much older than you, is he?'

Angela nodded.

'Well, I wonder what she's playing at then? She's in a right state as well. I'm fast becoming convinced that only nutters come into police stations. Although to be fair, she's still a good-looking woman—more my age than young Davy's I would think though.'

'What did she actually say, Sarge?'

'Well, she claims they are engaged but I noticed she's already wearing a wedding ring. What's the set-up?'

Angela sighed deeply and, with the back of her index finger, wiped back a stray tear. 'Davy was . . .' She appeared to search for words. 'Well, he was very close to her. In fact, to be honest, Sarge, he was nuts over her. Then she broke it off some weeks ago and he hasn't seen her since. Whenever he has spoken to me about it . . .' She shrugged. 'Well, he seemed to have got over it. Davy has been very ill, Sarge, and he's come on a lot in the last few days. I don't think it would be a very clever idea if Brenda descended on him now.'

'No, nor do I,' agreed the sergeant. 'Look, Angie, I know it's been a hell of a night, what with one thing and another, but will you do one further thing for me?'

'Sure, Sarge.'

'You don't know what it is yet!'

She forced a smile. 'Perhaps I'd like to get it all over in one go. What is it you want me to do?'

'Have a chat with her, reassure her a little. Let her down lightly if you have to, but take her in the interview room and have a sisterly tête-à-tête. But just pick your words carefully because that woman is one wrong word away from a neurotic explosion.'

'Thanks, Sarge. We should make a fine pair.'

Angela pushed the door quietly closed. 'Sit down at the desk, Mrs Flynn. Now, what can I do to help?'

Brenda fiddled anxiously with her rings. 'It's my fiancé, PC Ducker. I understand he's in hospital and I would like to see him—I have a right to, you know.'

'I see,' nodded Angela. 'But why have you come here? I mean, if he's in hospital, why haven't you called there?'

'I don't know what hospital he's in. They won't tell me.'

'Who won't tell you?'

'The hospital people. They say if I want information about injured policemen, then I must get it from the officer's own police station. That's why I'm here.'

'When was the last time you saw PC Ducker, Mrs Flynn?'

'Er, a few days ago I think it was.'

'He's been in hospital for a week, love.'

'Well, perhaps it was longer than that then. So much has happened lately that I've lost track of time.'

'Look, I can't keep calling you Mrs Flynn. May I call you Brenda?'

The woman sat up in anxious surprise. 'Yes, certainly—But how did you know my name?'

'I'm a close friend of David's myself. We were at training school together and he has spoken quite a lot about you.'

'You must be Angie then?'

'That's right. Look, Brenda. I don't wish to be cruel but before I can even start to help you, you are going to have to be honest with me. I happen to know that you are *not* engaged to Davy. I do know that he wanted to *become* engaged but as he told it to me, you refused. Is that right?'

Brenda lowered her head. 'That's right. Although it seems a million years ago now. It was when I had some pride. But now? I'd grovel for him now. I bet I look a pathetic creature chasing my—What do they call them nowadays, "Toy-Boy"? I bet they had a good laugh in that front office. "Look at the blousy old cow. Mutton chasing lamb." Do you know, I once forbade him to say the word "love". Do you know that? Now I love him so much I degrade myself and come lying and simpering into a police station at four in the morning because I can't even sleep without him. You know what maddens me most—Well, do you?'

'No.'

'I *knew* this would happen! That's what maddens me. I bloody *knew* it! I had a lifetime of love securely bottled up inside me, then that bugger comes along and takes out the cork. If only—' Her words were cut short by an eruption of tears. She laid her head on the table in front of her and simply gave in to what had obviously been building up for days. The hinges creaked as the station officer put an enquiring head around the door. Angela gave him a quick, reassuring nod as she eased her chair next to the woman and slipped a comforting arm around her quivering shoulders.

For several minutes Brenda was inconsolable. Finally the sobs became fainter and fewer. She slowly raised her head as Mary eased a cup of steaming tea across the polished desk. 'Thank you,' she whispered to the already

227

departing telephonist. Ignoring the heat, she raised the hot cup to her lips, clinging to it desperately as if some unknown force was about to snatch it from her grasp. With her swollen eyes and her tear-stained face she looked a very sad figure. Eventually, and with slow deliberation, she lowered the cup inch by inch to the table-top. For a few moments she ran her wedding-ring finger idly around the chipped rim.

'I bet you think I'm a complete fool,' she said, raising her head.

'Nothing of the sort,' assured Angela. 'In your circumstances I'm sure I would be exactly the same.'

'I feel better now . . . anyway, thank you for listening. Look, I realize you must be quite worried about my seeming lack of control—' She raised a quick hand to stifle Angela's protestations. 'But please, love, listen to me. You see, more than anything else I need to know David is all right. I don't even need to speak to him.' She shrugged helplessly. 'Perhaps if I could just see him from a doorway or something it would at least put my mind at rest, and if nothing else it would be a tidy finish. The way things are at the moment I wouldn't even know if he was alive or dead.'

'Brenda,' faltered Angela, searching desperately for words. 'Brenda . . . Well, David has been very ill and although he's recovering, it could easily be a long time before he is anywhere near back to normal and . . . Well, you know what I mean.'

Brenda stared at the girl for a moment before rising to her feet. 'Listen, Angie, all I want to do is to assure myself that he is okay. Will you see him for me, and when you think he is well enough, just tell him I asked, nothing more? I still love him, Angie—' She gave a rueful smile. 'But don't tell him that, of course. Just let me know how he is.'

'But how will I get in touch with you?'

'Ring me at the launderette. Here's my number. I'll be no more problem now, I promise. I'm going back to just being a mum. I'll tell you one thing, love. It'll be a lot less trouble.'

'I'll have a quick word with the station officer, Brenda. Perhaps he'll let us give you a lift home.'

'No. Thank you all the same, love, but I can do with the walk.'

'But it's four in the morning and it's almost five miles away!'

'It'll clear my thoughts. Heaven knows, they could do with it. Anyway, I've never minded a good walk.' She reached out and took the girl's arm. 'Don't look so worried, I'm much better now.'

'Are you sure?'

'Of course, nothing like a good cry, you know—and do you know why I cried?'

'Well, you were very upset and—'

'Bless you, love, that wasn't the reason at all. Most of my life has been an "upset" one way and another. I'm quite used to upsets, upsets I can take. No, I cried because of something I suddenly found myself saying. I could hardly believe it was me I was hearing. I said—or rather I started to say—"if only".' She gave a short, mirthless laugh. 'Just about the two most pathetic words in our language. I've always found "if only's" to be such snivelling little creatures. "If only this" and "if only that". Well, for a minute there I came very close to being one of them—and that would have been very silly indeed. You see, in spite of my tears, that boy was very good for me. He reminded me of something I'd almost forgotten. He reminded me that I was still capable of actually loving someone. You have no idea how important that is to me.' She gave a slight chuckle as her eyes began to recover some of their old vitality. '*If only* I hadn't met him I wouldn't have known that, now would I?' Bending forward she planted a quick kiss on Angela's cheek. 'Thank the lady for her tea and don't forget to ring me about Davy, eh?'

Angela nodded.

'Good-night, love, and do be careful out there.' She gestured towards the open door. 'After all, you're only a scrap of a thing.'

Angela watched Brenda all the way to the corner of the street before turning thoughtfully back into the front office. The door to the yard swung suddenly open and Heather Williams and Jill Kent from panda two struggled in with a yelling drunk. 'Urinating over passing cars, Sarge,' panted Jill. 'We've nicked him for drunk and indecent.'

'That's a bit of a feat, isn't it?' marvelled Tomlinson. 'Urinating over passing cars! I could never get a range like that when I was in primary school and *I* was the "Up-the-Wall" champion!'

The young WPC gave an exaggerated sigh. 'He was *attempting* to urinate over passing cars then, Sarge, put it that way.'

'That's a lot better! Cuts out third-party envy, you might say. So therefore he's not "drunk and indecent"? Just drunk perhaps?'

'Just drunk, Sarge,' agreed the girl acidly. 'Unless, of course, you think he was innocently directing traffic with the tip of his penis? In which case perhaps you should give him two quid out of the poor box and we'll take him home.'

'That is a point, Sarge,' agreed Heather Williams. 'Why don't the pair of you have a sort of play-off for the Cabul Lane Up-the-Wall championship? You could always say you were representing the police if anyone asks. We'll draw chalk lines and award a small prize for the winner.'

'You shouldn't be sarky to the sergeant, especially when he's about to be very nice to you. It's not good manners— nor is it wise,' added Tomlinson darkly.

'You?' asked Jill incredulously. 'You are going to be *nice* to *us*? What's happened, Sarge? You only got a day to live?'

'Okay, enough of the jokes. Listen carefully, you lot,' announced the sergeant. 'With your arrival back in the building, it now means that, together with the other two pandas, my entire shift of dedicated young Amazons are now back in base, as you might say. In addition to that, your arrival also coincides with the first total clear-up of messages we've had in the week since the riots began. In other words, we've finally caught up.' Both Jill and Heather gave a sarcastic cheer. Tomlinson raised his hands for silence. 'I've not finished yet. Now, Mary has made some tea and, because it is now nearly five hours into my birthday, I have provided a "bottle"—in fact, a couple of bottles. You are therefore invited to join the rest of the station staff in putting your feet up and toasting my continued health and prosperity.'

'Sergeant!' exclaimed Jill warmly. 'I'll never have another word said about you! Where are the glasses?'

'Glasses? We don't have glasses, but if you don't mind using cups you are very welcome to commence just as soon as your prisoner is banged-up.'

Angela had felt emotional ever since Brenda's departure and a generous half-cup of cream sherry simply compounded the feeling. The truth was she felt quite ashamed. Whilst offering Brenda a great deal of sympathy, she was beginning to realize that her own thoughts were more and more about David. She had also now realized just how tired she was. It was not until she had sat down that the full impact of her weariness had struck. Slowly her eyes closed. Oblivion was imminent as Tomlinson's voice cut through to her consciousness. 'Okay, ladies!' he sang out. 'Party's over! You can't sit around here boozing all night. It's time you were back on the streets—if you'll pardon the expression, Miss Kent.'

'Jane! Angela!' called the telephonist. 'Do you have any outstanding calls?'

Jane shook her head.

'Will you pop over to Brixton then and pick up Chief Inspector Hill? They are very short of transport and if you can't pick him up he'll be there for hours yet.'

The reminder of the chief inspector's impending distress placed a sobering air on the small group. 'Come on, Angie,' urged Jane. 'Drink up and let's get it over with. I've got some peppermints in the panda—might kill the smell of that sherry on your breath. It beats me how you can drink that stuff this time in the morning anyway!'

Angela reached the car still carrying an inch or so of the drink in the cup before she realized she had lost the taste. 'I was enjoying that sherry until Mary mentioned Ron Hill.' She gave a long sigh. 'It tastes like quinine now.' She threw the remnants into the yard and balanced the now empty cup on a convenient dog kennel.

A good cupful of Scotch had placed Sergeant Eric Tomlinson in a philosophical mood. 'Y'know, Mary,' he called across to the telephonist. 'If anyone had said to me that half a dozen plonks could run this nick every night for a week, I would have thought they were barmy. Don't you tell them I said so, but I think those six kids have done absolute wonders. They've been entirely on their own with no possibility of any back-up at all. Take the Weasel, for example. I wouldn't have liked to face him on my own— and without a weapon of any sort! I tell you, my old arse would have been making buttons—and that's a fact!'

'I'd be more than surprised if the lady wishes to know of the peculiarities of your bowel movements, Sergeant,' said an all too familiar voice.

The sergeant rose to his feet to welcome the superintendent, at the same time using his foot to quietly close the double drawer of the desk that contained both celebratory bottles, plus another half-cup of Scotch.

'All correct, sir!' snapped Tomlinson, in the time-honoured Met Police greeting.

Once he had recovered from the shock of seeing a superintendent before five in the morning, Tomlinson began to feel particularly relieved that he had not arrived some fifteen minutes earlier, when the entire night-duty relief had been either sipping sherry or drinking tea.

'Understand you have had some drama during the night, Sergeant?'

'Yes, sir. Mr Bromley is still in his office if you'd like to see him. I dare say he could put you in the picture better than me, sir.'

The superintendent sniffed and nodded his head thoughtfully. Eric Tomlinson had a gut feeling that he had not been listening to a word he had said.

'Tell me, Sergeant. When you came on duty last night, what time was it?'

'Six forty-five, sir.'

'I see. And what time did you sign to say that everything was in order when you took over responsibility?'

'At the same time, sir—six forty-five.'

'And was it?'

'Was it *what*, sir?'

'Was it in order, man! Did you check *everything* before you accepted the responsibility for it? In other words, when you *signed* to say it was correct, did you *know* it was correct?'

The reason for Tomlinson's vagueness was deliberate. He knew full well that Heath was laying a trap for him but as yet he had no idea what it could be. If a station officer checked everything he signed for, then every police station would grind to a halt in hours. It was reckoned that the changeover alone would take ninety minutes. On the other hand, he had no choice. He *had* taken over—and he *had* signed.

'Yes, sir.'

'Yes *what*, Sergeant? I want us to be precise about this. It is a matter of great importance. Now for the last time, did you check everything before you signed?'

'Yes, sir.'

'Ah ha! I suspected as much! Then come with me, Sergeant, I have something to show you.'

The superintendent then turned swiftly on his heels and strode out of the open door. Tomlinson followed closely behind but not before he had turned up his palms and given a bewildered shrug to the telephonist. The pair clattered down the steps that led into the yard and threaded their way through the numerous stolen cars that clutter up every police station. The first of the birds were singing in the old tree that grew on the factory forecourt next door, but as yet no dawn could be seen.

'There, Sergeant! See it?' The superintendent pointed dramatically to the corner of the yard.

'No, sir, I don't.' This time Tomlinson's vagueness was not deliberate. He neither saw it nor had he the faintest idea what 'it' could be.

'Are you blind? The dog kennel, man, the dog kennel!'

'I can see the kennel, sir, but we haven't had a dog in it for days. The only one we had handed in was claimed by its owner yester—'

'I'm not talking about *dogs*, you fool! I'm talking about teacups! There's a teacup on the roof on that kennel, Sergeant. You realize, of course, the implications? If you checked everything that you claim at six forty-five last evening, then that cup was placed there deliberately by one of your own men. *Your* man, Sergeant, no one else's!'

Tomlinson's first thought was to pound the superintendent into a pulp—and so was his second. After a moment's pause he gained just a little more composure. 'I have not had any *men* on my relief tonight, sir, nor any night for a week now.'

'The sex is unimportant, Sergeant.'

'The sex is *anything* but unimportant, sir. We have been policing this manor, one of the busiest in London I might say, every night for a week with five young girls and a mum-to-be. To my mind, they each deserve the Queen's Police Medal. Now I don't know where you've been, sir, but all I can say is that we haven't seen you. At least not until now. Pretty soon Chief Inspector Hill is going to come in that back gate a broken man, sir. His boy, an unmitigated shit of the first order, has just finished his career for him. I have nine prisoners in the cells and a constable with twelve stitches in her mouth. My relief are so tired they can hardly stand up and two miles up the road a war is taking place. I am forty today, sir, and as if that is not bad enough, my wife's just written off my car! So you see, when you come in here like some pompous prick and start crapping on about teacups, well, quite simply, sir, with all due respect to you and happily away from witnesses, I don't give a fuck! SIR!'

Heath's stunned face was suddenly illuminated by the headlights of the panda as it swung into the yard. As it braked to a halt, a uniformed figure could be clearly seen slumped in the rear. Angela slid from the front of the car and tilted her vacant seat forward to assist the emergence of the chief inspector. He thanked her politely and smoothed down his crumpled uniform. He then adjusted his cap and wearily climbed the staircase to the detective inspector's office. Sergeant Tomlinson and Superintendent Heath paused from their confrontation. Heath was the first to break the respectful silence.

'Sergeant,' he said curtly. 'I shall return to this subject and your attitude—which I consider insubordination of the worst possible kind—just as soon as I have offered my condolences to Mr Hill.'

'I think you may be well advised not to, sir—If you don't mind me saying so.'

'I mind very much, Sergeant! You have been grossly impertinent to me and—although I appreciate you have been under a certain stress—that is still no excuse for your boorish bad manners and flagrant dereliction of duty.'

'Sir, I have no desire to prolong this conversation except to say this. You are my superintendent and as such you are entitled to my loyalty. That you have. However, I did feel it was about time that your obsession with trivia was brought to your own attention. Firstly, it does neither you nor the force any credit, and secondly, the whole damn station is laughing at you behind your back. I hate to say this, sir, but in the context of current police priorities, teacups are nowhere.'

'You miss the point, Sergeant! Teacups are—'

'Sir!' Tomlinson almost yelled. 'There you go again! Will you bloody forget about teacups and try to do something positive about the morale at this station? I've been here for ten years now and it's never been so low. Might I ask, sir. Have you visited any of the men who are injured? They range from broken legs to fractured skulls and one young lad who's lost his memory. And how about those six girls, sir. Have you given them one word of thanks? I repeat, you're the guv'nor at this nick and as long as you are you have my official support—but *unofficially*, and just between you and me, you're the greatest tosser who ever put on a uniform. Now, if you have nothing further to say to me, I have a front office to run.'

'Before you go, Sergeant, I would like you to detail one of your officers to assist me for half an hour or so.'

'Very well, sir.' Tomlinson turned his attention to the panda that was now reversing across the yard. 'Hold it you two!' The two girls, who had heard every word of the argument and were about to swear they hadn't, wound down their windows simultaneously.

'Miss Helms, the superintendent has a job for you. In the meantime, Miss Robins, will you begin patrolling the manor on your own,' he said pointedly.

Angela strode briskly towards Heath and, when still a pace or two away, stopped still. She was never sure if one saluted or not in such circumstances. As a result her right arm quivered like some fiddler's elbow.

The superintendent glanced swiftly at the numerals on the girl's shoulder. 'Right, get yourself a clipboard, 590. We are going to search this station from top to bottom and I need you to list the position of every cup that we find.'

Tomlinson, who by now had reached the office steps, froze momentarily in his stride and closed his eyes in despair.

Thirty minutes later, the searching pair entered the front office. The superintendent could scarcely conceal his triumph. 'Well, Sergeant Tomlinson, I thought you might be interested in the results of my search. 590, if you please.' He gestured towards the girl. 'Call out exactly what we discovered.'

Angela shuffled uncomfortably. 'Er, well, sir. We found sixteen cups in all. There were three in the female rest-room, two in the collator's office, six in the CID, two in the sergeant's room and—er, one on the dog kennel, sir.'

Tomlinson remained unimpressed. 'That's fourteen. You said sixteen.'

'Er, yes, Sergeant,' agreed the crimson girl. 'But there were two more in the—er, gents' toilet.'

The station officer locked his gaze on to the superintendent but addressed his remarks to the young WPC. '*You* searched the gents' toilet, Miss Helms?'

'Well . . . Yes, Sergeant, but only in company with Mr Heath.'

'Uh-huh. Tell me, did you find anything else on this search?' Still his eyes did not budge from those of Heath.

'Well—er, yes. We found half a dozen empty beer bottles in the locker room, three PCs asleep in the female rest-room, and two more asleep on the snooker table.'

'How did you manage to see the two men on the snooker table? It's pitch dark down there at night.'

Angela looked quite puzzled. 'Well, we put on the lights of course.'

'I see,' said Tomlinson. 'And did the men wake up?'

'Yes.'

'Did they say anything to you?'

The girl made no reply.

'Well, did they?'

'Yes, they did, Sergeant. Or at least, one of them did.'

'And what did he say to you, Miss Helms?'

'He told me to "fuck off", Sergeant.'

'And did he see the superintendent alongside you when he told you to fuck off?'

'I don't think he saw anything but the light, Sergeant. It was shining right down in his eyes.'

Heath, who had been listening intently to the questioning, finally broke in. 'Well, Sergeant, in spite of your outburst in the yard, perhaps you can now see what a state we have reached. Sixteen teacups indeed! That's not "trivia", Sergeant, that's total indiscipline! In future, no more men are to sleep on these premises. The building is not suitable for it.'

'So where should they sleep, sir?'

'At home, of course—where else?'

237

'But the reason they are sleeping here is that they could not *get* home. Most of them finished around midnight and they are back on duty at seven in the morning—and that's after working seventeen hours! If they don't have their own transport there's no way they can get home and back in time—sir!'

Up to that moment, the superintendent had at least appeared rational but at last he changed. Snatching the clipboard from Angela, he pounded it down on the desk. 'Then they shouldn't live so damn far away, should they? When I joined the job we could only live five miles from the station and we never had any trouble toing and froing from work. But now they never seem to be happy unless they live in the damn stockbroker belt!'

'But you never worked fifteen hours a day!' pointed out Tomlinson. 'While hordes of bloody rioters were chucking bricks, spears and petrol bombs at you!'

'Could I see my son, Sergeant? Mr Bromley has no objections.' The calm, quiet voice of Ron Hill cut across the discord. The mere tone of it caused all of Tomlinson's anger to vanish instantly. It was only the clicking of Mary's knitting needles that broke the embarrassed silence.

'Yes. Yes, of course, sir,' answered Tomlinson finally. 'Miss Helms, here are the keys. Take the chief inspector down to number eight cell. You'll have to lock him in, I'm afraid.' He turned a little shamefacedly towards the chief inspector. 'Sorry about that, sir.'

'That's all right, Eric. I'll give you a buzz when I'm through.'

As the pair receded down the corridor towards the cells, so the sound of Mary's needles finally stopped.

'That's put your arguments in some sort of perspective, wouldn't you say?'

CHAPTER SIXTEEN

For the fifth time in as many minutes, Michael Butler stared into the bathroom mirror and for the fifth time he groaned. What a haircut! He had tried brushing it forward, hanging it down the sides and ruffling it everywhere in general, but it still looked what it was—a round tuft of hair on an otherwise shaven head. Just my luck, he thought. Two weeks off sick, able-bodied, the free use of David's van—but an appearance so comic it reduced most observers to a state of hysteria.

He had given a passing thought to trying his chances with Trixie again but his haircut had finally deterred him. Anyway, win, lose or draw, he was about to call on two ladies for whom he had more than a passing fancy. The problem was that neither of them were unduly interested in him. For Michael, this response would always be a challenge. What, he wondered, would Brenda do now? He knew enough about the relationship to realize that, barring a miracle, David and Brenda were finished. David was both stubborn and pig-headed but had, Michael considered, picked a real winner in that woman. He had sometimes wondered if David had realized just how good she was. For any twenty-year-old staid, naïve lad like David, Brenda Flynn was manna from heaven. He had hooked himself a voluptuous, experienced beauty and then ruined the whole thing by asking her to marry him! One thing was sure, Brenda Flynn had been totally wasted on young David. Then there was Angela. Heaven only knew what had got into her, but it was pretty obvious that in the last few weeks she had slowly become nuts over David. Given the slightest excuse, she would be either calling at the hospital or telephoning. Well, now he had good news for both of them. It would be interesting to compare their reactions. Michael enjoyed giving good news to women, it could occasionally be a very good start to a relationship. One thing was sure—given the slightest opportunity, he would never spoil it by proposing!

He wondered who to call on first, then, remembering that Angela was working nights, decided to let her sleep for as long as possible. Making one last rearrangement to his curls, he headed towards the launderette. On entering the door, he heard the sound of scrubbing coming from the small office at the rear of the shop.

'Brenda! Is that you?' he called as he strode purposefully into the room.

A blue-overalled figure was on her knees leaning forward with a bucket of soapy water at her side. It was a pose Michael had grown up with. Even as a twelve-year-old he had enjoyed looking at the backs of a good pair of strong female thighs. Well, if Brenda's thighs matched the rest of her, this could be an interesting start to the day.

All in all, Alice Sledge had kept in reasonable shape, considering ten children and her seventy-three years. But not even in the first bloom of her youth had she thought her thighs to have been any great attraction. Now if they had contained no special magic in 1930, grey winceyette and another fifty-six years of wear and tear had not improved them one iota. It was rare that Michael was at a loss for words, particularly when speaking to a female, but the sight of those thin, straight legs in those scruffy, twisted stockings seemed to place a certain restriction on his vocabulary.

Alice turned stiffly towards the young man, with dripping brush poised. 'Yerse, mate?'

'Oh—er, I'm sorry, I thought you were Brenda.'

'She ain't in this mornin', mate. She ain't well. Fact is, she ain't been well any mornin' this week.'

'I see. Er—what's the matter with her? Nothing serious, I hope.'

The old lady sniffed and cuffed her nose with the sleeve of her overall. 'Depends what you'd call serious, I s'pose.

Havin' another at her age though, well, I wouldn't a'thought that was too clever, would you?'

'Having a—! Do you mean she's having a baby?'

'Well, not right at this moment she ain't, no, but she's certainly got herself bleedin' pregnant—silly cow. You'd a' fort she'd know better at her time a life, wouldn't yer?' Alice's eyes suddenly narrowed as she craned forward to peer at him. ''Ere, you're not her *bloke* are yer?'

'No, no!' assured Michael hastily, fearing the wrath of the old lady.

'Only he's s'posed to be about your age.' She peered even closer, this time from beneath her raised spectacles. 'Oh no, I'm sorry, mate. This bloke who's put her in the family way is s'posed to be a copper. I s'pose you're wot they call a "punk", are yer?'

Michael's hands went instinctively to the sides of his head. This hardly augured well. He had planned to turn on the charm with both Brenda and Angela, but if Alice Sledge thought he was a punk, perhaps he should abandon the whole idea? He finally decided to put Alice's assumption down to senility. After all, his hair may have been high but he still had the old profile and charm.

'No,' he replied curtly. 'I happen to be a friend of Mrs Flynn. Can you tell me her address? I have to speak to her about something rather important.'

Alice's first instinct was to ask why, if the newcomer was a friend, he did not know Brenda's address. But the addition of the words "something rather important" changed all that. Other than her tribe of ten children, nothing "rather important" had happened to Alice Sledge in all her seventy-three years. How she envied people who had rather important happenings. She told him the address eagerly. After all, if it was *that* important Brenda might even disclose exactly what it was when she returned to work. He blurted a quick thanks and ran to the van.

After the fourth futile ring on Brenda's door, Michael returned to the vehicle and sat for a moment in quiet contemplation. What now? It was still too early to wake

Angela. He was assessing his next move when he heard the sound of running footsteps. 'Davy! Davy!' cried the voice. 'Oh! It's you, Mickey. I'm sorry, I saw the van and, well, I just thought . . .' The woman, white as a sheet, was swaying on her feet. Crashing back the sliding door, Michael caught her as she stumbled.

'I'm all right, really I am. I'm just—'

'You're anything *but* all right, Brenda. Come on, give me your key. I'll take you upstairs.'

It was a measure of her condition that she agreed. Some ten minutes later, Brenda lay on the settee whilst Michael rummaged diligently in the kitchen.

'The tea caddy's on the shelf,' called Brenda. 'The milk's in the fridge, the pot's on the draining board—and I don't take sugar.'

'Shut up and don't talk to me while I'm cooking,' he said. 'I lose all powers of concentration.' A few minutes later he emerged with a laden tray and placed it on the floor at the side of her. 'How d'you feel now?'

Brenda made no reply for a moment but just stared at him. 'Firstly,' she said. 'Will you please tell *me* something?'

'Fire away.'

'What've you done to your bleedin' hair? You look like a deranged Mohican.'

'Now, look,' he chided, waving a finger at her. 'I've come round here to be good to you, not to be insulted. If you must know, I sustained this haircut by protecting the life and limb of your old boyfriend.'

The smile faded from the woman's face. 'Yes,' she whispered. 'That term does have a certain air of finality about it, doesn't it—your old boyfriend?'

'I'm sorry, Brenda. I was only joking and . . .' He shrugged.

'Oh, that's okay, it's something I'll get used to no doubt.' She gave a wry smile. 'I'm a big girl now. Anyway, what's fetched you around here? If you're sniffing around for my Sandra, you're unlucky. She's in love.'

'Brenda, I had a phone call this morning from the hospital.'

She froze with her cup an inch from her lips. 'And?'

'Dave has come to his senses. It was actually him who phoned me. I went straight round to see him and it was just as if he had been asleep for ages. He still looks a little glazed around the eyes but in most other respects he appears normal.'

'You say, "appears"?'

'Yes. You see, he remembers nothing of the riots or even how he got injured. In fact, he remembers nothing that's happened in the last month or so. He has asked to see you and there is no doubt in my mind that he has no recollection of your parting. For heaven's sake, Brenda, either drink that tea or put it down. You've held it in the same position for ages.'

She looked down at the cup, almost in surprise that it was there at all.

'Anyway,' he continued. 'After hearing that you called in the station a few nights ago, I thought I'd put you in the picture. You see, it struck me that if you did see him, you'd both be speaking about two different things. He would still be thinking there was a relationship between you, and you'd be thinking he was an insensitive sod for treating your bust-up so lightly.'

'Yes, I see. Thank you very much, Mickey.' She swung her legs around and took up a sitting position on the settee. 'But there is another complication,' she began.

'You're pregnant?'

She looked at him, stunned. 'How on earth did you know that?' she asked incredulously.

'It's a virus that's running around the nick. You're the third case we've had.'

'Seriously, Mickey, *how* did you know?'

'I called in at the launderette and spoke to some old dear who thought I was a punk-rocker.'

'Oh, Old Alice,' she sighed. 'Yes, she sussed me out in days, I'm afraid. I suppose when you've had ten of your own you can spot a pregnancy three streets away. Of course, being evilly sick every morning hasn't helped.' The colour had returned to her cheeks and Michael began to understand why David had fallen so heavily for her. There was something powerfully sensual about the woman.

'Mickey, what am I to do?'

'It's got to be your choice, love, I'm afraid. All I can do is present you with all the facts. At the end of the day, though, it will have to be you who makes the decision.'

'What do you think Davy will say when I tell him I'm going to have his baby?'

'He'll go barmy with delight, that's a dead cert! Now if it was me for instance, I would sod off to the Foreign Legion or somewhere safe, but Davy was born for nappies and babies. The silly bugger will be in his glory. Actually, I would feel really sorry for any bird daft enough to marry him. He'll doubtless knock her up half a dozen kids before she—.' He stopped suddenly, realizing that at her age, the chances of Brenda having six children were remote to say the least.

'You didn't have to stop, Mickey. I got the picture, you know.'

Michael suddenly looked very uncomfortable. 'Look, Brenda, can I speak frankly? *Really* frankly, I mean?'

'I wish you would.'

'If it is possible for any marriage between a woman of *your* age and a fellow of *his* age to work, then there is no doubt at all that it would work with you pair. He would worship you and be around you so much he'd probably send you barmy. On the other hand, every time he went to work you'd be a mass of insecurity. It would have nothing to do with the perils of the job, but it would have everything to do with who he would be meeting, and who he would be working with. He might well come home at seven in the morning having spent the night with some sweet-smelling, tight-arsed little plonk in a panda car. Being the woman you are, I should think the uncertainty of that would drive you to distraction.'

She nodded. 'So what's the alternative?'

'You did say I could speak frankly, didn't you?'

'I dread to think what's coming—but go ahead.'

'Well, I think Davy has opened you up, as you might say. You were like a dormant little flower—' She raised her eyebrows. 'Well, all right, perhaps not quite so little. Anyway, you have unquestionably blossomed out in the last few months. Now, the way I see it, you have no real ties. I mean, you're not married or anything and your children are growing up. You're good company and most women of your age would give their eyeteeth to look like you and—'

'Mickey, I'm bloody pregnant!'

'Well, yes, I know that of course. But surely you could . . . well, you know.'

She leaned back against the cushions and raised her eyes in disbelief. 'Oh, you don't understand, do you?' She shook her head repeatedly. 'Mickey, I'm sure you're quite a smoothie with young girls but you are a million light years away from a woman like me. I now have the chance to get out and play the field—Is that what you're saying? I can do all the things at forty-four that I was prevented from doing at twenty-one—eh?'

'Something like that, yes.'

'Perhaps you for instance? You think that if your mate moves on to pastures new, you can take over for a while? This is, of course, until you get tired of me. Then I suppose you might pass me on to another police recruit? Perhaps I could even be part of the final exam, eh? "Yes, PC Bloggs, your probationary report has been excellent. All you now have to do is give Brenda Flynn a good seeing to and you will be the recruit of the year." You never know, perhaps if he could make me come twice in a session, he'd get a good-conduct medal, or whatever it is they give you coppers for being outstanding.'

'I didn't mean anything like that, Brenda!' he protested.

'Listen, Mickey, I am going to tell you something that you simply won't understand. Perhaps one day, when you're just a little less self-centred, you may do. Davy would certainly understand it but then Davy is far more adult than you.' She sat proudly erect and smoothed down her belly. 'There is absolutely no way I am going to get rid of this child. That's not even a matter for debate. My only decision to make is whether or not I breeze into that ward and say, "Okay, Davy, name the day." Having explained that, Mickey, now can I speak frankly to you? Really frankly, I mean?' she mimicked.

He nodded apprehensively.

'In spite of that haircut you're a good-looking boy, Mick. You're not only good-looking but excellent company. You're usually considerate and, I hesitate to say this, quite sexy. If I was under nineteen and looking for a good time, I would look no further than you. But if I was over twenty then it would be a totally different matter. At the moment your feelings for the opposite sex are about as shallow as anyone's can be. They are *intense*—but shallow. I have faith in you, Mickey, and I am convinced that you'll change—when you grow up, that is. So, if you can come back and see me when you are middle-aged—say around forty-five—I'll grab you like a shot. Mark you, I'll be around sixty-three then, so some of my fires may be dampened a little. Still, I could doubtless manage a brief smoulder.'

Michael began to look very angry.

Brenda rose to her feet and leaned forward, kissing him lightly on the forehead. 'Don't be offended, love. We are all different, every one of us. It's just that *you* are Michael and *he* is David. Sadly for you, and no doubt sadly for me, it's David that I love.' She shrugged. 'End of story.'

Michael also rose to his feet, his anger subsiding as quickly as it appeared. 'I'll file that little lecture away for twenty years in my things-to-do tray.' He stood back a little and eyed her up and down. 'I bet you'll be a right raver when you're sixty-three, touching up all those old boys in the pension queue. Anyway, do you want a lift in to see David or not?'

'No thanks, love. I must have time to sort myself out. I'm a mess at the moment. Give me a day to think things over, eh?'

'Sure.'

'But you'll ring me at the shop and let me know how he is?'

'Of course.'

Having waved goodbye to one of David's girlfriends, Michael decided it was time to call on the other. It was as he steered the reluctant van through the twisting streets that he realized the only complication he ever experienced with girls was usually with other people's. There was Helen's carpet salesman, Trixie's Arab, and now an emotional Brenda. Who, although he fancied her more than ever, was barmy about his best friend. One thing was sure, he was now determined to be completely detached about Angela.

With the arrest of the Weasel, the guard had been removed from White Stone Park hostel and the old informality had returned. Michael breezed through the open entrance and put his head around the kitchen door. 'Is Angie Helms about yet?' he asked.

A tall dressing-gowned redhead stood bent over a gas stove, a boiling saucepan in one hand and an egg-timer in the other. 'It's much too early,' she said, without even turning her head.

'Can I leave a message for her?'

'Not with me you can't, I'm off soon. Listen though!' Michael stood stock-still and did as he was bade but he heard nothing. 'You're in luck, that's Angie.'

'What was? I didn't hear a thing.'

'The toilet, didn't you hear it flush? Listen again.' Once more he remained immobile as he waited for a second flush. Once more he heard nothing.

'There you are! What did I tell you? If you pop upstairs sharpish, you'll catch her before she drops off again.'

'What'd you hear this time for heaven's sake? There wasn't the resemblance of a flush.'

'Floorboards—hear 'em? There ain't one in the place that don't creak.'

'Oh yes, of course,' he lied. 'What room is she in?'

'Room three,' said the dressing gown. 'And knock quietly, nearly everyone on that floor is "nights".'

'Angie!' hissed Michael, as he tapped softly on the flaking green door. 'It's me—Mickey.'

A muffled, sleepy groan came back in response.

'Angie!' he repeated with a shade more urgency. 'It's Mickey.'

Once more came the groan but this time of longer duration. For Michael that was close enough. He turned the handle and let himself into the room. The sound that Michael had interpreted as 'Come in' was obviously 'Just a minute'. He realized this as soon as he saw the naked Angela reaching for a towelling robe. The girl was far too tired to protest, however. She threw the garment loosely around her shoulders and, with her eyes closed, keeled over sideways on to the bed.

'Sod you, Mickey Butler,' she mumbled through a mouthful of bedcover. 'Go away and come back in a year when I'm not tired.'

'Listen to me, kid.' He moved his hand forward and, for the first time he could remember, actually covered up a part-nude female. 'Davy is conscious and he's asked to see you. I'm sorry to wake you but if I left it any later you wouldn't have time to visit him before you started work.'

The girl's eyes flashed open. There was no transition. One second she was stupid with fatigue, the next she was wide awake.

'Davy! How is he? Is he all right? When can I see him?' She swung her feet down from the bed straight into a pair of pink fluffy slippers. 'Oh, Mickey, when can we go?'

'Well, the staff nurse said that if you could leave it until about six this evening she would be obliged. Apparently there are quite a few tests they have to do. I thought if everything was satisfactory, I would pick you up from here and take you to the hospital—then on to night-duty for seven o'clock. Suit you?'

'Mickey, that's wonderful. That's absolutely perfect!'

'I did think of waiting until you had woken but you would have had no time to have visited Davy before you left for work.'

'I'm so pleased you didn't! Oh, you lovely man, you!' She seized Michael around the waist and tiptoed up to plant a sleepy-tasting kiss full upon his lips. 'Mickey?' she suddenly asked, leaning back from his face.

'Uh-huh?' he said, enjoying her proximity.

'Mickey—what's the matter with your bloody hair?'

He made no reply at first but simply locked his arms around her and stared for a moment down her gaping robe. 'Angie Helms, if I hear one more word about my haircut, I'm going to stitch you up a treat.'

'Oh yes?' she said saucily, as she wrested an arm free and gathered together the lapels of the parted robe. 'And how would you do that?'

'Well, in a general conversation with Davy, I might casually mention that you have symmetrically perfect nipples.'

She shook her head in mock despair. 'Yes, you would too, you bugger, wouldn't you? Okay, let me have one last little laugh to get it out of my system. I promise I'll not mention it again.' Her last few words were obscured by a happy, deep-throated chuckle.

As he relinquished his hold, he secretly marvelled at the girl's appearance. Minutes before she had been a sleep-starved, exhausted individual. Now, here she was, not just lively, but a positively radiant young girl, full of the zest of life.

'I'll pick you up at a quarter to six—all right?' he asked.

'Can't you make it half past five, Mick? It's not so long to wait.'

'You're just like a big kid! All right, five-thirty it is.'

Having two hours to kill, Michael wound his way back to the section-house. David had asked him to contact the two girls. Well, he had and he remained unconvinced as to the wisdom of that request. He was only pleased that it was David's problem and not his own. As an impartial observer, he was quite looking forward to the outcome. For a time, he had considered not approaching either of the two women—at least, not before he had the chance to hold a serious conversation with David. But even that approach had complications, for David did not take advice readily. It was best, he decided, for his friend to make his own mistakes, for mistake it would certainly be, whichever choice was made. The fool was too young and too intense for his own good.

Three teas, two games of snooker and six biscuits later, Michael set off once more for the White Stone Park hostel. There was to be no semi-nude welcome for him this time. Instead, a small note was pinned to the door of number three. 'COULDN'T WAIT, SORRY. ANGIE. PS. WOULD STILL APPRECIATE A LIFT TO WORK. X'

Michael cursed his own stupidity. Of course the girl would go straight to the hospital, he should have realized that. She had probably gone there just as soon as she had dressed. As far as Michael was concerned, he now considered his part was over. He had done everything a friend could be reasonably expected to do. The fact that the daft cow had dashed off on her own wasn't his fault, although he did wish she had shown just a little more restraint. Anyway, he was quite looking forward to seeing his old friend again. Besides, after two hours of Angela's drooling, David would doubtless be yearning for a little male company.

Lady Grant Ward was on the third floor and led off a long, narrow corridor. On leaving this corridor, the visitor would pass several rooms before arriving at the large double doors that led into the ward proper. One of these doors would be pinned back open but the other swung freely to and fro. It was at this location that one waited for a 'quiet word with Sister' or adjourned to be out of harm's way while a nearest-and-dearest received a bedpan. On reaching this door Michael paused momentarily. On his previous visit David had languished in the first bed on the left. The bed was now empty. 'Excuse me,' he asked of a passing nurse. 'Can you tell me where Mr Ducker has moved to?'

The nurse made no audible reply but pointed with a towel-covered bedpan to the opposite side of the ward where, halfway down and oblivious to all, two young lovers sat holding hands on a bed. Michael instinctively froze.

These two were not 'just friends', they were a fusion. He stood and watched for a minute or so. Occasionally the boy would take the girl's hand and press it softly to his lips. There was no stronger display of affection, nor did there need to be, it radiated from them.

It had taken Michael only seconds to realize that the slightest interruption would have been an intrusion and he wanted no part of it. He was about to tiptoe away when a familiar voice spoke from behind his shoulder.

'It solves a few problems, wouldn't you say?'

He wheeled round to face Brenda. Brenda, who was supposed to be taking a day or two 'to think things over'. Brenda, who had obviously spent the afternoon working like hell on her appearance. Brenda, who with a new loose-combed hairstyle and a white, fitted trench coat, looked an absolute stunner. And finally, Brenda, who now knew exactly what she wanted—but also knew from the second she had reached that door that she was never going to achieve it. Michael took her by the arm and moved her from the happy couple's line of vision.

'Brenda! How long have you been here?'

Tears had filled her eyes but as yet had not spilt on to her cheeks. 'Since I was fifteen, I think. I seem to have spent my whole life watching from doorways.' She gave a wry little smile. 'Or if I haven't, it certainly feels that way.'

'Come on,' he said. 'Let's get out of this place.'

The corridor was like a long, never-ending canyon and the clip-clip of her high heels seemed to echo more than most. Suddenly she stopped and turned to Michael.

'I'm bleedin' potty I am, ain't I?'

'Why?'

'Why? Well, look at me! All tarted up and chasing a starry-eyed boy. I need me bleedin' head examined. Not only that, but this bloody hairstyle cost me a bomb!' For the first time for weeks a genuine smile fashioned itself on her face. 'Come on, you. Yours cost you nothing —you can buy me a drink.'

'Brenda,' he said, slipping a comforting arm around her shoulder. 'I've been thinking.'

'Oh yes,' she answered, her eyes narrowing suspiciously. 'And what's coming now?'

'Well, you remember when you blasted me about "recruits" this afternoon?'

'Very clearly.'

'Well, you were right of course—but we've overlooked something.'

'And that is?'

'I'm no longer a recruit.' He slipped his arm from her shoulder and tightened it around her waist. 'That must make a difference, surely . . . '